MURDER, SHE WROTE: THE QUEEN'S JEWELS

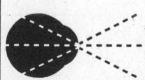

This Large Print Book carries the
Seal of Approval of N.A.V.H.

MURDER, SHE WROTE: THE QUEEN'S JEWELS

JESSICA FLETCHER & DONALD BAIN

Based on the Universal television series created by Peter S. Fischer, Richard Levinson & William Link

THORNDIKE PRESS
A part of Gale, Cengage Learning

GALE
CENGAGE Learning·

Farmington Hills, Mich • San Francisco • New York • Waterville, Maine
Meriden, Conn • Mason, Ohio • Chicago

Thorndike Press, a part of Gale, Cengage Learning.

Thorndike Press® Large Print Mystery.
The text of this Large Print edition is unabridged.
Other aspects of the book may vary from the original edition.
Set in 16 pt. Plantin.

LIBRARY OF CONGRESS CATALOGING-IN-PUBLICATION DATA

Fletcher, Jessica.
  Murder, she wrote: The queen's jewels / by Jessica Fletcher & Donald Bain. — Large print edition.
    pages ; cm. — (a Murder, she wrote mystery) (Thorndike Press Large Print mystery)
  "An Obsidian book."
  "Based on the Universal television series created by Peter S. Fischer, Richard Levinson & William Link."
  ISBN 978-1-4104-7927-3 (hardcover) — ISBN 1-4104-7927-7 (hardcover)
    1. Fletcher, Jessica—Fiction. 2. Women novelists—Fiction. 3. Women detectives—Fiction. 4. Jewelry theft—Fiction. 5. Large type books. I. Bain, Donald, 1935– author. II. Murder, she wrote (Television program) III. Title.
PS3552.A376Q44 2015
813'.54—dc23   2015026365

Published in 2015 by arrangement with New American Library, an imprint of Penguin Publishing Group, a division of Penguin Random House LLC

Printed in Mexico
2 3 4 5 6 7 20 19 18 17 16

For P. D. James, whose novels set a standard that inspires every writer of crime fiction.

JESSICA FLETCHER

For Phyllis James, my apt pupil at the *QE2*'s craps table and a reluctant idol to all writers. Renée and I treasure her friendship, as we do that of Rosemary Goad, her astute editor and dear friend.

DONALD BAIN

And for Captain Nick Bates, master of the *Queen Mary 2,* whose delightful book, *With a Pinch of Salt,* serves as a reminder of the rich nautical lore that exists. Not only is Captain Bates a superb seaman, he's a gifted storyteller.

PROLOGUE

London

Slowly, methodically, he dialed in the numbers until the telltale *click* indicated that the proper combination had been inputted. He looked back at his guest, smiled, and pulled open the heavy lead door. He reached into the wall safe until his fingers touched the small box, which he removed.

"Ready?" he asked.

His guest nodded.

Walter Yang sat on the love seat next to his guest. He placed the box on a glass coffee table, pulled off the top, extricated the soft black leather pouch, and placed it alongside the box.

"This is exciting," said his guest.

"Yes, it is very exciting," Yang said as he untied the black cord that secured the pouch. He probed inside until he found what he sought, and allowed his fingers to play with it before taking it from the pouch. It came to life as it caught the room's overhead light and sparkled as though on fire, reflecting and refracting from within, a diaphanous wonder of nature as it rested in the palm of his hand.

There was perspiration on his forehead and upper lip, like water beads on a recently waxed surface. He started to laugh. It began as a snigger but soon turned into a silly, childish giggle. "Want to hold it?" he asked.

"Yes."

He handed it to his guest.

"It's beautiful."

"It's so perfect," he said, "in every way, the clarity, the blue color. It's like the sky just before sunrise, wouldn't you say?"

"How poetic."

"More than seven carats of poetry. Look. See its static sparkle, the way it continues to throw off reflected light even when it's at rest? It's perfection. I've never seen a diamond with greater brilliance." He looked up and smiled. "They say a curse will fall on whoever owns it. Such nonsense."

He took the gem back from his guest and peered at it, as though able to penetrate its dazzling core, so engrossed in his appreciation of what he held that he didn't hear the muffled sound coming from the hallway outside his study. The intruder had entered through a back door leading to the kitchen, dressed all in black, a ski mask obscuring the face. The door to the study drifted open without a sound, but allowed a soft breeze to ruffle the drapes.

Yang's guest leaped from the love seat and moved behind a table. Startled, Yang turned. The intruder was on him in an instant.

"No," he pleaded, "no, no."

The intruder brought a fist to his face, breaking his nose, then spun him around and gripped him from behind in a violent choke hold. The diamond fell to the floor and rolled under the table. The arm around his neck squeezed tighter and tighter; a gurgling sound erupted from his mouth. His legs sagged. Still, the pressure on his neck intensified until it had compressed all life from him. The grip loosened; Walter Yang slid down his assailant's body, collapsing into a limp heap, lifeless, blood from his nose and mouth dripping onto the white carpet, leaving a stain the color of cardinals.

"Where is it?"

"Under there."

The diamond was scooped up and the attacker left the house, climbed into a Mercedes S400 hybrid vehicle, and rolled silently away.

Yang's guest left, too, walking slowly, quietly, through the open back door and out to the dimly lighted mews that ran behind the elegant town house in Belgravia, disappearing into the soft fog of the night.

CHAPTER ONE

"Did you hear about the big diamond robbery in London?"

The question was asked by Maniram Chatterjee as we shared a table in Mara's dockside luncheonette. Maniram and his wife, Hita, had recently moved to Cabot Cove from Detroit, where they'd owned and operated a successful jewelry store. A cousin who'd settled in Cabot Cove a few years earlier had persuaded them to experience the joys of small-town living. They'd sold their Detroit shop and opened one here, joining a small but growing Indian community.

"I certainly did," I said. "You couldn't miss it. It was on all the TV newscasts, and the front pages of the *Boston Globe* and *New York Times.*"

Maniram leaned forward. "That diamond was originally from my country. It is called the Heart of India. Only the most valuable stones are given a special name. This one was from the Kollur mine in the Golconda region. Many famous diamonds came from this mine."

"So you knew about this one before it was stolen?"

He nodded. "I even saw it once," he said. "In all the years that my family has been in the jewelry business, we'd never before seen a blue diamond of that color, quality, and size. It's extremely rare."

"Seven carats?" I said.

"Slightly more," he said.

"I read that it's worth ten million dollars," I said.

"Yes, that was what it was appraised at before it disappeared."

According to media reports, the heart-shaped diamond had been stolen from the home of a wealthy London businessman. Unfortunately he lost more than his precious gem. He also lost his life during the theft. The *Globe* article reported that not only was Scotland Yard involved in the investigation, but Interpol had also been brought into the picture, because it was suspected that the robbers, now also murderers, might be part of a network of globe-trotting jewel thieves that had been operating over the past six years with seeming abandon. And the *Times* story ended by pointing out that authorities had long suspected the slain businessman, Walter Soon Yang, of using a portion of his wealth to fund terrorist organizations around the world, although that charge had never been verified.

"Might make a nice ring, Maniram," Mara said, holding up her coffeepot as Dr. Seth Hazlitt pulled out a chair and joined us.

"Decaf for me, please," Seth said.

Maniram cocked his head and smiled wryly. "It would be quite a beautiful ring, Mara," he said. "But this gem carries a curse. It is said its owners will have great happiness or great misery. But you will not learn which until it is in your possession."

"Like the Hope diamond," Seth put in. "That one was said to curse its owners, too."

"Exactly," Maniram said, "and for good reason. The Heart of India was cut from the same stone as the Hope diamond."

"You mean there was an even bigger diamond?"

"Yes. Yes. When it was stolen from the mine in the seventeenth century, it was more than one hundred twelve carats. A French trader, Jean-Baptiste Tavernier, was believed to have taken it, and it was known for many years as the Tavernier Blue."

13

"Why was it cut down?" I asked.

Maniram shrugged. "Tavernier had sold it to the king of France and it was part of the crown jewels, but it disappeared during the French Revolution and was never found. Instead, we have the Hope diamond and the Heart of India, both the same blue, and with a similar curse. And there was a third, I believe, which was owned by the empress of Russia. I don't know if it was given a name."

"That must have been some rock," Seth said. "How big is the Hope diamond?"

"It weighs forty-five carats."

"Too big for my finger," I said, smiling.

"That's in the Smithsonian, isn't it?" Seth asked.

"Yes. The Museum of Natural History," Maniram replied, "but if it were on the market today, it could fetch more than three hundred million."

"That's too rich for my blood," Mara said, returning with her decaf pot. She handed Seth a menu and said, "One of you can buy me the ten-million-dollar ring for my next birthday."

"I'll do that," I said, sliding over my coffee cup for her to fill.

"Is your daughter feeling better?" Seth asked Maniram, referring to the eldest of his three children.

"Oh, much better," Maniram said, "thanks to you, Doctor. The chicken soup was like a miracle drug."

"Never fails," said Seth, looking pleased. He closed his menu and handed it to Mara. "I'll have the usual."

Mara left to get Seth his usual breakfast of her legendary blueberry pancakes — legendary at least in Cabot Cove and its environs.

"We're talking about that diamond robbery in London, the one where the owner was murdered," I said.

"So I gathered. I'm sure you'll pick up plenty of inside scuttlebutt while you're there," Seth said. "I imagine your friend Inspector Sutherland will fill you in."

"I hadn't even thought of that," I said. "But you're right. I'm sure he knows plenty."

"When do you leave?" Seth asked.

"A week from today."

"I heard you were going away," Maniram said.

"Oh? Who told you?" I asked.

"My wife. Hita said you would be traveling on the *Queen Mary Two.* She heard it at the bakery last week."

"No secrets in Cabot Cove," Seth said

15

playfully.

I shook my head. "Word does get around. It's true. I'm flying to London, spending a few days there with friends, and then six days coming back across the Atlantic on the *Queen Mary Two.* I'm looking forward to it so."

Over the years, I'd enjoyed plying the Atlantic on the *Queen Elizabeth 2* when I'd been invited to lecture during crossings — the crew always reminds you to call it a "crossing," not a cruise — and I'd been wanting to repeat the experience for a long time. Unfortunately the *QE2* was retired, slated to be a floating hotel in some Middle Eastern country, putting an end to that plan.

But then the *Queen Mary 2,* the *QM2,* had been launched, and I'd received invitations to lecture again to fellow passengers about my books, the murder-mystery genre in general, and the future of publishing. I'd heard nothing but raves about the huge new ship, and although my writing commitments made it difficult to block out the time, I decided that it was too good an opportunity to pass up. It would give me a chance to catch up with friends in London before sailing back home from Southampton. With the help of my travel agent, Susan Shevlin, whose husband, Jim, is Cabot Cove's mayor,

I booked my flight to London and my hotel in that wonderful city, which ranks high on my list of favorite places in the world.

A sly grin crossed Seth's lips as Mara delivered his breakfast.

"You look amused at something," I said. "Is my mascara running?"

"No, nothing to do with your makeup. I was just thinking about you traveling alone for six days on that ship. Perfect atmosphere for a shipboard romance."

"Oh, Seth, don't be silly. You know that isn't even a possibility."

"Well, just a thought."

"Ignore him," I said to Maniram. "He's being foolish."

Maniram grinned. "I have learned. The doctor, he likes to make fun."

"That he does."

Seth grunted and concentrated on cutting his pancakes and pouring syrup over them.

"I'm glad I didn't miss you before you left," Maniram said.

"Why's that?"

"Hita wanted me to tell you about our cousin Rupesh, who has just taken a job on the *QM Two* as a room steward. His mother received a postcard from him. Rupesh is — how can I put it? — Rupesh is a bit of a character. Over the years he's worked at too many jobs around the world to keep track of — computers, restaurants, tourist offices, teaching. He even spent a few months as a karate instructor back in India. A strange way to use his college degree."

I had to laugh. "A true jack-of-all-trades."

"Oh, yes, definitely that. We just wanted you to know about him in the event you and he should happen to meet on the ship. If you do, please say hello for Hita and me, and tell him to call his mother back in Delhi. A postcard is nice, but she likes to hear his voice every now and then. He isn't very good at keeping in touch with the family at home, and my aunt worries."

"I'll certainly say hello for you," I said, "and I'll scold him for not calling his mother."

"Oh, don't be too harsh with him, Jessica. He's an incorrigible free spirit, really quite charming. His name means 'god of beauty.' "

"Quite a lofty translation."

Maniram laughed. "All Indian names mean something wonderful. My name means 'jewel of a person.' "

"Sounds like you were fated to go into the jewelry business," Seth said.

"Maybe so," he replied. "Hita's name translates into 'lovable.' It's very true."

"Well," I said, "your cousin may be a god of beauty, but he still owes his mother an occasional call. I'll gently remind him of that, provided I cross his path."

"Wonderful, Jessica. Thank you, and *shubhyatra*. That means I hope you have a safe trip."

"Yes," Seth said, forking up the last of his pancakes. "Make sure you don't fall overboard."

CHAPTER TWO

"Ah, Jessica, how wonderful to see you again," my British publisher, Thomas Craig, said as he greeted me at the door of his home off Cadogan Place in London's tony Knightsbridge section. "Good journey, I assume?"

"Smooth and without hitches, Tom. Thanks to my frequent-flier miles, I flew first class."

"Nice to hear that someone enjoyed their flight. I find the whole flying experience these days to be dismal."

"It isn't what it used to be," I agreed.

"Come in, come in. The other guests have already arrived with the exception of one. My wife won't be here. She's off on an African safari communing with wild beasts, all from the sanctum of an air-conditioned tree house. Whisky? A martini? I promise to make martinis the way you do in the States, mostly gin and just a hint of vermouth."

"A friend of mine says he just whispers the word 'vermouth' over the glass. But no martinis for me, thank you. Sparkling water will do."

He gave my order to a young uniformed woman and led me to the terrace, where the others had gathered. Craig brought a halt to their conversation to introduce me.

The wife of one couple, Cynthia Walthrop, a woman of approximately my age, was a member of the House of Lords. I later learned she had been honored with a life peerage for her work with charities, which enabled her to be addressed as Baroness Walthrop. Her husband, Jacob, who appeared to have already enjoyed a few of Craig's American-style martinis, did not share her title. Mr. Walthrop was one of those fellows who tended to talk and laugh at the same time; his words were filtered through throaty chuckles. Between that and his British accent, I had to listen hard to understand him even though we were supposedly speaking the same language.

The second couple was Asian. Kim Chin-Hwa was introduced to me as a Korean venture capitalist who'd lived in London for many years, and who owned an office building in the financial district. He was a short, thin man with a chiseled face, and wore oversized horn-rimmed glasses. His companion, Betty LeClair, was a beautiful Eurasian woman with long, lustrous black hair. Her classic silk sheath clung to her lithe figure, the deep bronze color harmonizing with the large gold and onyx pin she wore at her shoulder. She was considerably younger and taller than Mr. Kim.

"Here's Paula Simmons," Tom said, gesturing toward a striking brunette with sky blue eyes, "a name with which I'm sure you're familiar."

"Of course," I said, shaking hands with my British editor. "How nice to meet in person at last." We'd exchanged a number of e-mails since Tom Craig had bought the British rights to my latest novel, and she and I had spoken briefly on the phone a few times.

"Paula's arguably the most beautiful book editor in London, not to mention that she beats the boys in the office at their game," Craig said. "She's a fan of your work."

Paula waved away his compliment. "I love your books, Jessica," she said. "There's a refreshing, old-fashioned attention paid to solid writing and inventive storytelling."

"I appreciate the compliment, Paula," I said. "Coming from someone with your editorial skills makes it all the more meaningful."

Madge and Gerald Wilson, an American documentary film team who looked to be barely in their thirties, were the last guests with whom I shook hands. They were in London for the premiere of a documentary they had produced based upon a nonfiction book Tom Craig had published several years back.

"It's about smuggling drugs into Great Britain from northern Africa," Gerald said, handing me a DVD. "Part of our promotional package," he added. "I'm telling Tom his book sales will soar once the film gets distributed."

"One can hope," Tom said drily. "If they do, I'll paste a sticker on the cover boosting the film."

"It's a deal," Gerald said.

It didn't take long before the conversation found its way to the recent theft of the rare blue diamond, and the murder that had accompanied it. Baroness Walthrop raised the subject. The moment she did, a silence fell over the group and all eyes went to Mr. Kim.

"Any leads?" Paula asked him.

"None that I'm aware of," he responded.

Tom Craig noticed my perplexed expression and explained. "Kim's business partner was the owner of the diamond. He was killed during the robbery, Jessica."

"Oh. I'm so sorry," I said.

Mr. Kim smiled. "Thank you, Mrs. Fletcher," he said. "The loss was traumatic to be sure, but I have been working at overcoming my grief. Walter Yang was not only a valued business associate; he was a dear personal friend. It is my hope that those who took his life are brought to justice swiftly."

"I'll drink to that," said Jacob Walthrop, raising his glass. "To justice being served!"

The mention of "justice" reminded me that the first person I'd called upon arrival in London was George Sutherland at Scotland Yard. I'd caught him as he was running out of his office, but we talked long enough for me to learn that he was working the diamond heist and murder case, and that he would fill me in when we met for breakfast the following morning. I've always been sensitive to the prohibition placed upon George when discussing an ongoing case, and never pressed for more information than he was allowed to give. But I also knew that he'd do his best to satisfy my natural curiosity without exceeding his professional boundaries.

I was tempted to ask Mr. Kim a number of questions that I'd formulated since hearing about the crime, but didn't want to appear insensitive. It turned out my reticence was unnecessary. He proceeded to speak at length about his relationship with his slain business partner and friend. As he did, I recalled that the articles I'd read about the theft and murder had mentioned that Yang had been suspected of funneling money to terrorists. Naturally I wasn't about to raise that issue, but I did eventually ask, "Have you ever seen the diamond, Mr. Kim?"

He managed a smile. "Oh, yes, Walter showed it to me shortly after he'd purchased it at auction at Sotheby's. It was — how can I say it? — it was *among* the most beautiful things I've ever seen." He glanced in Betty's direction, and she smiled. "It had been put up for sale by Petra Diamonds."

"It was a blue diamond?" filmmaker Gerald Wilson asked.

Kim nodded.

"The rarest of all diamonds," Jacob Walthrop pronounced.

"That's not quite accurate," Betty, Kim's companion, said. "Red diamonds are the rarest."

"Is that so?" Walthrop said, obviously piqued at having been corrected.

"Betty is right," Kim said. "But red or blue, any diamond of that size and purity is to be treasured."

"What did your friend Yang intend to do with it?" Madge Wilson asked.

Kim shrugged. "Keep it until its value had increased to the point that he could sell it again on the open market for a handsome profit."

"It certainly wasn't a secret when he bought it at Sotheby's," Tom Craig said. "I read about it in the local press."

"Which meant that whoever stole it knew exactly where to look," the baroness opined.

"Obviously," said Gerald Wilson.

"Where did Mr. Yang keep it?" I asked.

"He moved it several times to thwart would-be thieves. However, it was taken from a vault at his home," Kim replied. "A very secure one."

"Not secure enough," Jacob Walthrop offered. The baroness nudged him with her foot.

"That's obvious, too," Wilson said through a sigh. He was a young man who wasn't shy about throwing verbal jabs.

A sudden clap of thunder caused everyone to look up.

"Time to move inside," Craig suggested. He glanced at his watch and muttered, "I wonder what's keeping him."

We made it through the terrace doors just moments before the skies opened and rain came down in sheets. Craig led us to the large dining room, where the table was elaborately set with heavy crystal and flatware on a starched white tablecloth. Tall tapered candles in gleaming silver holders cast a warm, welcoming glow over the scene. Two household servants stood ready to serve: the young woman who'd delivered my drink and an older, tuxedoed gentleman with the quintessential bearing of an English manservant from central casting.

As we found our places, the door chimes sounded.

"Ah, that must be our missing party," Craig said, his face brightening as he headed for the front door.

At first, I was certain that I was confused. No, it couldn't be. But it was. Craig returned to the dining room followed by Michael Haggerty.

I'd first met Michael years ago at Brittany Bay, on the island of Jamaica. I'd flown there at the urging of a friend, Antoinette Farnsworth, who'd written me that she feared for her life. Unfortunately I wasn't able to prevent her death, and spent the ensuing days attempting to solve her murder. Michael, a charming Irish rogue with a brogue, kept getting in the way of my investigation. Still, he had proved helpful with the final resolution of the case.

We'd crossed paths after that on other occasions. By then, I'd learned what Michael truly did for a living: He'd been a secret agent for British intelligence, although he was officially retired when we met. But he always seemed to be called back into service by MI6 for assignments that demanded his particular skills and experience, including being a master at assuming different identities depending upon the circumstances. It had been a few years since we'd last touched base, and to say that I was surprised to see him come through the door is an understatement.

"Ladies and gentlemen," Tom Craig announced, "may I introduce our better-late-than-never and final guest for the evening, Mr. Wendell Jones."

Haggerty met my quizzical expression with a broad, charming smile and raised eyebrows. I'd seen that look before. It said, *Don't ask questions; I'll explain later.*

After everyone had been introduced to "Wendell," aka Michael, we took our seats, and the first course — a delicate shrimp and tomato bisque — was served. Michael, who is never at a loss for words, immediately threw himself into the conversation, charming everyone with tales of his life as a Dublin antiques dealer specializing in old theatrical and motion picture posters and handbills. I had little to say; I was still taken aback by his appearance and the identity he was using.

"Jessica and I have met before," Haggerty said. He flashed me his most winning smile. "In Dublin, wasn't it, Jessica?"

"I — I, ah, believe it was, Mr. Jones."

"The world gets smaller with every passing year," he said. "It is wonderful to see you again. You haven't aged a day."

"But I have aged a few years," I said. "You look the same, Mich— Mr. Jones."

"You've always been such a flatterer," he said. "And please call me Wendell." He turned away to respond to something Baroness Walthrop had said about the political situation in Ireland.

As the dinner wore on, I had the feeling that my publisher was trying to sort out my previous relationship with Haggerty. He cornered me in the library, where after-dinner drinks were being served.

"I'm sure you're wondering about Mr. Jones, Jessica," he said in a low voice.

"You're adept at reading thoughts,

Thomas."

"Interesting that you two have met before. I assume therefore that you are aware that his real name is —"

"Michael Haggerty," I filled in.

"Yes, of course. You would know that." His tone became even more conspiratorial. "You do know that he's been a special agent for MI6."

I nodded.

"I've signed him up to write a book for us about his remarkable undercover career."

"Really? That's wonderful."

"Yes. He tells me that he's retired from the intelligence service, gave up the life of chasing spooks and other assorted bad types around the globe."

"Fascinating," I said, "but why the false name tonight and the made-up background?"

He now spoke in a whisper. "Between you and me, Jessica, he's been called back to duty to work one last, very big case, something to do with terrorists and the like. He asked that his real name not be used tonight, and, of course, I obliged. Service to country and all that." He gave me a wink.

"I see," I said. "Thanks for sharing it with me. At least I now know that I'm not hallucinating."

He laughed, and we joined the others.

I found a seat next to Betty LeClair and complimented her on her beautiful dress and its unusual color.

"Thank you," she said, smoothing the fabric with a delicate hand. "It's a special silk that was made for me."

"Well, it's lovely," I said, "although I'm sure that everything looks good on you. You carry yourself like a model. Have you ever modeled?"

"I have," she said, showing a rare smile.

Mr. Kim was more forthcoming. "Betty was a top fashion model in Paris," he said with understandable pride.

"I don't doubt it," I said. "Did you enjoy modeling?"

"Not really. It is so — well, I suppose you could say I found it boring."

I laughed. "Too much waiting around for the photographers to set everything up."

"Yes, that is exactly right. Good fashion photographers work so slowly."

Jacob Walthrop joined us, a large snifter of Cognac in his hand. "I understand you're returning to the States on the *Queen Mary*, Mrs. Fletcher," he said.

"That's right. I'm really looking forward to it."

"When do you leave?" Haggerty asked.

"This coming Saturday. From Southampton."

"Jacob and I crossed on it shortly after it was commissioned," Baroness Walthrop said. "It's a floating palace, everything top-drawer."

"You're whetting my appetite even more," I said.

"What an interesting coincidence," Kim Chin-Hwa said. "I'll be on the ship with you."

"You will? That's wonderful," I replied.

"Yes," he said. "Betty and I and a few of my business associates will be fellow passengers. I trust that we'll have a chance to get to know each other better before we arrive in Manhattan."

"Actually we'll be docking in Brooklyn," I said, "but Brooklyn and Manhattan are both parts of New York City after all. Brooklyn is just a different borough."

"Strange. On my last crossing, the *QE Two* docked in Manhattan."

"Yes," I said, "but the *Queen Mary* is too big for the berths on Manhattan's West Side. It would stick out too far into the Hudson River."

"Brooklyn is not too far from Manhattan, as I understand."

"Just a short hop across a river," I said,

neglecting to mention that New York City traffic could make the trip more like a long haul than a short hop.

An hour later, guests started to depart, which pleased me. Although I'd gotten some sleep on the plane, I was still suffering from jet lag; the vision of climbing into my bed at the Grosvenor Square Hotel exerted a powerful pull.

Michael Haggerty suggested that we share a taxi, but I declined. As much as I was fond of him and admired his work as an under-cover agent — and as much as I appreciated all the help he'd provided me in certain murder cases in which I'd unfortunately, and inadvertently, found myself immersed — I wasn't eager to extend this most recent encounter. Michael can be as long-winded as he is charming, and I knew any extension of the evening would tax my weary bones.

"It was good seeing you again, Mr. Jones," I said with a twinkle.

"Thank you for keeping my secret, Jessica. You see —"

"I know — you're working a case *and* writing a book for Tom Craig."

"You approve?"

"About the case or the book?"

"Either, or both."

"You don't need my approval," I said.

"Oh, but I do."

"Then you have it. But for now, good night. I'm sure we'll be bumping into each other again."

"It's my most treasured hope," he said as he kissed me on the cheek, and was gone.

Tom Craig called for a taxi and waited with me by the front door. The rain had abated somewhat; it was now a quintessential London mist that created eerie patterns in the glow of the streetlights.

"Other plans while here in London?" he asked.

"A few," I said. "Dinner was lovely. Please give my best to your wife."

"I certainly shall, provided she hasn't become a snack for some ravenous lion."

The square black London cab arrived, and Craig walked me to it holding an umbrella, or "brolly" in British-speak, over my head. He leaned through the open door and said, "If you should run across a large blue diamond in your travels, please give me first crack at it."

I laughed along with him. Outlandish, unrealistic quips are often so amusing.

CHAPTER THREE

I was asleep minutes after my head hit the pillow in my suite at the hotel on Grosvenor Square. I awoke at seven the following morning — two a.m. back in Cabot Cove — and despite the sleep I was groggy. It took a long shower to clear my head.

I glanced out the window and saw that the storms of the previous night had passed and that the sun was shining brightly. Buoyed by the promise of fair weather, I dressed and headed downstairs to meet George in the hotel's dining room. He was already there when I arrived, and had secured a prime table next to a window.

Handsome as ever, he was wearing what is almost a uniform for him — Harris Tweed jacket with leather elbow patches, blue button-down shirt, muted maroon tie, tan slacks with a razor crease, and low brown boots polished to a mirror finish. Wrapped in that outfit was a six-foot-four-inch-tall man with eyes the color of Granny Smith apples, rugged but not coarse features, and brown hair with just the right touch of gray at the temples.

"Hello," I said as he stood and kissed my cheek.

"Hello to you," he said, pulling out my chair for me. "Well rested?"

"Not really. My circadian rhythms are still adjusting."

"You'd never know it by looking at you."

"Thank you, sir. I've reached an age where I don't casually dismiss compliments. Speaking of compliments, you appear to have lost a year or two."

"Must be the lovely weather we're having this morning in London, aided by the flattering lighting in this room. But I agree with you about graciously accepting compliments. I accept, and thank you."

He smiled broadly, and so did I. It was wonderful being there with him, as it always was when we got to see each other after a long absence. "Maybe this diamond robbery and murder has brought out the boy in you," I said.

He rolled his eyes and grinned. "It certainly has," he said. "I'm sure you've seen the headlines in the tabloids."

"Just a fleeting glance here in London,

36

but I read fairly detailed accounts back home. I had a bit of an inside look at the case last night."

"Oh? How so?"

"One of my fellow dinner guests was a partner of the man who was killed during the robbery."

"Kim Chin-Hwa?"

"Yes."

"What was *he* doing there at your dinner party?" George asked, his eyes wider.

"The host was my publisher, Tom Craig. He told me that Mr. Kim is considering investing in Tom's plan to take over a small publishing house that's up for sale. You're obviously aware of Mr. Kim's connection with the victim."

"Very aware, indeed. I questioned him at length shortly after it happened."

"And?"

"He has an airtight alibi, which doesn't mean he wasn't involved from a distance."

I tipped my head. "Is that the theory you're operating on, that he might have been involved in some indirect way?"

"Just one of many possible theories, Jessica."

We gave our order to the waiter: an English muffin and a bowl of fruit for me, fried eggs, tomato, and bacon for George.

"You were saying," I said after the waiter had left the table.

"Oh, yes. Kim Chin-Hwa. I don't know if you're aware that the victim, Walter Soon Yang, has been suspected for some time of funneling money to the Maoist Communist Party of India and other terrorist groups."

"It was in the papers I read back home. Any truth to it?"

George shrugged. "All I know is what I hear. The intelligence chaps are reportedly looking into it, but I haven't been informed of any progress on their end. Mr. Kim's name has also come up in that regard."

"Did you know he'll be on the *QM Two* with me?"

His expression was a meld of exasperation and concern. "Yes. We're aware of that at the Yard."

"I hadn't known, of course, when I first met him at dinner," I explained. "He announced it toward the end of the evening. He's traveling with some business associates, he said, and a beautiful young Eurasian woman who was his companion last evening."

"Ms. LeClair."

"You've spoken with her, too?"

"We have. She was at Mr. Kim's home when we went to interview him. The back-

38

ground check we ran on everyone, including Ms. LeClair, turned up some interesting facts about her. She was born in Shanghai, father a French soldier-of-fortune type, off fighting for one cause or another until one of those causes killed him. Mother was Chinese, moved to Paris with her daughter when she was nine years old. It seems the mother got herself involved in a smuggling operation that was broken by French authorities. She was convicted and sentenced to a lengthy incarceration, although she didn't last long. Died in her cell a year or two into her confinement. The daughter, Ms. LeClair, was raised by a distant relative of her father and went on to a successful modeling career, high fashion, that sort of thing."

"You learned quite a bit about her."

"There's more. More recently she's achieved a reputation for herself as a party girl."

"A girl who likes parties?"

He laughed. "No, hardly that. She evidently uses her exotic good looks to entice wealthy men into relationships. A few years ago one of these men, who was well into his eighties, changed his will six months after meeting her, leaving a hefty portion of his estate to her. A son challenged it in court, but the will was ruled valid."

"Do you think that Mr. Kim is one of those men who've been seduced by her looks and charm?"

"It's not out of the realm of possibility, although I doubt she needs his money now that she's an heiress."

"Some people are never satisfied with how much money they have," I said.

"True. We're keeping an eye on her, too, but I'd wager that Kim has a motive in Yang's murder. We just haven't uncovered it yet."

Our breakfasts were served, and conversation ceased for the moment. One of many things I love about London — all of England for that matter — is the homemade jams and jellies, which I liberally applied to my muffin.

I broke the silence with, "How was Mr. Yang killed, George?"

"He was found on the floor of what you might call his library. At least it contained walls of books. It appeared he'd been beaten, although the official cause of death was strangulation. He'd evidently put up a struggle, but the room was relatively intact aside from the door to a large wall safe left swinging open."

"Where he kept the diamond."

"Precisely."

"I wonder . . ."

His raised eyebrows invited me to continue.

"I was just wondering why the safe would have been open. According to Mr. Kim, it was a very secure safe."

"It was of a type that would have made it extremely difficult for the thieves to break into. Too heavy to have been removed from the wall and carried away, although I've been involved in cases where heavier safes have been removed by particularly muscular thieves. The assumption, of course, is that either the thieves forced Mr. Yang to open the safe, or he had already opened it and was enjoying fondling his precious gemstone when the thieves entered, which we understand he was wont to do. I rather favor the latter theory."

"Why?"

"A man can't give directions to open a safe while he's being strangled. Or call for help. I think the thieves killed him quickly and then walked off with the goods."

"Perfect timing, wouldn't you say, knowing when he'd removed the diamond from the safe?"

"Raising the possibility that someone from within Mr. Yang's inner circle knew when he would have the rock in his hands and alerted the thieves to that moment."

George fell silent as he finished what was left of his breakfast.

"Am I asking too many questions?" I asked.

"No, luv, not at all. I don't have any problem sharing this with you. I trust your discretion."

"I appreciate that, George. I assume the diamond was insured."

"Oh, yes, for its full value."

"The estate will want to collect the insurance money, of course. Do you know who his heirs are?"

"Not yet. There's a question of a missing will, allegedly made later than the one on file with his solicitor. There's also some confusion about whether his various business entities might be involved in ownership of the diamond. The insurance chaps have their hands full trying to sort things out."

"I would think that a man of his wealth would have a sizable household and professional staff."

"We questioned them all. No one claims to have heard or seen anything that night. A few of the household help were off for the evening."

"No security?" I asked, incredulity in my tone.

"He had four security men assigned to the house. They worked in shifts. The bloke on duty the night of the robbery — a formidable fellow with a neck the size of my waist — claims that his boss informed him earlier that evening that he was not to be disturbed. He assumed that Mr. Yang was entertaining a woman in the library, which he said wasn't unusual. If that's true, his lady friend enjoyed perfume, and plenty of it. The scent lingered in the room. One of our female investigators at the scene said she couldn't identify the name of it but was certain it was expensive."

"How did the thieves enter the house?" I asked.

"A back door leading into the kitchen."

"No alarms, no sirens going off, no video cameras?"

"Oh, yes, the place was nicely alarmed. But the system had been deactivated."

"Convenient," I said, my expression of disbelief overt enough to cause him to laugh.

"You have the genes of a top-shelf criminal investigator, Jessica. Murder brings out the best in you."

"I'm not sure that's a good thing," I said,

"but enough of diamonds and murder. Tell me everything that's been happening in your personal life since the last time we were together."

We left the restaurant an hour later and went to the curb, where a line of taxis waited.

"I'm always impressed with how easily the conversation flows between us," he commented. "I'm sure we could have stayed at the table for the rest of the day."

"I always love our conversations."

"It says something about us, Jessica."

"And what might that be?"

"It says that — well, it says that we're always comfortable together. I observe too many couples these days who sit in restaurants and have absolutely nothing to say to each other except 'Please pass the salt,' or 'I wish you wouldn't chew with your mouth open.' "

"Well," I said, "I don't use much salt, and neither of us chews with an open mouth."

"I think you're evading the point I was trying to make."

"I'm sorry. I suppose I was. Will I see you again before I go to Southampton on Saturday?"

"I'll make certain of it. I'm tied up tonight

and all day tomorrow. Dinner tomorrow night?"

"Love it."

We embraced, and I watched him climb into the back of the next available cab and ride off. It was always so wonderful to see him — and equally sad when he went away.

CHAPTER FOUR

I learned years ago from a veteran world traveler that the first things you pack when taking a trip are plastic bags of various sizes, which I've been doing ever since. The second item on my packing list is comfortable walking shoes. This is especially important when visiting London because no other city in this world that I know of is so conducive to walking. Well, Paris is wonderful, too, and New York City. But there's something about London that especially appeals to me, and I try to take in as much as possible whenever I'm there.

Of course, my penchant for walking means spending less time in London's fabled taxis. London cabs and their drivers are the best in the world. The boxlike vehicles provide spacious comfort for passengers, and the consummate professionals who drive them spend three to five years preparing for the stringent exams they must take in order to earn a license. They immerse themselves during those years in learning the location of thousands of buildings, hotels, and restaurants, as well as myriad out-of-the-way destinations their customers throw at them; they tool around the sprawling city on motorbikes until they know London cold and can prove it to their examiners.

But on this day, with perfect weather — bright sunshine coupled with a cooling breeze — I was in a walking mood and set off to explore the area around my hotel, Grosvenor Square. I'd done some brushing up on my history before leaving home, particularly the World War II era. Not only is London made for walking; you're surrounded by history with each step you take.

During World War II, Grosvenor Square and its immediate surroundings were home to the headquarters of the U.S. command in Europe, as well as to General Eisenhower's headquarters. Locals called it "Little America." Today, it's the site of the American Embassy, the largest embassy in Britain, with almost six acres of floor space.

I stood outside the embassy and looked up at a gigantic bald eagle on its roof. My guidebook said its wingspan was approximately thirty-five feet, a huge, soaring symbol of my country, the business of which is conducted inside. A stroll through the square itself brought me to William Reid Dick's magnificent bronze sculpture of Franklin Delano Roosevelt. My walk took me as far south as the famed Hyde Park Corner, where I ducked into the Four Seasons Hotel for a light lunch. From there I headed northwest to Berkeley Square, home to some of London's wealthiest families, and proceeded back to my hotel to kick off my shoes and rest my tired feet.

I'd asked Tom Craig during dinner to recommend a play for me to see while in town. London's vibrant and easily accessible theater scene is inevitably thought-provoking, and I always try to catch a few shows, often seeing them before they transition to Broadway. He had suggested the new revival of Ibsen's *A Doll's House* that had been set in Edwardian England rather than in Ibsen's Norway. I'm a fan of Ibsen, and I've always liked that particular work. Tom also had said that its focus on political scandal had special meaning in its new English setting because of the current uproar over members of the British parliament obscenely padding their expense accounts.

I was about to call the concierge to see if tickets were available when the phone rang.

It was George.

"Jessica," he said, "bad news. I've been called out of town to follow up on a lead in the diamond case. I'm afraid I'm going to have to cancel dinner tomorrow night. I feel terrible bollixing up your plans."

"Oh, that's a shame, George, but I certainly understand. A promising lead?"

"Hard to know at this juncture, but of course every lead must be followed, promising or not."

"Of course. When do you think you'll be back?"

"I don't know that either; hopefully before you head for Southampton. When is that?"

"Saturday morning."

"I'll do my best to be back before then."

"I know you will. Be safe."

"You, too, Jessica."

We'd no sooner ended the conversation than the phone rang again.

"Is this the famous Jessica Fletcher?"

I knew immediately that it was Michael Haggerty.

"Hello, Michael."

"You knew I'd be calling."

"I recognized your voice."

"I'll have to work harder at disguising it, maybe develop a Maine accent like yours."

"Somehow, I don't think you could muster

a Down East accent. Why are you calling, Michael?"

"Jessica, why this standoffish tone? It was wonderful seeing you last night."

"I'm sorry, Michael. I don't mean to be standoffish. I've just come back from a long walk and —"

"I know, I know — your feet hurt."

"Well, as a matter of fact, yes." What I didn't say was that my disappointment at not being able to see George again was probably coloring my tone of voice.

"A good soak in cold water and you'll be tip-top in no time."

"I beg your pardon."

"Mother Haggerty's recipe for ailing tootsies. Look, Jessica, I really would like to see you again while you're in London. Do you have plans for this evening?"

"No, I — I thought I'd take in some theater."

"A musical?"

"No. As a matter of fact —"

"There isn't any better theater in London than the Ivy."

I knew that he was referring to the celebrity-driven restaurant that has long been a favorite of London's theatrical and motion picture crowd. I'd been there before as the guest of an actress friend and enjoyed

50

it very much.

"We'll see all the stars in London's entertainment firmament, but unfortunately you won't be able to prove it to the folks back home. You can't bring a camera to the Ivy," he continued. "Taking pictures there is prohibited. Got to protect the celebs from the paparazzi. Always quite a show, however. How about we have dinner there tonight?"

I couldn't help but laugh. Reservations had to be made at the Ivy weeks, if not months, in advance. He sounded as though we could just pop in and have our choice of tables. I mentioned this.

"Not to worry, Jessica. I'm a charter member of the Club at the Ivy. You can do theater any night, but an invitation to the Ivy comes along only now and then." He broke into song: *". . . and we will cling together like the ivy."*

I sighed.

"A popular song of yesteryear, Jessica; that's where the Ivy got its name. They say a table at the Ivy is the most sought-after piece of furniture in all of London, and the sticky toffee pudding with vanilla ice cream is divine, worthy of sainthood."

"I get your point, Michael."

He turned serious. "Jessica," he said, "it's really important that I spend some time

51

with you. I have a favor to ask."

"Which is?"

"Not on the phone," he replied, his voice dropping.

"Michael, I —"

"Swing by to pick you up at nine? I know that's late, but the action really doesn't get started until then. The Ivy. My treat. Think of all the famous folks you'll see prancing about in their thickest makeup and latest designer togs."

"All right," I said, laughing.

"Wonderful. We'll have ourselves a deadly time."

"Deadly?"

" 'Deadly.' A *good* time. You've allowed your Irish vocabulary to slip. Be at your hotel at nine sharp. Toodle-oo."

". . . and so there I was, Jessica, trapped between a ruthless gang of drug-smuggling terrorists and a rogue intelligence agent determined to blow me away."

"You obviously escaped your predicament," I said.

"Well, naturally. Here I am, hale and hearty, sitting across the table at the Ivy from a lovely woman who also happens to be one of the world's best crime novelists."

"You've been kissing the Blarney Stone

again," I said. "So, how did you escape?"

"I maneuvered myself so that the terrorists and the rogue agent ended up firing at each other. They killed the agent, but not before he took down two of them. I handled the rest."

"A fascinating story, Michael."

"Do you think I should lead off my memoir with it? Is it strong enough to draw the reader in?"

"Definitely, although that's between you and Tom Craig."

"Nice fellow, isn't he?"

"Very nice. Now, you said that you wanted to ask a favor. I've been waiting all evening to hear what it is."

Dinner at the Ivy with Michael had been enjoyable. The food was excellent, the service good, and the ambience pleasant. Michael had pointed out a few celebrities, none of whose names rang a bell with me, nor were their faces ones I recognized, but I accepted his claim that they were stars in London's entertainment industry. The only problem was that the tables were impossibly close together, ensuring that whatever you said was heard by a dozen others. Michael was apparently aware of that because he said in response to my question, "Let's go to a place where what we say stays between us."

That place was a quiet pub down the alley from the Ivy, where the loudest noise was the thud of darts hitting the board. We nestled in a deserted corner. Michael ordered a lager; I opted for nothing.

"I learned at dinner last night that you're taking the *QM Two* back to the States on Saturday," he said.

"That's right."

"When I heard the news, I thought back to those moments when we worked together to solve a murder. Those were exciting times, weren't they, Jessica?"

"Yes, I suppose they were, although I think 'unfortunate' is a better choice of words."

"Come on, now, my girl; you loved every minute of it."

"We could debate that point, but speaking of points, please get to it. You said you wanted a favor from me."

"Right. You'll be on the ship with the gentleman who was also at dinner, Mr. Kim Chin-Hwa."

"So I understand."

"What I'd like you to do is stay close to him, get him to talk, take in everything, forget nothing, and report back to me."

"You can't be serious, Michael."

"Oh, I am very serious, Jessica. Mr. Kim is — well, I suppose you could say that he's a person of interest to MI6."

"That may be so, but it's nothing to do with me."

"It has to do with the funding of terrorists."

"If that's true — if Mr. Kim is involved in something as terrible as that — then I hope he gets his just rewards. But again, it doesn't concern me."

"Doesn't *concern* you, Jessica? How can you possibly say such a thing? Terrorism concerns every decent, peace-loving person."

"For goodness' sake, Michael, stop twisting my words. I'm not a spy, and not remotely qualified to act like one. It's you and others like you who are trained to do battle with terrorists. Me? I'm just a former English teacher who writes murder mysteries. Besides, this is a working trip for me. I'm sailing on the *QM Two* as a lecturer. When I'm not lecturing, I intend to enjoy my first true vacation in years, my first holiday *without* intrigue. Sorry, but it's out of the question to even think that I'd act as a spy for you."

He fell into an exaggerated pout that I'd

55

seen many times in the past.

"Thank you for a lovely evening, Michael," I said. "The Ivy was wonderful, and as always I enjoyed the stories of your most recent escapades. But I think it's time for me to get back to the hotel."

He downed what was left of his lager, stood, and held the back of my chair. "I am forever at your service, Jessica."

My eyes rolled up to the ceiling, but I said nothing.

We found a taxi waiting outside the Ivy and climbed in the spacious rear compartment.

"Where to, sir?" the driver asked.

"Dukes Hotel," Michael instructed.

"I'm staying at the Grosvenor Square," I said.

"I know that, Jessica. Trust me."

We pulled into the cul-de-sac in front of Dukes, a small jewel of a hotel on St. James's Place. Michael paid the driver and hustled me into the lobby.

"Michael!" I said loud enough for a desk clerk to turn to us. "What are we doing here?"

"Just a necessary precaution, Jessica."

We stood in the lobby and looked out at the cul-de-sac where another taxi pulled in. A heavyset man with a long, bushy beard and wearing a long, black raincoat and yarmulke paid the driver, stepped away from the cab, and stood in the shadows, his attention fixed on the hotel entrance. I felt Michael tense.

"Do you know him?" I asked.

"Yeah. It's Uri."

"Uri?"

"One of Israel's undercover intelligence agents."

"He seems very much on top of the covers," I said.

"Come on," Michael said, taking my hand and leading me to a service entrance at the rear of the hotel. We exited to an alley and hailed a passing taxi that took us to Grosvenor Square.

"I had a feeling we were being followed, Jessica," Michael said, squinting at the view through the rear window. "Can't be too careful."

"Why is he following you?"

"Us."

"Us? He can't possibly even know me."

"He does now," he muttered.

Vintage Michael Haggerty.

"Sure you won't change your mind?" he said as we neared the hotel. "About finding out what you can about Mr. Kim?"

"Positive!"

"You wouldn't be alone, Jessica."

The cab pulled up in front of the hotel, and a uniformed bellman held the cab's door open for me.

"What do you mean by that?" I asked. "About not being alone?"

"I'll be there at your side," he said with a wide smile.

"You'll be — ?"

"I've decided to join you on your voyage, Jessica. Of course, it will be Wendell Jones, Dublin antiques dealer, making the crossing, but we'll have our little secret to share."

The driver glanced back to see if either of us was interested in exiting.

"All I can say, Michael, is —"

He placed his index finger on my lips.

"It will be a joy sailing with you, Jessica Fletcher, like old times. Go get your beauty rest, and don't forget to buy patches for seasickness. The Atlantic can get rough this time of year — v-e-r-y rough. See you in Southampton."

CHAPTER FIVE

My final day in London proved to be somewhat disappointing. I received a call from George Sutherland, who said that the lead he was following would necessitate his being out of town for at least another two days. That meant, of course, that we wouldn't see each other again before I set sail from Southampton.

After exchanging regrets that getting together wasn't in the cards, I asked whether there was anything new in the case.

"I'll know more tomorrow," he said, "although the ties the victim is suspected of having with terrorist groups are coming into focus. According to what I hear, your U.S. intelligence blokes are taking a more active role in the investigation. The Israelis, too."

I immediately thought of the fellow who'd followed Michael and me the previous evening. Michael had said Uri was an Israeli spy. I was going to mention it, but George sounded rushed. I didn't want to waste our call trying to make sense of that episode. Nor did I bring up Michael Haggerty's sudden reemergence into my life, both at the dinner party and in his last-minute decision — was it last-minute? — to book passage on the *QM2.*

"I suppose all that's left to say, Jessica, is bon voyage. I regret not getting back to see you off. Were I in London, I'd have driven you to Southampton."

"I know you would have, George, but the good folks at Cunard offered a car service, a perk of my being a lecturer on the ship. That'll work fine."

"Have a pleasant crossing, lass, and be in touch when you arrive safely home."

Faced with a day without plans, I tried to shake off my sadness at not seeing George again by setting out on another round of sightseeing. I don't know how far I walked — it must have been miles — and happily headed back to my hotel in late afternoon, both well exercised and in a lighter mood. I was a block away when I stopped to admire an exquisite sterling silver tea set in a shop window. A reflection in the glass caught my eye; it was a figure across the street attempting to read the *Observer. Odd,* I thought, *to be standing on a breezy street with a broad-*

*sheet newspaper opened wide, trying to keep
the wind from sending it sailing.* Then, a current of air tore the paper from his hands to
reveal the Israeli intelligence agent Uri. I
looked around for Michael Haggerty. Surely
Uri wouldn't be following me. But there
was no sign of my old friend from MI6.

I considered crossing the street to introduce myself, but thought better of it. I'd
once taken an FBI-sponsored course in
surveillance techniques. If he was really following me, Uri would have flunked. But
while I found his clumsy presence almost
amusing, there was also an unsettling aspect
to it.

I walked the rest of the way to the hotel
and stopped to chat with the doorman, one
of several whose top hat and tails, gentlemanly demeanor, and loud, shrill whistles
when luring a taxi extended the hotel's
charm to the outdoors. I took advantage of
standing with him and looked back to where
I'd seen Uri, who was still trying to tame
his newspaper.

"Do you know that gentleman?" I asked
the doorman.

"No, ma'am, although he has been about
today. He's walked past quite a few times.
Is he bothering you?"

"Bothering me? Oh, no, not at all — just

curious. Thank you."

My intention upon reaching my suite was to draw a hot bath and enjoy a luxurious soak. But there were two phone messages awaiting me, one from Seth Hazlitt in Cabot Cove, the other from Tom Craig. I called Seth and caught him as he was leaving his office for lunch. It was noon back home, five o'clock London time.

"Just wanted to wish you a pleasant and safe voyage, Jessica," he said.

"Thank you."

"I assume you've spent some time with George. Hope you gave your Scotland Yard friend my regards."

"A hurried breakfast was all the time we had, I'm afraid. He's away working the diamond theft case."

"From what I hear, he'll be kept busy."

"Oh? Was there more about it in the news?"

"According to the BBC, there's been another robbery of precious gems, a lot of 'em, as a matter of fact." Seth is fond of tuning in to the BBC late at night on an elaborate shortwave radio he has in his bedroom. "Seems a jewelry store somewhere in London was robbed last evening."

"I hadn't heard."

"Whoever did it walked away with a bagful of diamonds worth a million or more. That's all I know."

"I'm sure the newspapers here will have something about it, Seth."

"I imagine so. You all right, Jessica?"

"Yes, I'm fine. Why do you ask?"

"Oh, it's just that whenever you're off somewhere and some sort a' crimes are taking place, you too often end up in the middle of things."

I laughed. "Seth," I said, "in the first place, that sort of thing is past tense with me. Second, there is no earthly reason that I'd become involved with these robberies here in London. And third —"

"Just thinkin' out loud," he said, returning my laugh. "You take care, Jessica, and send a postcard."

"Hard to do in the middle of the Atlantic," I said.

"Have yourself a pleasant crossing."

"If the captain were here, he'd be proud of you. Most people call it a cruise."

"Whatever they call it, enjoy it, give a good lecture, and don't stray too close to the railings. Don't want to hear you fell overboard."

That dire warning ended our conversation.

I reached my British publisher at his office.

"Do you know where Michael Haggerty is?" Tom asked.

"You mean Wendell Jones?" I said, mirth in my voice.

"Whatever he calls himself. I've been trying to locate him all day — a contractual matter having to do with his book."

"I have no idea where he might be, Tom, although it's possible he's in Southampton."

"Why would he be there?"

"To catch the *Queen Mary Two*."

"He's on your trip?"

"So he told me."

"Well, that's a bit of interesting news. Now, I don't mean to pry, but are you and he — well, are you and he . . . ?"

"Are you suggesting that — ?"

"No, no, just a thought. You said you've known him for years. Never mind me. If you see him, please tell him I need to speak with him as quickly as possible."

"I'll be happy to relay your message — if I see him," I said stiffly. "With more than twenty-five hundred passengers aboard, there's a good chance I may miss him."

"Have a wonderful trip."

"Thank you. I'm sure I will."

Which had been my intention all along.

When I accepted Cunard's invitation to lecture on the crossing, I viewed it as a chance to get away from the rigors of writing and the grind of everyday life — no telephones, no e-mails to answer (although I would check mine a few times during the trip), and no pressure to turn out pages for a book every day. I recalled with such fondness those trips on the now mothballed *QE2*, speaking to a theater filled with interested men and women, signing my books for them in the ship's well-stocked bookstore, and interacting with them at meals and on the decks when I wasn't at the podium. Mostly I remembered all the downtime I enjoyed during those six days at sea, the salt air tickling my nostrils, brisk walks around the ship on the exercise deck (five circuits equaled a mile on that ship), a quiet glass of wine on my stateroom balcony while watching the sun set on the horizon, sleeping as late as I wanted, and getting in plenty of reading for pleasure. In other words, six days of true relaxation despite my obligation to deliver three forty-five-minute lectures.

Of course, I hadn't planned on Michael Haggerty showing up and sharing my voyage, nor had I anticipated that the business partner of a man who'd been murdered while his precious blue diamond was being stolen would also be aboard.

But those surprises wouldn't get in the way of my enjoyment of the crossing.
I simply wouldn't let them.

CHAPTER SIX

First Day at Sea

My driver navigated the maze of streets leading to where the *Queen Mary 2* was docked in Southampton, the ship's distinctive red and black funnels rising imposingly into the crystal clear blue sky. As we drew closer, the ship's immense size became increasingly apparent. It was, I knew, the world's longest passenger vessel, 1,132 feet in length, longer than the Eiffel Tower is tall; it would stretch the length of four blocks on Manhattan's Fifth Avenue.

"She's a beauty, isn't she?" my driver said as we pulled up in front of the sprawling terminal.

"She certainly is. I can't wait to get on board."

The driver helped deliver my luggage to a porter, wished me a pleasant voyage, and drove off, leaving me to enter the huge terminal, where I was handed a card indicating the section in which I was to wait. The place was chockablock with passengers. I knew the ship accommodated 2,620 passengers from having read the literature that had been sent me, and that this particular crossing was sold out. That meant that there were probably 2,619 other souls with me in that building, all happily anticipating their trip.

I scanned the room for Michael Haggerty but didn't see him, nor did I see Kim Chin-Hwa and the beautiful Betty LeClair. It wasn't unexpected with so many passengers waiting to board. Many were undoubtedly already in their staterooms. I sat down to wait, wondering how many hours it would be, but the process was surprisingly quick and smooth.

Fifteen minutes later, I was called to a string of positions where my photo was taken, and I was issued a special charge card to use when accessing and paying for the ship's amenities not included in the basic fare, including the Canyon Ranch Spa, which I fully intended to explore. As a lecturer, my trip was compliments of Cunard, but all incidentals were my responsibility.

With that bit of logistics out of the way, I walked a long, twisting gangplank up to the ship and was greeted by a line of sharply dressed young crew members, one of whom directed me to my stateroom. But first I paused for one of the shipboard photographers to snap my picture. Every arriving passenger was photographed, the printed results to be displayed and for sale in the ship's photo gallery.

My stateroom on Deck Eleven was large and airy. Glass doors led to the balcony with two lounge chairs and a table. Waiting for me in the cabin were a bucket of chilled champagne, chocolate-covered strawberries, and two notes: One was from the captain welcoming me aboard the *QM2;* the second was from the ship's recreation director, informing me of a five-thirty cocktail party for lecturers in the Commodore Club.

My luggage had already been delivered; how they managed to do that so fast was beyond me. I'd started to unpack when there was a knock on my door. I opened it to be face-to-face with a handsome young man in uniform.

"Mrs. Fletcher?" he said.

"Yes."

"I'm here to help unpack your luggage, madam."

"Oh, that won't be necessary," I said, "but thank you. I'm an old hand at unpacking when I travel."

He showed me where my life preserver was located; I'd have to take it with me for the safety drill that was coming up shortly.

"Thank you," I said.

"My pleasure, madam. I am Rupesh, your cabin steward. If there is anything you need, please call me." He pointed to the phone and gave me his extension.

"I'll do that," I said. "Thanks again."

He bowed and left. But the minute he was gone, his name registered with me. Rupesh! Maniram Chatterjee's cousin?

I opened the door and beckoned to him when he emerged from the cabin adjacent to mine. "Rupesh," I said.

"Yes, madam?"

"Do you happen to have cousins living in Cabot Cove, Maine? Maniram and Hita Chatterjee?"

His large black eyes opened wide, and he broke into a smile exposing a set of exquisite white teeth. "You know Maniram and Hita?"

I explained.

"How are they?" he asked, his voice animated, which added to its lilt.

"They're fine," I said. I adopted an exaggerated stern expression. "But they tell me you haven't been keeping in touch with your mother back in India."

His sheepish expression, too, was exaggerated.

"I promised them that I'd remind you to call or write her," I said, lightening my voice. We were going to be together for six days across the Atlantic, and I didn't want him to consider me an old scold.

"I will, Mrs. Fletcher," he said. "I will write her tonight."

"Good. Maybe we can find some time during the crossing to have a chat. From what your cousins tell me, you've lived quite an interesting life."

"It has been — let me just say that I have enjoyed it."

"Which is so important," I said. "Well, I'd better get to the safety drill."

After reporting to the assigned deck, where crew members explained the routine should an emergency arise, I dropped my life preserver back in my cabin and hastened to attend the cocktail party. The ship's staff captain, second-in-command after the captain, was on hand to greet us as we entered the Commodore Club. One of his myriad duties was commanding shipboard security, he told me. His staff of sixteen security officers not only maintained day-to-day security; it could be called upon to act as a seagoing police force should troubles of a criminal nature arise.

Our host was the ship's entertainment director, a charming fellow who'd once been a British TV and film actor. My fellow lecturers made for a pleasant group — an expert on global warming, an astronomer, a college professor who specialized in rare plants, and a musical duo, a man and woman who performed historic British sea shanties and songs of the sea. I learned that my first lecture was scheduled for eleven o'clock the next morning in "Illuminations," the *QM2*'s very own floating planetarium. An actual working planetarium on an ocean liner. What would they think of next?

I returned to my stateroom just as the ship was beginning to pull away from the dock, stood on my balcony with a flute of champagne, and watched as the dock became smaller and we headed for the open sea. I felt at peace with the world at that moment. Any tension I'd experienced over the past few weeks seemed to vanish immediately, blown away in the bracing breeze that mussed my hair. The champagne's bubbles tickled my nose and caused me to laugh.

An hour later, dressed to reflect that evening's semi-formal dress code, I made my way to Deck Seven, where the Princess

Grill was located, at the rear of the ship —
no, make that the "stern." I reminded myself
that I'd better get comfortable using nautical terms.

One of the grill's hosts escorted me to a
table against a large window that afforded a
lovely view of the ocean. It was a table for
six, but I noticed it had been set for five. I'd
no sooner been seated than the first of my
dinner companions arrived. He was a tall,
handsome man whom I judged to be in his
late seventies or early eighties. His face,
tanned and quite wrinkled, was that of a
man who'd spent much of his life outdoors.
He wore a blue, double-breasted blazer with
brass buttons, white slacks, and a bright
white shirt open at the throat.

"Hello," I said as he came around to a
chair next to me.

"Hello to you," he said in a deep voice
tinged with gravel. He sat in the chair the
host held out for him, drew a deep breath,
looked at me, smiled, and extended his
hand. "Harrison Flynn," he said. "Call me
Harry."

"Jessica Fletcher," I replied.

"The mystery writer," he said. "They told
me I'd be having the pleasure of dining with
you."

"I hope it's as pleasurable as they said it

would be."

We looked up at the next arrival, a young British couple. Harry stood and accepted the husband's and wife's outstretched hands, and I greeted them from my chair. They introduced themselves as Richard and Marcia Kensington. Richard had a face that hadn't been creased by too many smiles. Even so, he was nice-looking — sandy hair worn fashionably long for his age, pale blue eyes, and thin lips. Marcia was considerably shorter than her husband. He stood six feet; I doubted she topped five-two. They were dressed more casually than Mr. Flynn and I were, although not blatantly so, Richard in a multicolored pullover sweater over a blue button-down shirt and khaki slacks, Marcia in a loose-fitting white blouse over a dressy pair of jeans. She had a shy smile, which she directed at her husband while he held her chair; I had the feeling that when it came to decision making, Richard ruled the roost.

We fell into an uneasy conversation. Richard Kensington wasn't the talkative type, nor did he seem especially interested in what others had to offer.

"We're on our honeymoon," Marcia said without being prompted.

"Oh! Congratulations," I said. "What a

wonderful honeymoon, crossing the Atlantic on this magnificent ship."

"It isn't all a honeymoon," Richard corrected his wife. "I have business in New York."

"What do you do for a living, Richard?" Harry asked.

"Ah, I work alone." No smile, no apparent pride in his occupation. He seemed to address the white tablecloth, avoiding eye contact.

"Richard is very successful," Marcia said, smiling proudly and touching his arm.

"I believe this gathering of kindred souls calls for champagne," said Flynn. He waved over the wine steward and ordered a bottle of Krug Grande Cuvée. "Not the most expensive," Flynn said, "but a particular favorite of mine. I first tasted it in Hong Kong years ago. I ended up there as a guest of the government for a week; something to do with my papers not passing muster."

"What business were you in?" I asked.

"I'd hardly call it a business," he replied pleasantly. "I was captain on an oil tanker."

"How marvelous! Were you always a ship's captain?" I asked.

"As a matter of fact, I was. I started out with Harland and Wolff in Belfast —"

We were interrupted by the arrival of the

last of our tablemates, Michael Haggerty, dressed in a nicely tailored tuxedo complemented by a muted orange, white, and green striped bow tie and matching cummerbund.

"Good evening, ladies and gents," he said as he took the fifth chair. "A pleasure dining with you. My name's Wendell Jones. And you are?"

Richard and Marcia introduced themselves, Richard without enthusiasm. Harry Flynn eagerly shook Michael's hand and said, "That's a handsome tie you're wearing. Same colors as the Irish flag."

"An astute observation," Haggerty said, his brogue thickening. "That's exactly what it is — orange for the Irish Protestants, green for Irish Catholics, and white in between as a symbol of hope for peace between them. I had the tie and cummerbund specially made in London." He turned to me. "And I know this lovely lady. Jessica Fletcher, my favorite writer of crime novels. We've met on several occasions."

"So we have." I took Michael's hand and said, "And how is the antiques business in Dublin, Mr. Jones?"

Michael flashed his best winning smile. "We'll have none of this 'Mr. Jones' formality, Jessica. But to answer your question, business is splendid. There seems to be an insatiable demand for historic theatrical and motion picture memorabilia." He turned to Mr. Flynn. "Did I hear you worked for Harland and Wolff? Some mighty fine ships were built by them."

Harry beamed. "And I've served on a good number of them."

"Obviously not the *Titanic,*" Haggerty said pleasantly.

"My good fortune to have missed *that* one," Flynn responded with a laugh.

Our champagne was delivered and opened with a flourish by the wine steward. We clinked our flutes. "Here's to a long life and a merry one," Harry said, "a quick death and an easy one. A pretty girl and an honest one, a cold pint — and another one!"

Haggerty and I joined Flynn's hearty laugh. Richard Kensington grimaced. His wife's smile was guarded. Haggerty proclaimed, "Down the hatch!" before he drained his glass.

"Yes, indeed," said Flynn. " 'Down the hatch.' Does anyone know the origin of that phrase?"

No one responded.

"Well," he said, warming to his tale, "cargo ships have large hatches through which the crew can access cargo below. In rough weather, if those hatches aren't securely closed, great amounts of water can pour into the hold, sometimes enough to sink a ship. Crew members began toasting each other with 'Down the hatch,' meaning opening up one's gullet for large amounts of alcohol."

His story was well received by everyone at the table except for Richard, who stifled a yawn and checked his watch.

I noticed that another table in our section of the grill was set but unoccupied. It wasn't until we were halfway through our main courses that its occupants arrived: Mr. Kim Chin-Hwa; his companion, Betty; and two strapping young Asian men who I assumed were his "business associates." They were seated, but Mr. Kim got up almost immediately and came to our table.

"Ah, Mrs. Fletcher," he said, "it is my good fortune to see you again."

"Hello," I said.

"And Mr. Jones," Kim said, acknowledging Haggerty, who stood and shook his hand.

"This is Richard and Marcia Kensington," I told Kim, "and Mr. Harrison Flynn."

Richard simply nodded; his wife smiled. Flynn stood and gave Kim a hearty greeting, offering a large, calloused hand that

78

engulfed Kim's smaller, almost delicate one.

"My apologies for interrupting your dinner," Kim said. "But perhaps we'll have the opportunity to enjoy your company later this evening." He looked at me.

"I'm sure we'll have plenty of opportunities to spend time together over the next six days," I said.

"I look forward to it," Kim said, and rejoined his party.

As the meal progressed, Richard Kensington became more sullen and noncommunicative. He seemed perpetually bored with the conversation, which became quite spirited at times. Michael Haggerty was in his usual ebullient mood, and Harry Flynn reveled in telling stories of his many years at sea, and in relating bits of wisdom.

". . . and so I believe in the old adage that before you criticize someone, you should walk a mile in his shoes. Not only will you be a mile away from the bore, you'll also have his shoes."

Richard wiped his mouth with his napkin and said to his wife, "Let's go."

"No dessert?" Flynn said. "Cunard's sweets are reputed to be the best."

"No, we have things to do," Richard said, standing and pulling his wife's chair out. I looked into her eyes and saw a certain sadness reflected in them, and resignation.

"See you tomorrow night," I said.

Richard nodded, and we watched them walk away.

Flynn leaned close to me and said, "Not especially happy honeymooners, are they?"

"No," I said. "Too bad."

We'd finished our coffee and those fabulous desserts Flynn had raved about, and we were in the process of leaving when Kim Chin-Hwa and his party approached. "Might I suggest, Mrs. Fletcher, that we extend the evening with a nightcap and dancing in the Queens Room?" he said. "I understand the orchestra is excellent."

I shook my head. "Oh, no thank you, Mr. Kim. I don't think that —"

"Why, Jessica, the night is young," Haggerty said. He turned to the others. "We can't have any wet blankets, can we?" He leaned close to me and lowered his voice to barely above a whisper. "Besides, Jess, I need a favor from you."

Flynn weighed in with, "I think a nightcap and a few spins around the dance floor are exactly what we need to work off this wonderful meal."

"I really thought that I would —"

Haggerty took my elbow and said over his shoulder, "We'll see you there." He guided

80

me to the foyer.

"You're incorrigible, Michael," I said.

"As my dear departed mum used to say, I am difficult but adorable. Come on, now. Drinks are on me." He continued to lead me away from the Princess Grill and the others toward the elevators, talking all the way. "It would be a crime to hide alone in your cabin and waste that lovely dress you're wearing, Jessica." He pushed the down button. "What do you call the color? Coral? It's striking on you." The elevator door opened. "Glad to be rid of that sour young couple, huh?" We stepped inside. "I like the old fellow, a real gentleman. . . ."

We reached Deck Three and left the elevator. Music came from the direction of the Queens Room, the ship's grand ballroom. "I bet you still do a wicked two-step, Jessica."

I sighed and followed him into the huge, elegant room, where couples doing the foxtrot already filled the dance floor.

"Tom Craig was looking for you," I said. "Did he reach you before you left?"

"Yes. Thanks for letting me know."

We found a table large enough to accommodate everyone from dinner, including Mr. Kim's party. Minutes later they joined us. His two tough-looking, expressionless associates sat together at a table two removed from ours. After drink orders had been given to the waiter, Harry Flynn addressed me: "Dance, Mrs. Fletcher?"

"Thank you, but no, Mr. Flynn," I said through a smile. "Perhaps another time."

"I look forward to it. And please, it's Harry." He looked at Betty, who turned her face away, then directed his gaze across the dance floor to where several women were seated together. "Excuse me," he said. He crossed the floor, chatted with them for no more than a minute, then extended his arm and led one to the dance floor.

"I like his style," Haggerty said to me.

"I think we, too, will take advantage of the music," Kim said, rising and inviting his lovely companion to join him. Betty, whose long black hair swayed across the back of her tight-fitting red dress, attracted all eyes, male and female, as she and Mr. Kim joined the dancers.

"They make an attractive couple," I said to Michael.

"He's too old for her. And too short. But she's an eyeful. I'll give you that."

"She was a top fashion model in Paris."

"I don't doubt it."

"Mr. Flynn dances beautifully, very smooth."

"Perhaps he plans to apply for a job as a gentleman host."

"He'd make a good one," I replied.

Many ships hire "gentlemen hosts," whose function is to provide dance partners and social companionship for single women traveling alone. They are generally middle-aged men, although some are older. Before they're hired, these immaculately groomed and dressed gentlemen must prove to the management that they are good dancers and conversationalists. They are required to seek out as many unaccompanied women as they can, and work under a stringent set of rules that limit their interaction to dancing and talk — nothing more — although I remember one gentleman host from a previous crossing who'd wooed a wealthy Palm Beach widow. By the time we'd reached our destination, they'd announced wedding plans.

"You said you had a favor to ask me," I said to Michael. "I hope it's not the same one you proposed before."

"What do you think of Mr. Kim?"

I shrugged. "I don't know him sufficiently well to form an opinion. He's nice enough, I suppose."

"He was the partner of the murder victim,

Yang, who owned the Heart of India diamond."

"Yes, I know."

"He seems to have taken a liking to you."

"Don't be silly, Michael."

"No, I mean it. This favor I'm asking of
you — well, it would be a help to me if
you'd get to know him better, flirt a bit,
flatter him, apply that keen insight into
people for which you're known."

"Michael, I already told you —"

"You're a writer, Jessica. Writers are supposed to have a special understanding of
what makes people tick."

"Even writers are allowed a holiday," I
said. "Aside from my lectures, I'm on vacation. If you think that —"

Michael ignored me. "Well, well, well," he
said, eyes on the dance floor. The orchestra
had changed tempos, from the fox-trot it
had been playing to a rumba. "See that?"
he asked, pointing to where Flynn now
danced with a different woman, a statuesque
blonde, whom I'd noticed earlier sitting
next to a thickset woman all in black, her
closely cropped hair the same color as her
outfit.

"As I said, he's quite a dancer."

"And she's quite a beauty."

"She certainly is." *And is well aware of it,* I

thought as the blonde tossed her head back in a laugh, eyes flashing, hips swinging to the Latin tempo.

"I'd like to get to know her better," Haggerty said through a devious grin.

His interest in her didn't surprise me. Michael Haggerty, aka Wendell Jones, had always had an eye for dazzling, self-possessed women.

He smiled, stood, pulled on his lapels, and bounced up and down a few times on his toes. He leaned over and said, "You'll excuse me, of course, Jessica. I think I must cut in on Mr. Flynn."

CHAPTER SEVEN

Michael tapped Harry Flynn on the shoulder, exchanged what appeared to be a few pleasant words, and whisked the blonde out to the middle of the floor. As I watched them, Flynn rejoined me, a satisfied smile on his ruggedly handsome face.

"You look like you're elsewhere," I heard him say.

"What? Oh, just daydreaming."

"Daydreaming is good," he said, sliding into his chair. "People ought to do more of it."

"You dance beautifully," I said.

"Thank you for the compliment," he said, dabbing a drop of perspiration from his upper lip with a neatly folded white handkerchief. "One of the perks of traveling the world," he added. "I've learned from some of the best dancers around the globe. Of course, I was rudely interrupted. Oh, I don't mean to sound as though your friend's cutting in bothered me. All's fair in love and war, especially on a dance floor. Lovely woman. Her name is Jennifer."

"I love her dress and jewelry," I said. "She has very good taste. Did she say what she does for a living?"

"No. Sure you don't want to dance?"

"Not at the moment, but thank you for asking."

"I assure you I'll ask again before we reach the States."

I kept my eye on Haggerty and his dancing partner while chatting with Harry. Kim and Betty were still on the dance floor.

"Do you have family?" I asked.

Harry's face brightened, one foot tapping in rhythm to the band's music. "I certainly do: a splendid daughter named Melanie, the apple of my eye. She's a nurse in New York City, works with the disadvantaged. I've had a few wives, three to be exact, but those marriages didn't last. Not easy for a woman to be married to a man who's always off on a ship somewhere in the world."

"You live in New York?"

"I really haven't lived anywhere since my last divorce. I have a room in my daughter's apartment in New York, but I'm seldom there. Always on the sea, it seems."

"Are you still working?"

He shook his head. "No, but once you've enjoyed traveling the globe, it's hard to break the habit. Some of the freight companies I've worked for give me free passage whenever I ask. Of course, traveling as a passenger on a freighter is a far cry from this magnificent ship, but I must say that I probably enjoy them more. Opulence has never been my style, although I admit that I could get used to it."

"You seem to be very much at home on the *Queen Mary Two*," I said.

"I'm enjoying it. I felt it was time for me to indulge myself before it's too late." A shadow of melancholy crossed his face but was gone as quickly as it had appeared.

"I thought I'd stroll past the casino and test the waters," he said. "Would you like to join me?"

"I think not, Harry. I'm about to call it a night. Besides, I'm not much of a gambler."

"Smart thinking, Jessica. I hate to think of how much I've lost betting on some damn fool thing or other. My first captain used to say that sailors work like horses while at sea, and spend their money like asses ashore. I'm afraid that definition fits me."

I was tempted to suggest that at his age, he should do whatever it was that gave him pleasure, but I wasn't sure he'd take it the right way.

Kim and Betty returned to the table.

"Mrs. Fletcher?" Kim said. "May I have this dance? They're playing 'The Tennessee Waltz,' one of my favorites."

"I was just telling Harry that I'm going to retire for the night," I said, rising.

Kim took my hand. "I insist. Just one dance."

I allowed him to lead me away, hoping Harry wouldn't be insulted that I'd turned him down. But he'd started up a conversation with Betty and didn't seem to notice. Kim was shorter than I, but it didn't pose a problem any more than it had with Betty. He was a graceful dancer, easy to follow.

"You and Betty looked as though you could be professional dancers," I said.

"We've practiced," he said. "Betty has given me ballroom dance lessons."

"What made you interested in dancing?"

"It's a useful skill," he said quietly, swirling me around so that I had to concentrate on my feet instead of his answer.

We glided past where Haggerty and the stunning Jennifer were dancing. Michael smiled at me and winked. I was sure he was pleased, thinking that I'd put myself in a position to find out something constructive from Kim, but that was the last thing on my mind. Not stepping on my partner's feet was more important to me.

Kim executed a final spin and, before I knew what was happening, pressed his hand into my back, tipped me into a quick dip, and smoothly pulled me upright.

"My goodness," I said, laughing. "I haven't done that in a long time."

"Dancing relaxes me," he said as the music came to an end. He took my elbow and said as he steered me off the dance floor, "Do you intend to write about this crossing, and the fact that the partner of the murdered owner of the Heart of India was also a passenger?"

"Heavens, no. Aside from my lectures, I'm aboard purely to relax."

"I'm pleased to hear that. I would hate to think that the unfortunate death of my partner and the theft of his precious diamond would become the basis of popular fiction."

I was taken aback.

Up until then, he'd been a man who laughed easily, his demeanor pleasant and charming. When he said those words, however, his face darkened briefly, his eyes hard, as though to reinforce his point, but his expression immediately melted into its usual affable smile. I wondered if I had caught him in an unguarded moment.

"No offense meant, of course. Thank you for the pleasure of the dance," he said, delivering me to the table, where Harry was preparing to leave.

"So soon?" Kim asked him.

"Off to try my luck at the craps table," Harry replied. "I tried to convince Jessica to accompany me — I've always had better luck with the dice when a beautiful woman is at my side — but she's declined."

"Perhaps another night," I said.

"How about you, Mr. Kim? Care to take your chances with the dice this evening?"

Kim looked at Betty, whose stern face said that the answer would be no. He shook his head at Harry, one eyebrow raised in mock regret.

"Another drink, Mrs. Fletcher?" Kim asked me.

"No, thank you," I said, picking up my purse and making my good-byes. "I'm looking forward to a good night's sleep," I said as Harry and I walked away.

"The motion of the ship will ensure that," Harry said. "The seas are calm right now and the ship's movement always lulls me to sleep. Enjoy it while you can."

"What do you mean?"

"I spoke with one of the young officers

this afternoon. We're in for some rougher weather tomorrow."

We passed the table where Michael was now sitting with the blonde and her friend. I thought I could make my escape without engaging in another conversation with him, but that wasn't to be. Harry and I were almost out of the Queens Room when Michael hustled over. "Are you leaving?" he asked, pulling on my arm.

"Yes, Wendell," said Harry.

"I'd like a word with Jessica if you don't mind."

"Not at all," Harry replied. "Have a pleasant evening. See you both tomorrow, I'm sure."

"Did you find out anything from Kim?" Haggerty asked me once Harry was gone.

"Of course not. We only had one dance. Besides, Michael, I told you I'm not up to getting involved in whatever investigation you're conducting. You and that pretty lady seemed to be hitting it off quite nicely. Why don't you ask her to dance again?"

"Nothing like a few spins around the floor to establish rapport. But she'll be here tomorrow. Have a nightcap with me, Jessica?"

"Not tonight, Michael."

He grinned. "Come on, I'll walk you to

your cabin."

"That's not necessary."

"Oh, indulge me, Jessica, for old times' sake. Let's spend a few minutes on the deck, take in some sea air."

"No, I —"

He lowered his voice to a conspiratorial level. "I'll fill you in on some very juicy information concerning the robbery of that famous diamond and the murder of its owner. Ten minutes — I promise. Then you can head for your cabin. Deal?"

It was no use trying to resist Michael Haggerty. He was very convincing, and to tell the truth, I *was* mildly curious about what he knew of the diamond theft in London and the killing of its owner — maybe a bit more than mildly.

Had Seth Hazlitt been privy to our conversation, he would have shaken his head and given me a long-suffering sigh. He would have said he'd known immediately that I would agree to hear Haggerty's story. My inquisitiveness when it comes to crime is deeply embedded in my psyche, often to my chagrin. I have no idea where it comes from. Had my mother and father possessed that curiosity gene and passed it along to their daughter? Was there something in my DNA, or a section of my brain that released some hormone whenever a crime had been committed in my sphere? Or was it environmental? Had my years in New York City sharpened my need to know about crime and criminals? No, I was exactly the same in Cabot Cove long before I'd moved temporarily to an apartment in Manhattan. Perhaps writing so many murder-mystery novels triggered my fascination with crime from real life to the page — or the other way around. Whatever the answer, it was impossible for me to walk away from Michael Haggerty's tantalizing promise.

We took the elevator up to Deck Seven and stepped out to the deck that skirted the *Queen Mary 2,* where in the daytime joggers and walkers alike take their exercise, and where strollers try to keep out of their way. The ship was making good time, causing a stiff breeze to slap our faces and toss our hair. A few other intrepid people were on the deck, too. I spotted the Kensingtons, who leaned over the railing, peering down into the churning seas below. Richard picked up Marcia and pretended he was going to throw her overboard. She screamed, just as he'd expected, and when he let her down, they laughed and hugged each other. It was nice to see some affection between them.

"Beautiful, isn't it, Jessica?" Haggerty said as we walked toward the stern of the ship, the wind at our backs.

"Very."

"Are you chilly?"

"No, not at all, but I am curious."

"As I knew you would be." He laughed. "I found just the right bait for this fish."

"You did," I said. "Here's a question: Why are you involved with the theft of the Heart of India and the murder of its owner? You're an intelligence officer. This is a police matter."

"You are absolutely right, Jessica. It is a police matter. But *if* rumors are true that its owner was using proceeds from his business dealings to fund terrorist groups around the world, it very much becomes a matter for MI6 and other intelligence agencies."

" 'If' is a very big word, Michael. My understanding is that that charge has never been proved. No one's been able to find a solid link from Walter Yang to the terrorist organizations. It could all be gossip and innuendo. I find it hard to believe that your agency would get you involved on so slim a pretext."

Michael cocked his head. "Ah, you're too smart for me, Jessica. But evidence seems to be mounting that makes it more of a plausible charge. I would tell you more, but my oath of secrecy means I must keep mum." He put his index finger to his lips and smiled.

"All right," I said, "I'll let you off the hook for now. Now get back to your dancing partner, and let me get a good night's rest."

He laughed gently and looked around to ensure that we were alone. "I think I might have fallen in love. She is very beautiful, and a wonderful dancer, I might add."

"You've always had a discerning eye when it comes to beautiful women, Michael."

"Which is why I spotted you in a crowd the first moment I saw you."

"You've also always been an inveterate flatterer."

He shrugged. "Part of my job description. Unlike that inaccurate old cliché, flattery will often get you far. And please call me Wendell. Too easy to have a slipup in public if you call me Michael in private."

"You're changing the subject, *Wendell.*"

"That I am, or at least I tried. But here's the gist of it. Did you know, Jessica, that there were three jewel robberies in London last night?"

"No. Oh, yes, I learned about one of them. Three?"

"Exactly."

"Do you think they're connected in some way to the theft of the Heart of India?"

"I think that it's a distinct possibility."

"Is that the juicy information you promised me?"

He shrugged. "You know the constraints of my business. Haven't I answered all your questions, Jessica?"

"Not at all; you keep evading them. But what strikes me is that I'm here on this lovely ocean liner, a band playing, superb meals being served, round-the-clock entertainment, even a planetarium on board, and more than twenty-five hundred happy people I could be enjoying myself with. Instead, I meet up with an undercover intelligence agent" — Michael tipped his head to the side and grinned — "and his quarry, a man who might be a killer, financing terrorism. It's not what I bargained for when I agreed to lecture."

"But you have to admit, Jessica, that it's more interesting than spending six days putting together a thousand-piece jigsaw puzzle, or taking a class in napkin folding."

"There are many more attractions on the ship than that," I said. "Time for me to head to my cabin. I have a lecture to give at eleven in the morning."

"I'll be there, of course, applauding your

efforts."

As we parted at the elevator that would take me up to Deck Eleven, I asked, "What about that Israeli agent, Uri, who followed us? Is he on board, too?"

"I haven't seen him, but if he is, he'll surface soon enough. He's not especially skilled at keeping a low profile. Oh, by the way, we'll be joined tomorrow at dinner by my new friend. Her name is Jennifer Kahn. Her traveling companion is Ms. Kiki Largent. That sour young honeymooning couple has requested a table for two, much more romantic than sitting with those of us on the wrong side of fifty. Sleep tight, dear lady. See you at breakfast."

CHAPTER EIGHT

Second Day at Sea

Harry was alone at the table when I arrived at the Princess Grill for breakfast. He was dressed in a bright blue and green shirt worn loose over white slacks. He looked none the worse for wear after his night in the casino.

"Enjoy a restful night?" he asked, rising as the maître d' pulled out my chair.

"As a matter of fact, I did. You?"

"I always sleep well at sea," he said, sitting again. "Did you notice? The swells are getting heavier."

The young officer's weather prediction had been accurate. The glasslike surface of the Atlantic from the previous day had been replaced by deep swells; a howling wind kicked up frothy whitecaps. The captain had announced over the ship's PA that areas of the decks would be closed until the weather improved.

"Looks like it could become a Force Eight," Harry said.

"Meaning?"

"Force Eight on the Beaufort scale. Admiral Beaufort created the scale to standardize the reporting of weather conditions. It's been adjusted over the years, but Force Eight generally means a wind speed of between thirty and forty knots, and swells of three to four fathoms. A fathom is six feet."

"It doesn't feel that bad," I said.

"That's because you're on a state-of-the-art ship, Jessica. She's got four big stabilizers that extend to counteract any rolling motion. On some of the freighters I've served on, a sea like this would have us bouncing around like a cork. This lovely lady just plows through it."

I noticed that Harry had barely touched his breakfast, and wondered if it was because he'd had a losing night at the craps table. I asked.

"To the contrary, Jessica. I walked away with over four hundred dollars." He lowered his voice. "It would have been a thousand had you been at my side."

I laughed. "Seems to me you don't need anyone to serve as a lucky charm."

"It never hurts to help luck along." He

chuckled. "Celebrated my winnings in the nightclub. They have a disc jockey. It's called a disco, I suppose. The music is terribly loud, but at my age, my hearing isn't what it used to be anyway. I admit that I enjoyed it."

I smiled. "Somehow, Harry, you don't strike me as the disco type."

"You'd be surprised. I've been to my share of them over the years. Anything to spice up life when you finally reach shore after battling boredom for weeks or months at sea." He sat back, folded his hands on his stomach, and closed his eyes. He'd gone to a different place for those few moments, possibly back to one of his many experiences as a merchant seaman. When he opened his eyes, he shook his head and said matter-of-factly, "I hate growing old."

"They say growing old isn't for sissies," I said.

"Yes, I've heard that. I had a dear friend, no longer with us, who was fond of saying that dying is the price we pay for living."

He evidently read my face, which said I was concerned as to why he'd raised this topic. He offered a small smile and said, "Enough of this dreary gloom-and-doom talk, huh? What's on your agenda today?"

"I have my lecture to give at eleven. Before

that, I thought I'd take an hour and explore the ship. It's so huge, I'm not even sure an hour will be enough. Later today — well, I might check out the spa."

"Sounds like an excellent plan. Ah, here's our antiques dealer," Harry said as Michael Haggerty joined us.

"Everyone tip-top this morning?" Michael asked.

"Couldn't be better, Wendell," Harry said. He stood and said to me, "I'll see you later at your lecture, Jessica. Have a good hike around the ship."

"Nice shot of you," Michael said, pointing to my picture on the cover of the *Daily Programme.* He opened it to see what was on tap that day, while I enjoyed a second cup of coffee. A schedule for the next day was left outside each cabin door the night before, and was chock-full of useful information. Michael put it down and glanced toward the empty table where the Kim party usually sat. "Late sleepers, huh?"

"Oh, look at the time. I need to get back to my cabin, Michael. I have things to do before I give my lecture. Excuse me."

"Call me Wendell," he said, looking around to make certain no one had overheard me. "Look, Jessica, before you go, I'm still counting on you to find out what you can from Kim."

"We're not discussing this anymore, Michael, ah, Wendell, whatever your name is."

"Ignoring terrorism won't make it go away, Jessica. If you ended up being instrumental in heading off funding for a terrorist organization, you'd have saved many lives, including Americans — *mostly* Americans."

His treading on my patriotism was annoying, but as he knew it would, it touched a chord somewhere inside. However, it was a reminder I hadn't needed. Before retiring the night before, I'd already gone over in my mind everything that had occurred over the past few days, thinking about the possible connections.

A rare blue diamond, the Heart of India, had been stolen. The legendary gem was said to bring its owner either great happiness or great tragedy. In the case of Walter Soon Yang, his happiness ended quickly, and the tragedy was his death at the hands of thieves who'd taken the prize he'd been so thrilled to have acquired. Yang was rumored to be connected to terrorist organizations. Was it true? And if so, who killed Yang? Jewel thieves? Terrorists?

I go to dinner at the home of my British publisher, who introduces me to Kim Chin-

Hwa, a Korean businessman, who just happens to be a business partner of the murdered owner of the Heart of India. Mr. Kim tells me he is booked on the *Queen Mary 2* along with his beautiful girlfriend, Betty LeClair, a former Paris model, the pair accompanied by two formidable-looking young men. Employees? Relatives? Bodyguards?

Michael Haggerty, a former MI6 intelligence agent and old friend, now back in the intelligence game, also shows up at my publisher's home, using an alias, Wendell Jones, antiques dealer. He tells me that he, too, will be joining me on the crossing to New York, and asks me to spy on Mr. Kim for him. We're tailed by an Israeli intelligence agent. Why?

It was an odd confluence of events, to be sure, but what did it mean? Haggerty had always had a knack for attracting trouble. It was as if he was a magnet for the bad guys. He wanted me to get close to the victim's partner in the hope that I'd pick up on something he said or did that might help the MI6 investigation. This man could be completely innocent and know nothing about either the theft or terrorists. He was a victim himself since he'd lost his good friend and partner. I refused Michael's request. Now he was suggesting that if I continued to refuse, I'd be aiding and abetting terrorists.

Ridiculous!

As I was about to leave the table, my cloak-and-dagger friend added, "And don't forget, Jessica, that the owner of the Heart of India was murdered, and that his murderer could be aboard this ship. Murder! Your specialty!"

I ignored the jab. What nagged at me as I walked away was that there was a modicum of truth to what he'd said. Not that I consider murder to be my "specialty." Sure, I deal with murder day after day as I sit at my computer and weave tales of mystery and mayhem, deeds most foul. But that's what I do for a living. I'm a writer. My fascination with murder and murderers has to do with the characters and plots in my books.

But I can't deny that I too often end up leaving my computer and the pages I've written and find myself immersed in murder of a more human and realistic type. Seth Hazlitt accuses me of seeking out those situations. Do I? I prefer to think not. But if I'm to be totally honest — and I like to think that I am — *real* murders exert a powerful pull on me. Is it because I'm able to take what I've learned from them and make use of it in my writing? I've used that rationalization at times. But truth be told, there's more to it than that.

The theft of the rare blue diamond the Heart of India, and the murder of its owner, Walter Soon Yang, had captured my imagination. No debate. And while I feigned disinterest in Michael Haggerty's involvement, I'd very much been interested in Inspector George Sutherland's take on the case. Should I bring these new wrinkles to George's attention? Would he welcome the information? Or would he think my vivid imagination — and Michael Haggerty's — was conjuring connections where none existed? What to do? I found myself mentally questioning every aspect of the case, and I had a lecture to give in two hours. Perhaps a good long walk would clear my mind.

My self-generated tour of the *QM2* was both interesting and tiring. I started at the ship's stern, where I'd just had breakfast, and checked out the outdoor Terrace Pool and Bar, although through a window because of the foul weather. I made my way down a few decks to the art gallery, where auctions would take place each day that we were at sea, then peeked in the Golden Lion Pub and other bars and restaurants, browsed the high-end shops, took in the huge Royal Court Theatre — a British theatrical troupe would be performing plays there later in the day — and finally looked into Illuminations, the floating planetarium in which I'd be delivering my lecture. I checked my watch. I was due there in an hour and realized that I'd better get back to my stateroom and review my notes.

As I approached my cabin, Betty emerged from the door next to mine, abject fury written all over her cameo face.

"Good morning," I said.

She ignored me — perhaps she didn't hear me — and strode away down the corridor.

My door had been propped open by Rupesh while he made up my stateroom.

"Good morning, madam," he said. "Did you have a pleasant night?"

"Yes, very much, thank you. I see that Mr. Kim has a cabin next door."

"You know him, madam?"

"I recently met him. I just saw his friend leave."

Rupesh raised his eyebrows but said nothing, and I had the feeling that he wanted to say something but decided it would be indiscreet to discuss a passenger.

"The woman with Mr. Kim is very beautiful," I said, hoping to elicit a further comment. He simply nodded and finished making the bed, then left with his cleaning materials. I closed the door behind him, but opened it again to a knock. Rupesh handed me an envelope.

"This was in your mail basket," he said. "Have a pleasant day."

"Yes, thank you, Rupesh."

My balcony had two comfortable chairs and a small table, but it was too rough and windy to sit out there. I cracked open the door to allow some air inside, but quickly changed my mind when the breeze scattered the papers on my desk, including all my lecture notes. I pocketed the envelope Rupesh had given me, and knelt to retrieve my papers, sorting them several times to put them in the correct order before securing them with a paper clip.

I reviewed my lecture from beginning to end, taking out one story and substituting another. I have always found that anecdotes are the best way to entertain a crowd, and I leave the details of my writing process — how long it takes to write a book, how many pages I write a day, and where I get my ideas — for the question-and-answer period when those topics inevitably arise. Satisfied I had everything in order, I checked myself in the mirror, reapplied my lipstick, and picked up my shoulder bag, sliding the paper-clipped notes inside. I looked around for my room key, but it wasn't on the desk. I patted my pockets and discovered the key along with the envelope Rupesh had delivered.

On the front was typed J. FLETCHER. I opened the envelope and pulled out a folded slip of paper. The message was also typed, and terse: CURIOSITY KILLED THE CAT!

CHAPTER NINE

". . . and thank you so much for being here. I hope to see you again tomorrow, same time, same . . . planetarium." A few people laughed. "In a few minutes I'll be signing copies of my latest novel in the bookshop on Deck Eight, at the front of the ship — or I should say the bow. Enjoy the rest of your day."

The lecture had been successful. I estimated that three hundred people were in the audience. They were attentive throughout, and had lots of questions at the end. I stayed for ten minutes to shake hands with the people who came forward, and then followed the cruise director to the bookshop, where a long line of people awaited me, my book in their hands.

Focusing on the lecture had kept me from dwelling on the strange note that had been left for me. But it had intruded on my thoughts a few times while I'd been speaking, and was very much with me as I greeted book buyers and personally inscribed their purchases. The signing took almost an hour, and I was glad when the last person in line reached the table. I love meeting my readers and finding out something about them, but the process can be tiring. I also knew that once the video of my talk played on TVs in every cabin, there would be plenty of passengers throughout the ship who'd want to stop and talk.

Curiosity killed the cat!

Who would have sent me such a message? Was it a joke? Could it possibly have something to do with the missing diamond, its murdered owner, and terrorists? Mr. Kim had asked if I planned to write about that, and expressed relief when I'd said I hadn't. Was he pressing his point? Couldn't be, I decided. He was more direct than that. Had he shared his concerns with Betty and had she taken it into her own hands to warn me off? I didn't see why. I hadn't asked provocative questions of anyone, hadn't done anything that even smacked of probing. No one knew — or at least I thought no one knew — that Wendell Jones was, in fact, an MI6 agent. But in any event, no one knew that I knew. Was I really the intended recipient? Perhaps the note should have been left at Kim's cabin next door. But, no, that wasn't right. It had my name on the envelope.

Kim and his two male colleagues — I kept thinking of them as bodyguards — were at lunch when I arrived. Haggerty was sitting alone at our table. I saw the Kensingtons at a table for two when I entered the grill and was pleased to see them talking easily with each other. Michael was right. As newlyweds, they probably hadn't been happy being consigned to dine with older passengers. The change would be good for them.

I was disappointed not to see Harry Flynn. I'd quickly developed a liking for him, and thoroughly enjoyed his stories of life on the high seas. He was the quintessential gentleman, well-spoken and kind, and reminded me of my late husband, Frank, who shared those same qualities. Then, too, his presence would have ensured that Michael refrained from pressuring me to spy on Kim.

"That went very well this morning, don't you think?" Michael said when I'd taken my seat.

"Yes. I do. I didn't see you. Were you there?"

"Of course. I said I would be and I was. You had so many admirers, you just didn't see me. I'll have to bring you a book to sign when there isn't a long line. You will sign one for me, won't you?"

"Anytime," I said, picking up the menu. I ordered the spa luncheon. Despite what Harry had correctly labeled my "hike" around the ship, I was acutely conscious that eating three full meals a day — plus sandwiches, scones, and pastries at the *QM2*'s afternoon tea, should I decide to take advantage of that appealing meal — would soon leave me unable to fit into my clothes. I was grateful that the ship provided diet selections, and was certain they'd be every bit as delicious as their more caloric offerings, which they were.

"I met Harry coming here," Michael said later. "He was on his way to the bridge. Apparently the captain invited him up."

"How nice for him. Perhaps they're old friends. I imagine sea captains know each other — or at least know of each other — the way, oh, say, captains of industry do."

"Or like mystery authors do?"

"Yes, that's true, too. I know many mystery writers personally, and have heard of or read the works of many more. Isn't that true of spies, as well?"

Michael gave me a mock scowl and glanced over his shoulder. "Shh. This table

113

could be bugged. See this salt cellar? It might contain the new crystalline eavesdropping device, indistinguishable from regular table salt."

"Another reason to avoid extra salt on my food," I said.

The odd note I'd received — was it a threat? — was in my pocket. I debated showing it to Haggerty. What could he tell me? It was innocuous enough, but clearly there was something calculated about it. A message behind the message. After a half hour of banter — Michael is good at banter — I decided to share it with him.

"I'd like you to look at something I received this morning," I said, reaching into my pocket.

He adopted a puzzled expression as he read it, turned it sideways and upside down, and ran a finger over the typed letters. Finished with his perusal, he handed it back to me with a shrug.

"Any suggestions?" I asked.

"Can't imagine who'd send it, Jessica, unless it's one of your many fans on the ship. Your picture was in the program this morning, and now that you have one lecture under your belt, your fan base will grow by leaps and bounds."

"Yes. But I received this before the lecture."

"It's probably nothing. I certainly wouldn't worry about it."

I decided that he was right. Some fan of my books may have thought it would amuse me to receive an anonymous note. Some friends at home had thought that once, too — sending me anonymous mail with letters cut from magazines — but once I learned of their prank, I quickly disabused them of the idea that it was amusing. Were I able to speak with the author of this note, I would courteously inform him or her that I'd just as soon not be on the receiving end of such well-meaning frivolity.

Kim came over to our table as we were finishing up.

"I thought you two might be up for a game of bridge," he said. "The weather is foul — perfect time to sharpen our wits. But I should warn you. I play to win."

"I haven't played bridge in ages," I said. "I'm more of a chess fancier."

"Like falling off a horse," Haggerty suggested. "You'll pick it up again in no time."

"And you, Mr. Jones?" Kim said.

"No thanks. Count me out. I've never gotten the hang of it. You two go ahead. I'm sure you'll find others looking for a game."

115

He slapped Kim on the shoulder. "Don't believe the lady that she's a novice, my friend. She's a cardsharp if I've ever seen one."

Do I go to the spa, or take Mr. Kim up on his offer?

"I'd be happy to play," I said, "provided you'll excuse my mistakes."

"Of course."

The cardroom was located in the Atlantic Room on Deck Eleven. On our way there, I asked Kim whether Betty wasn't feeling well. She hadn't appeared at lunch.

"She's fine, just a trifle weary, that's all."

Somehow, I didn't believe him but didn't press. When I'd seen her furious expression that morning, I assumed that they'd had a spat. Her absence at lunch might be her way of sending a message to him that she was still angry.

Kim's two associates rode up on the elevator with us.

"I don't believe we've been introduced," I said, and extended my hand. "I'm Jessica Fletcher."

My forwardness seemed to unsettle them. They awkwardly shook hands, mumbled their names, and said nothing else.

"Do you play bridge?" I asked as the elevator door opened on eleven.

"They're not cardplayers, Mrs. Fletcher," Kim said, and left it at that.

Finding two others to join us wasn't difficult. At least a half dozen bridge aficionados were in the room when we arrived, and two of them, a husband and wife, eagerly accepted our offer to make a foursome. Kim's "business colleagues" sat together in a far corner and picked up magazines.

Kim was as practiced and smooth at bridge as he was at dancing. At one point, he suggested we wager on the game — "to make it interesting" — small stakes, he assured us. I was relieved when the other couple declined: "We never play for money," said the wife.

My bridge skills improved as we played, but I was never able to match Kim's ability or his concentration. He was so engrossed in his cards that barely a word passed between us other than what was required for the game's bidding. I found it amusing that Haggerty had wanted me to cultivate a friendship with this man to elicit useful information. From what I'd seen of Kim Chin-Hwa, he rarely spoke beyond the social needs of the moment, and since we'd been introduced, I'd learned nothing more about him than that he liked to dance and play cards — hardly the stuff of valuable intelligence.

The game ended an hour later with a grand slam in our favor. Kim was willing to continue playing, but the couple announced that they'd had enough. Another couple offered to take their place, but I declined.

"Smoke?" Kim asked as we left the cardroom.

"Pardon?"

"Do you smoke? I'm in the mood for a good cigar. They have a special room for cigar and pipe smokers, Churchill's, two decks down from here. Please join me."

"I don't smoke," I said, "but I'll be happy to accompany you. I didn't get to see that room on my tour this morning."

Churchill's was a good-sized space that I now remembered seeing through its glass doors when I attended the welcoming party for lecturers that had been hosted at the Commodore Club. Kim held the door open for me, and we stepped inside. Four people sat in large leather armchairs that ringed the room, one smoking a pipe, one a cigar, and two puffing away on cigarettes. Smoking areas on the ship were limited, with the dining rooms and most bars smoke free. Only the casino and a few designated tables in the Golden Lion Pub accommodated those who still had the habit.

I stood with Kim as he admired an array of cigars in a locked glass cabinet. "They have Cuban cigars," he said. "You can't get them in the States because of your silly embargo on Cuba."

"Cuba is an interesting country," I said, wishing to avoid a political discussion. "I'd be interested in visiting it one day."

"If you have money to spare, Cuba is a good place to invest it," he said as he continued to survey the assortment of cigars in the case. "One of these days Cuba will open up again and become the next tourist Mecca."

Kim summoned a waitress from the club, who unlocked the case and handed him the Cuban cigar he'd chosen. We took chairs in a corner of the room, next to the pipe smoker. My late husband, Frank, used to smoke a pipe on occasion, and I must admit I still enjoy the aroma of pipe tobacco. As for cigars . . .

The ventilation in the room was impressively efficient, but not enough to totally cover the smell of cigar smoke. I've always had an especially keen sense of smell, and I knew my clothing would need airing when I got back to the cabin. Still, I'd decided that having a conversation with Kim might be enlightening. If nothing else, I could fend off Haggerty's next query by saying that I'd at least spent quiet personal time with the wealthy Korean businessman.

Shortly after we sat down, three of the others in the room finished their smokes and left. The gentleman with the pipe had nodded off in his chair. The waitress asked if we wanted anything to drink, but we declined. Kim deftly lit his cigar, taking care not to let the flame from his lighter touch the end of the cigar itself. He sat back, sighed contentedly, and allowed the smoke from his first puff to curl above us and disappear into the ventilation system.

"You play bridge quite well," he finally said after some additional draws.

"Thank you. It started to come back to me, although I admit I've forgotten much about bidding."

"You were fine. The other couple was no match for us."

After another pause, I said, "You were very forthcoming at Tom Craig's home about the theft of the Heart of India and your partner's death. Do you mind another question about it?"

"No, not at all," he replied with a discernible wariness in his tone. "It is a topic that seems endlessly fascinating to everyone."

"Is it not fascinating to you?"

"To the contrary. It is painful to explore. Walter was a friend as well as a business colleague. I cannot separate my grief at his death from the circumstances of it. It is all one."

"I'm sorry. If you'd prefer not to talk about it, I understand."

He waved the cigar. "No, go ahead. It will not be the last time someone wishes to dissect the details. Curiosity, it seems, is rampant when it comes to such crimes."

I was taken aback at his use of the word "curiosity." Had he or someone close to him been the one to send me the note? I waited to see if he would mention it, but instead he said, "Ask your question. Perhaps you will see something the police missed. Do you think your powers of observation are superior to those of the investigative authorities, Mrs. Fletcher?"

It was a trick question. If I answered in the affirmative, I could be accurately accused of pomposity. But if I said no, he'd be within his rights to ask why he should answer me in the first place. I decided just to forge ahead. "It's my understanding that your partner's alarm system was inoperative the night of the theft and murder."

He nodded and inhaled on his Cuban treasure.

"Do you have any idea why that might have been?"

"No. I wasn't there."

"One of his security men said that your partner had left instructions that he was not to be disturbed in his study that night. This security guard assumed he was entertaining a lady in there. He said that wasn't unusual."

Kim smiled. "My friend Walter appreciated many of the finer things in life."

"Like Cuban cigars?" I asked playfully.

"Oh, yes, and beautiful women, too. It would not surprise me that he entertained a woman the night he was murdered."

"Would you have any idea who that woman might be?"

"How could I possibly know that, Jessica? I wasn't there. Walter and I shared many things. We were intimately involved in business deals, and I knew a great deal about some of his personal preferences and habits. But we never discussed the women in our lives. That was off-limits."

"I can't help but wonder how those people who stole the diamond and killed your partner would know when the safe was opened. And how did they know the diamond was in his safe to begin with, if he, as you told us the other night, moved it around for the sake of security? Someone had to know he'd taken it home, and that someone also had to know him sufficiently well to assume he would take out the diamond, perhaps to show it to the woman he was entertaining."

Kim examined the end of his cigar, made a face, pulled out his lighter, and put the flame to it again. He said into the room, "You ask a lot of questions, Mrs. Fletcher, for someone who doesn't intend to write about it, and you also seem to know a great deal about this most unfortunate incident."

I wasn't about to mention George Sutherland and that he'd shared with me his knowledge of the case, so I said, "Many details were in the press." I then forced a laugh and added, "Just my natural-born curiosity." I looked directly at him. "I know that curiosity is supposed to have killed the cat, but I'm afraid I can't help myself."

If the curiosity-killing-the-cat reference registered with him, his face didn't express it.

"Do you mind if I ask you how the diamond was insured?"

"I really don't know," he said, stubbing out the cigar and rising. "It was probably with his personal casualty company. I'm going to get a drink. You're welcome to join me for a cocktail, if you like."

"Thank you, no. I think I'll go now. You've been very generous with your time. I enjoyed our bridge game, too. See you at dinner."

Rupesh was exiting Kim's room next door as I walked down the corridor to my cabin.

"Hello, madam," he said.

"Hello, Rupesh. I have a question for you. I need access to a typewriter or computer with a printer. Would Mr. Kim have either one in his cabin?"

"I don't know, madam, but we have a very fine computer center, which you are welcome to use, and there are even computers in the library next to the bookstore."

"Yes, but this would be so convenient. He's right next door. Would you ask the next time you see him?"

"Of course, madam. Is everything to your satisfaction?" he asked.

"Yes, everything is fine, thank you."

"You have a very pleasant evening, madam."

"I'm sure I will," I said.

CHAPTER TEN

While dressing for dinner, I watched the ship's channel on the TV in my cabin. Along with news of upcoming events, it ran a program over and over on safety information, including what to do should we witness a fellow passenger falling overboard: *Yell as loud as you can, "Man overboard," and throw the nearest life preserver at the person in the water.* The mere thought of someone falling into the Atlantic and being swept away and under sent a chill up my spine.

Because this was one of three formal nights on the *Queen Mary 2,* I chose my outfit accordingly. When I arrived in the lounge for a predinner drink, Michael — or rather Wendell, as I had to remember to call him — and his two female guests and Harry Flynn were already at the bar, drinks lined up in front of them. Unlike most of the men, who were decked out in black tuxedos, Harry wore a double-breasted white dinner jacket, black tux pants, and bloodred bow tie and cummerbund. He looked positively stunning with his erect posture, tanned face, and full head of salt-and-pepper hair.

Haggerty introduced me to Jennifer Kahn, and to her friend Kiki Largent. The contrast between them was striking. Ms. Kahn was dressed as though she were about to be introduced to royalty, a command performance before a queen or other head of state, although her green silk floor-length gown cut low in front and with slits up the side might have been considered a little too risqué in some royal circles. Her long, tapered fingers held a variety of rings that positively dazzled in the room's flattering light, and a necklace and pendant drew the eye to her décolletage.

Ms. Largent, on the other hand, wore a pair of black slacks and a black pullover shirt. Her acknowledgment of the evening's formal dress code was a large, heavy multistrand necklace of assorted seashells, and gold earrings that reached her shoulders. Her short black hair, almost a classic buzz cut, had some sort of gel in it that provided sheen.

Conversation flowed easily. Jennifer had a trace of an accent that I pegged as Slavic, Hungarian perhaps, or Czech. Her friend

Kiki said little, but what I did hear was absent any obvious nationality. She didn't smile much, and I had the feeling that her role was to fawn over Jennifer, perhaps act as a gofer and all-around assistant.

"Did everyone have a good day?" Flynn asked.

There was a unanimous nodding of heads.

"You?" Haggerty asked Flynn.

"An excellent day," Harry said. "I took a peek at the bridge, then spent an hour at the driving range — incredible, the use of technology to display an actual golf course on the ship — and then worked out in the gym. It even has a separate weight room, a far cry from the freighters I spent my working life on. And this is the perfect way to top off the day: a cold, dry martini." He'd just been served one, and he lifted his glass in a toast: "May you live as long as you want, and never want as long as you live."

"Hear, hear," said Haggerty.

"You'll notice that I remained seated while offering my toast," Harry said. "Toasts are usually offered standing up. But back in the sixteen hundreds, a British king was alleged to have stood to offer a toast while aboard ship and cracked his noggin on the low ceiling. That led to a decree that toasts at sea may be proposed from a sitting position.

That rule is still in effect."

I'd learned in the short time I'd known him that Harry Flynn reveled in telling sea tales, and would undoubtedly have many more to share as the crossing progressed.

Jennifer Kahn began questioning me about my books and how I write them. She had missed my lecture, but had read one or two of my books and seemed sincerely interested in what I had to say.

Kim, Betty, and their two bodyguards showed up as we were preparing to go into the dining room. He nodded at me, but his smile and outwardly pleasant demeanor were absent this time. His face was set in a scowl, and Betty's expression wasn't any more welcoming. Apparently, whatever they had been arguing about earlier in the day when I'd seen her storm from the room was still a matter of contention. They took a table in a far corner of the lounge.

After we'd been seated and we'd chosen our selections from that evening's menu, I asked Jennifer what line of work she was in.

"Design," she replied. "I design jewelry."

"Oh, and have you designed what you're wearing?" I asked, noting the elaborate garnet and diamond necklace set off by the green silk of her dress.

"Yes," she said brightly, her fingers fluttering near the diamond pendant. "Do you like it?"

"It's beautiful," I said, "but I would have thought pieces designed by such a young woman would be more modern. Your necklace doesn't look modern at all. In fact, it looks like an antique."

"I adore antique jewelry. I've collected antique pieces my whole life." She shot a wink at Kiki, who dropped her head and focused on buttering her roll. "They have so much more depth and grandeur, don't you think? I like to think my work would have fit in in the days of royal courts, pre–French Revolution, of course. Gems and jewelry from those days are my inspirations, although I confess I love all jewelry. I've always been attracted to sparkly things."

"How fascinating," I said, turning to her friend. "And you, Kiki? Are you a designer, too?"

"No," she said. "I'm Jennifer's assistant."

"I don't know what I'd do without her," said Jennifer.

"We can all use a good assistant," Haggerty said. "Makes life considerably easier, doesn't it?"

"I have some antique jewelry that my mother left me," Harry said, slipping off a small diamond ring he wore on his pinkie.

"I managed to keep this out of my last wife's hands during the settlement. Not nearly as valuable as your jewelry, of course, Jennifer." He turned to Haggerty. "But maybe Wendell here could tell me more about it. I've always wondered about its origin."

Michael had been sipping his drink when Harry addressed him. He sputtered and coughed, until Harry pounded him on the back. "You okay, old man?" Harry asked.

Recovering, Michael nodded. "Yes, of course. Thank you so much. Wrong pipe, I fear. You were saying?"

"I was asking you about my mother's ring," he said, holding it up.

Michael cleared his throat and nodded. "Movie memorabilia," he said.

"I beg your pardon."

"Posters, playbills mostly," Michael said. "My specialty. I'm not up to speed on" — he waved his hand toward Harry — "antique jewelry."

"I see," Harry said, returning the ring to his finger. "Don't know how you manage to have a shop with such a narrow focus. You must be a superb salesman."

"Wendell has very special clientele," I put in.

"He must have," Jennifer said. "By the way, Harry, that ring is Art Deco, platinum and diamond. It's pre-1940 and worth about twenty-five hundred dollars."

"It is? How nice to know."

We were well into our entrées when Kiki announced that she wasn't feeling well and was going to her cabin.

"She's been queasy ever since we left port," Jennifer explained as Kiki excused herself and left.

"She needs a stabilizer," Harry offered.

"Stabilizer?" Haggerty said.

"Half port, half brandy," Harry explained. "Works wonders. They call it the 'stabilizer' on most ships' bar menus. Of course, Sir Isaac Newton had the best remedy. He said that the perfect solution for seasickness was to sit under a tree."

This led to a discussion of how to prevent seasickness: Dramamine, wristbands, or ginger. The results were mixed.

I was well aware that unlike the previous evening when Kim made a point of coming to our table and suggesting we continue the night as a group, he stayed away this evening. I can only describe the mood at his table as somber, and at one point Betty snapped at one of the bodyguards, who left in a huff.

"Well," Haggerty said after we'd finished our desserts and coffee, "off to the Queens

Room for more dancing?" He directed the question at Jennifer, who, it seemed to me, had become smitten with my dashing friend from MI6. She had laughed at every one of his quips, including those that weren't funny, a sure sign of infatuation. The feeling was clearly mutual. Michael had obviously succeeded in establishing a flirtatious relationship with her.

"You, Jessica?" Michael asked.

"I think not," I said. "I read in the program that the ship's resident string quartet is performing this evening in the Chart Room, followed by a jazz trio. I'm in the mood for listening music, rather than dancing music."

"Mind company?" Harry Flynn asked.

"I'd love it," I said.

We caught the end of the quartet's performance and waited for the jazz trio to get set up on a small bandstand. Harry took advantage of the lull in the music to tell me a story about how he'd personally encountered pirates off the African coast, and how he and the rest of the crew had managed to fend them off. It was a gripping tale, and I hung on every word.

As the trio began to play its first tune, "Autumn Leaves," a song I've always loved, I saw a familiar figure enter the room. Kiki

Largent was obviously feeling better and had changed her mind about going to her cabin. I thought nothing of it, until a second familiar person walked in not far behind her. Then I sat up straight and took notice. It was Uri, the intelligence agent who'd followed Michael and me in London. What was he doing here? Was he still tailing Michael?

Harry noted my new focus and joined me in looking in their direction.

"Appears that she's recovered," he said. "Maybe she found a tree to sit under." He laughed at his own joke.

I raised my shoulder and twisted in my seat, hoping they wouldn't notice me. I must have succeeded because they both walked past without a sideward glance in our direction. Kiki moved with purpose, as though she wanted to get someplace in the shortest time possible without breaking into a run. Uri, who'd replaced his long black coat with a gray sport jacket worn over a black polo shirt, but wearing his yarmulke, plodded after her. I hadn't realized when seeing him in London just how big a man he was. His bearlike physique made it difficult for him to go unnoticed, but there were so many people in the bar, perhaps he was successful in concealing himself from his quarry.

"Would you excuse me for a few minutes, Harry?" I said.

"Of course. The powder room?"

"Ah, yes."

"Do you know where the term 'powder room' comes from?"

"No, I —"

"It has nothing to do with a place where women can retreat to powder their faces."

Kiki had stopped just outside the door to the room near the photo shop, where cameras and other photographic paraphernalia were sold. Uri turned as if suddenly interested in the musicians.

"The name originated in forts where certain rooms were designated as dry storage areas for gunpowder," Harry said. "I remember once when a woman mistook the sign over a door in an old fort as an indication that even back then they were concerned with providing proper accommodations for the female sex."

"Fascinating," I said, meaning it, but anxious to see where Kiki and Uri were headed. "Please excuse me."

"Of course," Harry said, rising as I vacated my seat. "I have a nephew who's a jazz musician. I'm especially fond of the music."

I went to the Chart Room's entrance but

hung back so that I could watch Uri tail Kiki without them seeing me. Kiki moved into the photo shop. Uri followed, pretending to peruse cameras in a display case. I fell in behind.

Kiki stopped and looked around, as though unsure where to go next, or possibly to see that she wasn't being followed. Uri turned his back to her. So did I. She then walked away in the direction of Sir Samuel's wine bar, a tribute to Cunard's founder, Samuel Cunard, with Uri in pursuit. I debated continuing. I didn't want to leave Harry Flynn alone for too long. But he seemed the understanding type, and also appeared to have settled in nicely to enjoy the jazz. He didn't need me for that.

The three of us proceeded through the Mayfair Shops to the Grand Lobby, where Kiki rang for an elevator. I took a box from a shelf in the store, pretending to look at it while checking Uri to see what his next move was. He did what I did, watched Kiki get into the elevator and disappear behind the closing doors. My eyes went to the floor numbers displayed above the elevator. It went directly to Deck Seven, the highest deck served by that bank of elevators.

"That shaving kit is usually meant for men," a saleswoman said to me. "I saw you

135

studying the label. Are you looking for a man's gift?"

"Not today," I said, returning the box to the shelf and hurrying from the shop.

When the next elevator door opened, I dashed in front of a group of people who had been waiting patiently and, ignoring scowls aimed at me, huddled in the corner of the cab as the others squeezed in, last of all Uri. Everyone exited at Deck Seven.

There was no sign of Kiki. Uri entered the area called Kings Court, a twenty-four-hour food court that served a wide variety of ethnic dishes — pizza, Chinese, salads, burgers, and other simpler fare than the formal dining rooms. I followed him. As I did, I saw Marcia Kensington sitting alone at a table far removed from where I was. I then spotted Kiki standing in front of a set of doors leading to the Outdoor Promenade. Uri saw her, too, and stopped. So did I.

Despite the captain's PA announcement earlier in the day that outdoor areas were closed until further notice, Kiki skirted a temporary sign that read DECK CLOSED DUE TO WEATHER, pushed through the heavy door, and stepped into the night.

Uri seemed confused about what to do next. I waited until he finally ducked into a bay of tables that were set up along a line of windows. I pulled a foldout map of the *QM2* from my purse and held it in front of my face as I positioned myself at another window, hoping not to be seen by him. But he was so intent on Kiki, I needn't have bothered.

The scene on the deck was straight out of a gothic movie. A dense fog had settled in, shrouding everything in ghostly gray and rendering the exterior lights almost useless. Kiki leaned into the fierce wind and made her way to a nearby alcove that shielded her somewhat from the gale. Engulfed in fog, she was almost invisible to me from my vantage point, but not completely. What surprised me was that there was another figure already in that alcove, a form so vague that it was impossible to determine who it was, even whether it was male or female. Kiki extended her arm, and the other person did the same. They'd exchanged something, but I couldn't tell who'd offered it and who was on the receiving end.

Kiki left the protection of the alcove and was buffeted by the wind as she made her way back to the door. I slipped behind a pillar and held my breath. The wind slammed the door closed, and she walked quickly past me, her black shirt and hair gleaming with water. I waited. Uri was next to pass. I turned back to the window in the hope of seeing who it was that Kiki had met with, but there was no sign of him, or her.

My final glimpse of the pair was at the staircase leading to the Grand Lobby. I saw the back of Uri's head as he descended the stairs, and assumed Kiki had preceded him. I considered following after them but decided against it. If Kiki had left the dinner table in order to rendezvous with this other person, she'd accomplished her mission and was probably on her way back to her stateroom. As for Uri, simply knowing that he was on the ship was discovery enough for the night. I glanced to where I'd seen Marcia Kensington, hoping I hadn't attracted her attention. She was gone.

I returned to the Chart Room to find that Harry had left. Our waiter from earlier that evening handed me a folded sheet of paper. "The gentleman asked me to give this to you should you return."

"The music is grand, Jessica, but I felt the pull of the craps table and decided it was useless to resist. I'll probably cap off the evening with a drink in the Commodore Club. Please join me in either place. But if not, I certainly understand. Hope you don't have a touch of mal de mer, but if you do, try a stabilizer. If not, see you in the morning. Harry."

It didn't sound as if Harry was annoyed by my sudden absence. However, I owed him an apology the next time we were together. I debated joining Haggerty and Jennifer Kahn, who were likely to be dancing in the Queens Room. Did Haggerty know that Uri was on the ship? If so, he'd never mentioned it. Why not? I'd have to ask him, but tomorrow was time enough to talk, particularly if I could get him alone for some frank conversation.

I went to my cabin and stepped out onto the balcony. It was cold and damp; would this foul weather stay with us for the remainder of the crossing? I retreated back inside, got into my pajamas and the fluffy robe provided by Cunard, and sat at the small desk, my mind still turning over the events of the evening.

Whom did Kiki Largent meet on the deck, and why had they chosen such an uncomfortable setting for their brief encounter?

Did Kim's sudden change in behavior toward me signify anything, or was he merely reflecting his companion's mood?

Why did Uri — and I wished I knew his last name — find Kiki to be of sufficient interest to follow her around the ship? Had he been following Michael in London in the hope that my MI6 pal would lead him to her?

My idyllic crossing on the *Queen Mary 2* was turning into something quite different from what I'd anticipated. Maybe I did carry some sort of curse that led me into these situations.

I checked out movies playing on the TV and found none of them to my liking, but when I returned my eyeglasses to my purse, I found the DVD given me at Tom Craig's dinner party by the husband-and-wife film-makers, Madge and Gerald Wilson. I slipped it into the DVD player provided in every stateroom and pressed play. It took only a few minutes for me to become captured by the documentary, which cut back and forth between British authorities and two North African drug smugglers, who appeared on camera with their faces obscured by an electronic pattern to conceal their identities. I'm always impressed with how documentary makers manage to convince law-breakers to speak freely about their nefarious activities, even with faces masked out. Halfway through the DVD Gerald Wilson interviewed two very young women who'd been enlisted by the smugglers to carry their contraband into the UK. Their stories were heartbreaking, girls no older than teenagers putting their lives at risk for money. They'd come from harsh, poverty-stricken backgrounds, the lure of the smugglers' money too tempting to ignore. Toward the end, one of the smugglers justified his use of these young, vulnerable women as drug carriers: "The trick is to use people who the authorities are not likely to suspect: young, pretty, wide-eyed women with no criminal backgrounds."

The documentary ended. It had been an emotional, wrenching story expertly told by the Wilsons, and had inspired me to get hold of a copy of the book on which it had been based.

I still wasn't ready for bed and pulled out my lecture notes for the next day's talk in the planetarium and soon became lost in them, a welcome respite from the dark thoughts with which I'd been consumed from recent events on the ship, magnified by the documentary I'd just watched.

But every now and then when I looked up, I wondered, *Who sent me that strange note?*

The curious cat — me — wanted to know.

CHAPTER ELEVEN

Third Day at Sea

I put on my robe and slippers upon awakening the next morning and went to the balcony to check on the weather. The fog had lifted, the seas had calmed, and ahead of us was blue sky.

I considered calling for room service — such service is available on the *Queen Mary 2* twenty-four hours a day at no additional charge — but decided I'd better look for Harry Flynn to apologize for having abandoned him last night. By the time I'd showered, dressed, and reached the Princess Grill, everyone else had eaten and departed, including Harry.

"Were the two ladies who were at dinner with Mr. Jones last night here this morning?" I asked our waiter.

"No, Mrs. Fletcher. Mr. Jones and Mr. Flynn were the only two at breakfast."

"Mr. Kim and his party?" I asked.

The waiter, a charming young Swedish fellow, laughed. "It seems no one was in the mood for breakfast this morning," he said, "unless they preferred to dine in their cabins."

"Well, then it looks as if I'll be having breakfast alone," I said.

I'd brought that day's program with me and settled back to go through it in search of activities that appealed. My photo was on the front page again promoting my eleven o'clock lecture. My topic that morning was the state of the publishing industry, including the impact of electronic books on book sales. I'd amassed a number of statistics to enhance my talk, including one that found that e-books accounted for only eight percent of all books sold. But I'd also gathered prognostications from industry leaders that promised an increase in the popularity of books read on a screen, rather than between covers. I still prefer to hold a printed book in my hands, but at the same time I didn't want to appear to be hopelessly mired in the past. I had boned up on "cloud computing" — which is expected to take the place of hardware and software — as the wave of the future, a future in which all we'll require is access to the Internet, which will provide all the services we want without the need to buy special programs or devices, an intriguing idea that is rapidly coming true.

After breakfast, I took a walk outside on Deck Seven. The improving weather had lured many people there, some power walking, some relaxing in lounge chairs, others taking a morning stroll. I fell into step with them and basked in the fresh air and views of the ocean. I hadn't been walking long before coming on the newlyweds Richard and Marcia Kensington, who stood at the rail, their attention on the sea. Richard wore a dark blue polo shirt and white shorts. Marcia looked cute in a yellow sundress that reached her knees. A large pair of binoculars tethered to a strap hung from her neck.

"Good morning," I said.

Richard mumbled a return greeting, but Marcia broke into a wide smile. "I'm looking for dolphins and whales," she said.

"I'd love to see some before we reach New York," I said. "I've seen quite a few on previous crossings on the old *QE Two*, but none so far on this trip. The weather hasn't been cooperative."

"Look!" Marcia suddenly shouted.

I looked to where she pointed and saw a slice of black back break the surface of the water a few hundred feet from the ship.

Then two more whales rose, sending plumes of mist from their blowholes into the air.

She raised her binoculars to her eyes.

"May I see, too?" I asked, but Marcia didn't answer. She kept watching until the whales disappeared from view.

"Those must be autofocus binoculars," I said. "I haven't seen that before. Would you mind?" I held out a hand.

"What?" Marcia said.

"Yes, they are," Richard said. To Marcia: "Come on. We have to go."

She gave me a slight smile and followed him away, and I silently hoped that his gruff, discourteous demeanor would soften with age — for her sake.

I returned indoors and wandered through the Images Photo Gallery on Deck Three, where photos taken of passengers as they'd boarded in Southampton, or snapped during dinner in the ship's various restaurants, were on display and for sale. The array of color pictures was staggering, hundreds of them grouped according to where they'd been taken. I looked for my boarding shot and found it. The photographer had caught me with a silly grin, and I decided this was not a photo I wished to keep for posterity. I perused others, men and women (and some children) with happiness written all over their faces as they embarked on what they anticipated would be a splendid vacation. I couldn't help smiling back at them.

I walked away from the boarding photos and had started to look at pictures taken in the Princess Grill when something drew me back. Could it be? I wondered as I leaned closer to a picture a few rows below mine. No, it couldn't be.

But it was.

The picture was of a man wearing a tan safari jacket and a blue British-type golf visor, its bill pulled low over his eyes. Hair sprouting from under the cap was silver, and his mustache was the same color. He looked as though he'd tried to shield himself as much as possible from the photographer getting a clear shot of him. But it was clear enough for me to recognize him.

Dennis Stanton!

Dennis was a reformed second-story man, a crafty jewel thief who'd gotten into that line of dishonest work following the death of his wife, Elizabeth, when the firm that insured the couple, the Susquehanna Fire and Casualty Insurance Company, refused to cover Elizabeth's medical expenses. Dennis took revenge by stealing jewels — but *only* jewels insured by that company. His ill-advised foray into crime came to an end, of course, although his punishment was mild, thanks to a judge who sympathized with Dennis's motive. Eventually he moved to San Francisco, where he became a successful insurance investigator for the Consolidated Casualty Company, specializing in recovering stolen gems. We'd ended up embroiled in a few murder cases over the years, but I'd fallen out of touch with him and often wondered what he was up to.

Like Michael Haggerty, Dennis was handsome, charming — and cunning, a little too much for my blood at times. I suppose "smooth" would adequately describe his persona; his British accent and love of fine clothes added to his aura of erudition. I admit to having felt romantic stirrings a few times when with him — they never lasted long — but I did enjoy his company; he was the perfect companion for tea when he wasn't off using what he'd learned as a thief to outwit other bad guys.

Seeing him provided a shock, and a sudden knot in my stomach. Obviously, he was a passenger on the ship, unless he'd decided at the last minute to abandon his plans after being photographed.

All right, I thought as I found a comfortable armchair near a window and sorted out my thoughts. I answered my first question, which was why Stanton had elected to be on that particular crossing. *Jewels!* A rare blue diamond had been stolen, and there had been a string of jewelry robberies in London just prior to our setting sail. Those factors could explain Dennis's presence on the *QM2*.

Did he know that I, too, was a passenger? He did if he read the daily program, on the front page of which my lectures were promoted, complete with photograph and my name in large type.

Why hadn't I seen Stanton on board? Of course, the ship was immense; it was easy to become lost in the more than two thousand passengers and thousand crew members. I wondered in which dining room he took his meals. Not the Princess Grill. I certainly would have seen him there. I'd been told by a crew member that there were those passengers who took every meal in the Kings Court, electing to opt out of dress requirements. Somehow I doubted that Dennis would have been one of them, not with his devotion to male sartorial splendor. It had taken me a day to spot Uri. Maybe I'd better become more observant of my fellow passengers from now on.

I left my comfortable chair and went down to the purser's office on Deck Two, where I fell in line behind some other passengers with business to conduct. When I reached one of the staff, I said, "I'm Jessica Fletcher, one of the lecturers on board."

"Of course, Mrs. Fletcher. Enjoying your crossing?"

"Oh, yes, very much. I, ah — I've been told that an old friend might be on board, and was wondering if you'd be good enough to check to see whether he's listed as a passenger."

The slight tightening of her face said what I'd expected: that it wasn't policy to release such information.

"I can't believe that it's possible," I said with a lighthearted chuckle, "that this old and dear friend actually ends up on the same ship with me. I'd hate to miss the opportunity to at least say hello."

A small smile crossed her pretty face. "What's his name?" she asked.

"Dennis Stanton."

She consulted her computer, looked up, and shook her head. "Afraid not, Mrs. Fletcher. No one registered by that name."

"Silly me," I said. "I thought it was too good to be true. Thank you so much."

As I walked away, I wondered whether Stanton had booked passage using a false passport. Haggerty was aboard with phony credentials. Working for MI6 had provided him with a variety of such ruses over the years. Stanton, as far as I knew, was still a private citizen without easy access to false documents. That didn't mean, of course, that he'd be unable to come up with a passport bearing a different name. Unfortunately that sort of thing happens all too often, with the wrong people.

The last time I'd been with Dennis Stanton was on a ship in the Caribbean. He'd signed on as head of security: "I needed more adventure in my life than just chasing down missing trinkets," he'd told me on that cruise. That was my final contact with him.

Until now?

I had time to return to my cabin before the lecture. As I walked down the narrow hallway, I saw two of the ship's officers conversing at the open door leading to Kim's stateroom. I recognized one of them from the cocktail party I'd attended. He'd been there to greet lecturers, and I'd had a chance to chat with him. He was the ship's staff captain, second-in-command after the captain, and head of the security force.

They stepped inside the door to allow me to pass. As I did, I paused to look beyond them into the room. Betty was seated on the edge of the bed talking with a woman wearing officer whites. It appeared to me in the brief glimpse I had that she was crying.

The staff captain turned, acknowledged me, stepped inside with his colleague, and closed the door.

I was naturally curious about what had happened to Kim's beautiful companion but pushed it aside as I freshened up in preparation for going down to the planetarium, where I would deliver my second lecture. I was taking a fast look at my notes when there was a knock on the door. It was Rupesh.

"Come in," I said.

He held the door open but remained in the hall. "I have checked about a typewriter or computer, Mrs. Fletcher," he said. "The party next door, Mr. Kim, has a small computer and printer."

"A printer?"

"Yes, madam, a very tiny one, no bigger than a loaf of bread." He smiled. "A small loaf, of course."

I'd wanted to know whether any of the few people I'd met so far had brought with them their own printer. The note left for me — "Curiosity killed the cat" — appeared to have come from a computer printer, an inkjet from the look of it, and I wondered whether one of those persons had originated it. Of course, the note could have been written and printed by anyone from the ship's computers, including dozens in the computer learning center.

"Is there a problem next door?" I asked. "I saw the officers and —"

"It has to do with something, or someone, missing. That is all I know."

"I hope it's nothing serious," I said.

"I wish that, too," he said. "Is there anything else I can provide for you?"

"Not at the moment. I'm giving another lecture this morning."

"Yes, I saw it in the program. You are a very popular speaker, I'm told."

"Thank you. I'd better run. Thank you for the information about the computer."

"My pleasure, madam."

The door to Kim's stateroom was closed as I passed it on the way to the bank of elevators, one of which I took down to Deck Three and the Images Photo Gallery. I plucked Dennis Stanton's photo from the display rack, took it to the counter, and paid for it. "My friend will love that I bought this for him," I said, not needing to explain my purchase but feeling better having done so. I went directly from there to the bow of the ship, a healthy walk, and entered the planetarium, where the social director awaited my arrival. The room had already begun to fill; it looked as though I'd draw an even bigger crowd than the previous day.

"Your first lecture was very well received," the social director told me as we went together to the podium, "very well indeed."

"That's always nice to hear," I said as I looked out at the arriving audience. I recognized Harry Flynn and waved. He returned it with an energetic smile. On the opposite side of the planetarium sat Michael Haggerty. He was alone; his new female friends evidently had something better to do that morning. Upon seeing me, he got up and approached the podium. "I've been waiting for you. We need to talk."

"Good morning, Michael," I said. "Can we get together after my lecture?"

"Yes," he said sternly. "Meet me in the Commodore Club."

"I have a book signing right after my talk."

"I'll wait."

He walked away. I'd hoped that he'd stay for the lecture, but instead he went up the aisle and left the huge room with its twinkling heavens above.

His demeanor was off-putting. I simply wanted to tell him about having seen Uri the previous night, to let him know that the

Israeli was aboard. But from the sound of Haggerty's voice, and the somber expression on his face, what he had on his mind was considerably more serious.

CHAPTER TWELVE

Harry Flynn came to the podium following the lecture, and we walked together to my signing.

"About last night," I said. "I owe you an apology."

"Nonsense! I stayed through the trio's first set — they were very good, by the way — and decided that you'd either gotten lost, become ill, or fallen into a more interesting situation. I hope you weren't ill."

"No, I seem to have my sea legs. That's not —"

I had to walk fast to keep up with him.

"So," he continued, never losing a step, "I made my usual foray to the casino, where I did quite well again at the craps table — a little over five hundred dollars — I have the feeling they'd rather not see me show up again — and I topped off the evening in the Queens Room, where I played gentleman host, unofficially of course, to a few charming ladies, a few of whom danced quite nicely. I considered putting out an SOS in the event you'd run afoul of something. You know, people think SOS means 'Save Our Souls' or 'Save Our Ship,' but it doesn't. It doesn't really stand for anything. An SOS is made up of three dots, three dashes, and three dots again, in Morse code. It became the international distress signal because its repetition could be heard over noisy engines. Plus it was simple to remember, and easy for the intended savior to understand."

I had to laugh. "Where do you get your energy?" I asked as we neared the signing table.

"You mean for a man my age?"

"No, I —"

"For your information, Jessica, I recently turned eighty-two, a proverbial spring chicken."

"Eighty-two going on forty-two," I said.

"Exactly. I enjoyed your lecture."

"Thank you, sir."

"You had the audience eating out of your hand."

"It was a good audience."

"Your fans are waiting, Jessica," the social director said as we reached the bookshop and library, where the line of people holding my newest novel snaked out the door and down the corridor.

"I'll leave you to your adoring throng," Harry said. "See you at lunch?"

"I hope I make it on time."

I watched him stride away, head up, arms swinging, whistling, a man at peace with himself and his world. But I was immediately reminded of the task that awaited me. I sat, pen poised, and began the enjoyable process of inscribing books.

After the last book had been signed and people dispersed, I thanked the social director and the wonderful bookshop staff and headed off to meet Haggerty in the Commodore Club. It was only two decks up at the same end of the ship as the bookshop, and I was there in minutes. Michael was seated at a window looking out over the expanse of water ahead of us. The fog over the ocean had lifted considerably, although Michael seemed immersed in his own grayness. I took an adjoining stuffed chair, exhaled, and said, "Uri is on the ship."

"I know," he said, not looking at me.

"You do?"

"Yes. I spoke with him this morning."

I was surprised, considering how we'd played cat and mouse with the Israeli back in London.

"I followed him last night," I said.

157

"Is that so? Why?"

"Because *he* was following Kiki Largent."

"Oh."

"You said you had something to discuss with me. It sounded serious."

"Yes. You might say that, Jessica. I think my cover has been broken."

"Oh? How do you know?"

"Someone went through my cabin last night while I was in the Queens Room with Jennifer."

I sat up straighter. "Do you have any idea who it could be?"

"No. I thought you might have an answer."

"Me?"

"Yes."

"Why me?"

He turned to face me. "Because you're the only one on this ship who knows who I really am."

"First of all," I said, lowering my voice so as not to be overheard, "to accuse me of revealing your true identity is ridiculous. Why would I 'break your cover,' as you put it? I haven't talked about you — even as Wendell — to anyone."

"Who else knows?"

I sat back and thought for a moment before answering. "Well, what about your spy buddy Uri? He certainly knows who you are."

"He's a professional. He'd never put a fellow agent in jeopardy."

And you think I would? I thought. But I didn't voice it. I didn't want to get into an argument with him. "What about a member of the crew?" I asked. "Is it possible that someone from your office informed Cunard of the real reason for your being on the ship?"

Michael grimaced. "We don't operate that way."

"Look, Michael, I'm sorry that someone went through your cabin, and I'm also sorry if your true identity may have been revealed. Frankly, I think a little personal introspection might be in order. You had a few drinks last night. Perhaps you wanted to impress Jennifer that you were more than an Irish antiques dealer, selling posters of *Gone with the Wind* and *Birth of a Nation.* Could it be that your male ego came to the fore?"

His grimace turned into an expression of disbelief. "I can't believe you'd even think such a thing of me, Jessica."

"And I can't believe that you'd think I'd go around telling people that you're a spook."

"I hate that term."

"Sorry."

"Did you find out why Uri was following Kiki?"

"No. She went out on the promenade on Deck Seven and met with someone."

"Who?"

"I don't know. She gave him, or her, something. Or maybe he or she gave something to Kiki. I couldn't determine that. It was too dark and foggy."

"Sounds like the opening of one of your novels. 'It was a dark and stormy night.' "

"Oh, Michael, please."

"Just joking. Having someone search my cabin is serious stuff, Jessica."

"You're sure it happened?"

"Of course I'm sure. I always apply a wet strand of hair on my door and drawers. No doubt about it. The hairs were broken or had fallen off. Someone entered and snooped around."

"Probably your cabin steward. They come and go all the time to service the staterooms. Where *is* your cabin, by the way?"

"Deck Ten, midship."

"The deck under mine. Michael, I have a question."

"Is there ever a time when you don't?"

I ignored his sarcasm. "You hinted to me that you believe the stolen Heart of India

and the person, or persons, who stole it —
and killed its owner in the process — are on
this ship. What makes you think that?"

He looked at me as though I'd said something stupid. "It's pretty obvious, isn't it?
Look who's on board. The diamond owner's
partner is here, and he's London-based."

"I agree that his presence is tantalizing,
Michael, but —"

"You see, Jessica? You did it again. I must
insist you call me Wendell."

"Very well, Wendell. My point is that
because this individual happens to be on
this crossing, it doesn't mean that he had
anything to do with the diamond's theft. It
could be sheer coincidence."

He shook his head. "There's more to it,"
he said, "things I can't share with you." He
leaned close after surveying our immediate
area and said, "We *know* that the diamond
is on the *Queen Mary Two.*"

" 'We'?"

"MI6. Israel's Mossad. The CIA. Scotland
Yard. The Yard has come up with some solid
leads and shared it with MI6. Doesn't
always happen that one government agency
shares information with another, but in this
case the stakes are sufficiently high to
demand it. Trust me, Jessica. We *know* the
diamond is on the ship, and that the person

who stole it, who happens to be a cold-blooded killer *and* a provider of funds to terrorist organizations, is also here. Satisfied?"

"I —"

"Not only that, Jessica. We've learned that precious gems previously stolen throughout Europe often end up being smuggled into the United States by people who prefer to travel by ship, rather than by air. It's become one of their MOs."

Until that moment, the whole business of stolen diamonds and terrorist funding had been somewhat vague and conceptual for me. But Haggerty's certainty cast a new spell over it for me, gave me a sense of purpose that I hadn't felt to date, and I didn't like it one bit.

I glanced at my watch; I'd promised Harry that I'd join him for lunch. "I'd better be going," I told Haggerty. "Oh, if you don't know, I guess I should tell you that when I went to my cabin this morning, there was some official activity concerning Mr. Kim's room. Our steward, Rupesh, said he thought it had to do with something or someone missing. The staff captain was there along with a few others, and I saw Betty sitting on the bed in their stateroom. She appeared to be crying."

"Something missing?" Haggerty said. "No idea what it was?"

"No. I've told you all that I know."

I stood. "Coming to lunch, Mi— Wendell?"

"No. I have something else on my agenda."

I reached into my purse, withdrew the photo of Dennis Stanton that I'd purchased in the photo gallery that morning, and handed it to Haggerty. "Have you seen this man on the ship?" I asked.

"No. Who is he?"

I said lightly, "I thought you might know. Just someone who looks like an old friend. I'm probably wrong."

Haggerty looked skeptically at me. "He looks like he didn't want his photo taken."

"It does appear that way, doesn't it? Well, I'm sure we'll catch up later."

As I stepped away, Michael said, "Take care, Jessica."

My raised eyebrows invited clarification.

"These are bad people, Jessica. Watch yourself, and let me know if you come across anything that might be of help."

I'd balked at helping Michael Haggerty when he'd first asked for my assistance.

I no longer felt that way. If he was right about the missing diamond, or diamonds, being on board, and that the person or persons responsible for stealing them and killing the owner of the Heart of India was a passenger — and if money from the gem or gems would go to finance terrorist groups — I now shared his sense of urgency.

CHAPTER THIRTEEN

". . . . and so I had the pleasure of another tour of the bridge while you were signing books," Harry told me as we were finishing lunch. "The master of this ship is a splendid fellow who was gracious enough to honor my credentials as a fellow ship captain. Quite an impressive array of equipment, and sharp-looking young male and female officers up there, Jessica. Everything and everyone spick-and-span. Do you know the origin of that phrase, 'spick-and-span'?"

"No, I don't think I do, Harry."

"Goes back centuries. Nails used to secure timber planks on sailing ships were called 'spicks.' They called the timbers themselves 'spans.' Brand-new ships coming out of shipbuilders' yards were said to be 'spick and span new.' They eventually dropped the word 'new,' and 'spick-and-span' came to mean something new and immaculately maintained."

Dining with Harry Flynn was, as I'd come to expect, pleasant, relaxing — and educational. Because I'd arrived late, we had the table to ourselves. Jennifer and Kiki had been there earlier but, according to Harry, had eaten a quick lunch and left.

"Was Ms. Largent feeling better?" I asked.

"She seemed to be; ate what little she ordered and kept it down."

"That's good to hear." I pulled Dennis Stanton's photo from my bag and handed it to Harry. "You get around the ship quite a bit," I said. "Have you seen this fellow in your travels?"

Harry pulled a pair of half-glasses from his pocket, the only acknowledgment to his age that I'd noticed since we set sail. "No," he said, "can't say that I have." He started to hand the photo back to me but pulled it back for another close look. "Wait a minute, now. Maybe I have seen him," he said, frowning down at the picture. "He looks like a fellow who has a cabin a few doors down from mine."

"Where is your cabin?"

"Two decks below us on Deck Five."

"Are you sure he's the same man as in this picture?"

"I'm pretty sure. Who is he, Jessica? Is he bothering you?"

166

"No, no, nothing like that. He looks like someone I once knew."

"A former suitor?" Harry asked with a knowing smile.

I shook my head. "Harry," I said, "you've spent some time with Jennifer and Kiki. Have they spoken about their jewelry-design business?"

"A bit. Nothing specific. Why do you ask?"

"Just curious."

He scrutinized me for a moment before saying, "Why do I have this sneaky suspicion that you're in the process of researching your next murder-mystery novel?"

"I can't imagine."

"When you look at people, it's as though you're attempting to read their minds, access their inner lives."

"Really?"

"And your friend Wendell. He certainly asks a lot of questions."

"I hadn't noticed."

"Well," he said, "let me fill you in on some scuttlebutt that you might be able to use in your next novel. You know Mr. Kim, of course."

"Yes."

"I've been told that he was the partner of the fellow murdered in London during the robbery of a very rare diamond."

I wasn't sure whether to acknowledge that I already knew, but decided there was nothing to be gained by feigning ignorance. "Yes," I said, "I'd heard that, too."

"Those two brutish fellows with him. Rough-looking chaps, wouldn't you say?"

"They do look formidable."

He came closer. "They use the gym. We were there yesterday, and I happened to overhear a bit of their conversation. Not that I was trying to, of course, but one of them was speaking in a rather loud voice. Hard to be heard over some of those machines. He was telling his partner that he wouldn't mind if 'the boss' — yes, that's what he called him — he wouldn't mind if 'the boss' got his the way Yang did."

"Yang? Oh, the murdered owner of the diamond."

"Exactly. I remember his name from newspaper accounts."

"Yes. I do, too," I said, purposely neglecting to mention my other sources of the story. "Did he say anything to clarify what he meant?"

"Not that I heard, but his meaning doesn't take much of an imagination, does it?"

I tried to make light of it. "Probably had a bad day, that's all," I offered. "A disgruntled employee saying he'd like to kill his boss."

"Well, I hope he doesn't act on his feelings. By the way," Harry added, "that young lady Ms. Largent was in the gym, too, lifting weights. I imagine she could hold her own against those big fellows. She raised those weights as though they were balloons."

I could easily have sat there chatting with Harry for the rest of the day, but I wanted to squeeze in some of the remarkable range of activities the *QM2* had in store before the trip ended and we pulled into New York Harbor. That included attending the afternoon production in the Royal Court Theatre of a classic British comedy, *Hobson's Choice.* A theatrical group from London's Royal Academy of Dramatic Art, known as RADA, was part of the ship's entertainment, and I was looking forward to enjoying a few hours of good theater, particularly since I'd lost my opportunity to see a play in London when I'd accepted Haggerty's invitation to the Ivy. I'd seen the David Lean film version of *Hobson's Choice* many years ago, starring one of RADA's most celebrated graduates, Charles Laughton, and thoroughly enjoyed it.

I invited Harry to join me, but he declined. As we walked out of the dining room, he said, "I mentioned that I'd heard scuttlebutt about Mr. Kim. Do you happen to know the genesis of the word 'scuttlebutt'?"

I smiled. "I haven't the slightest idea, Harry, but I'm sure I'm about to find out."

"I'm not boring you with my stories, am I?"

"Not at all," I said, meaning it. "They're very enlightening, and I'm eager to learn. But would you mind telling me how the term 'scuttlebutt' originated on the way to the elevator? I don't want to be late for the theater."

"Well, many years ago at sea, the water barrel that held the crew's drinking water was called a 'butt,' and the hole cut into the butt from which sailors drank was called a 'scuttle.' Sailors tended to gather around the barrel and pass on the latest gossip, so when the captain wanted to catch up on what was going on, he'd ask someone what 'the scuttle butt' was."

I laughed. "Like office workers congregating around the watercooler."

"Precisely."

"What are your plans for this afternoon?" I asked.

"Some golf — the captain has opened the decks now that the weather has cooperated — and some time in the computer room. I've just recently become interested in e-mail and other remarkable means of communication. Never too old to learn, are we?"

"Absolutely not. See you at dinner."

The theater was at the opposite end of the ship, and I had only a few minutes to get there before the curtain went up. I just made it, sat back as the house lights dimmed, and became lost in the deliciously funny antics on stage. But it was an abbreviated version of the play, and my afternoon's entertainment was soon ended. The lights came up, and I joined the throng slowly filing out of the theater. Up ahead, in the mass of departing theatergoers, I spotted a familiar face. It was Dennis Stanton.

"Yoo-hoo," I called out, frantically waving and bouncing up and down to see over those in front of me. "Dennis?"

I saw him turn around.

"Excuse me," I said, hoping to skirt several people who had stopped to greet one another. "I'm trying to reach my friend."

I waved and called again, but Dennis was too far away. "Pardon me," I said to a large gentleman in front of me, thinking I might squeeze by him.

"We're all trying to get out of here, lady. Wait your turn."

By the time I reached the theater doors, he was gone, of course. I retraced my steps the length of the ship, looking through the windows of the Mayfair Shops in case he had stopped to buy a souvenir. The day's art auction was over, but I wandered among the hundreds of works still to be sold, thinking they may have attracted his interest. No Dennis. Finally, I went to Deck Five on the off chance that he might appear from one of the staterooms, provided, of course, that Harry had accurately identified him. I knew it was a long shot, but on such a large ship, with so many places he could be, it was worth the effort.

After twice walking the length of the hallway on Deck Five without seeing my old friend, I went to the Grand Lobby and sat for fifteen minutes in case he happened to stroll by. No luck. All my perambulations had worked up a good thirst, and I stopped at the Golden Lion Pub on Deck Two, where I sat at the long, curved bar and ordered a club soda with lime. It was relatively quiet there, the daily pub lunch crowd having taken off for other parts of the ship. I heard voices from around the bend, people sounding as though they were engaged in some sort of contest or game. Curious, I moved to another barstool that afforded me a view of the goings-on. A dart game was in progress. Eight men and women surrounded a uniformed crew member who was conducting the tournament, keeping track of scores and advising players when it was their turn. Seven of the eight were dressed in afternoon casual wear, shorts and colorful shirts, sneakers and sandals. But one man who'd just been handed the darts was dressed in a white linen suit, pale blue shirt, and royal blue tie.

Dennis Stanton!

I decided simply to watch the competition until it ended before I approached him. I didn't have to. When a young man was declared the winner, and the others drifted away, Dennis walked in my direction. I said nothing. He stopped, cocked his head, and narrowed his eyes.

"Jessica?"

"Hello, Dennis."

"How marvelous to see you again." He gave me a brief hug, but his eyes avoided mine. "I knew you were on board, of course; couldn't miss your picture in the daily program," he said, defensively. "Terribly sorry. I meant to attend your lectures but got caught up with other things, I'm afraid."

"I was hoping to run into you," I said.

He took the stool next to mine. "How did you know I was here?"

"I saw *your* picture in the photo gallery,

the one taken when you boarded."

His expression turned sour, then brightened. "Imagine that."

"You looked as though you didn't want your picture taken."

"No, not at all," he said with a wave of his hand. "Whatever gave you that idea?"

I didn't answer and instead changed the subject. "So, what brings you on the *Queen Mary Two*? Vacation?"

"Yes, quite. I'm on holiday. Was due for a holiday. Haven't been on holiday in some time now. Great place for a holiday — don't you think? Bracing sea air and all that."

"You look well rested," I said. "Are you traveling under a different name?"

"Why would you say that?"

"When I saw your photo, I checked the ship's passenger manifest. They don't have any Dennis Stanton listed."

He forced a small laugh. "Must be a mistake. You know how bloody computers are always making mistakes."

I nodded.

"What about you, Jessica? On holiday?"

"Part holiday, part work. As you read, I'm lecturing."

"Oh, yes, yes, of course you are. Going well?"

"Very well. The last time we met, you were

serving on a much smaller ship in the Caribbean as security officer. Still doing that?"

"No. I had my fling with a tropical adventure."

"Back to investigating jewel thefts for that insurance company in San Francisco?"

"That's all in the past," he said, running a finger under his collar. "You have quite a memory, Jessica."

"Yes, I do. What dining room are you in? I haven't seen you."

"I'm booked at the Princess Grill level, but I've been taking meals in my cabin."

"Keeping a low profile?"

"No, just more comfortable there."

"Dennis — ?"

"Yes, luv?"

"The theft of the Heart of India diamond in London wouldn't have anything to do with you being on board — would it?"

"I'm not sure what you're talking about."

"It's been in every newspaper in the country, probably in the world for that matter."

His blue eyes lit up, and he raised a finger. "Oh, yes, *that* diamond. I have heard of it. The chap who owned it was killed, as I recall."

"Unfortunately."

There was an awkward lull, and I decided this wasn't getting me anywhere. I checked my watch. "I really should be going, Dennis," I said. "I'm so pleased to have bumped into you."

I swung around on the barstool and was about to step away when he said, "Jessica. Don't leave just yet."

I resumed my place at the bar.

"I, ah — I think we should have a private chat, but not here."

"A private chat about what?"

"Come to my cabin. We can talk safely there."

"I —"

"Please. Having you on board is — how shall I say it? — well, it's somewhat difficult for me."

"How so?"

"Please, I promise only to hold you up for fifteen minutes, twenty at the most. I have a nice little bar set up there and —"

"All right, Dennis, but I don't want a drink."

"Splendid. You don't mind if I have one, do you?"

We went to the stern of the ship and up to Deck Five. As we reached Dennis's door, Harry Flynn came from his cabin. "Hello there," he said. Seeing Stanton, he said to me, "Ah, I see you found him. Good for you, Jessica." He thrust out his hand to Dennis. "Harry Flynn," he said.

"My pleasure," Dennis reciprocated without mentioning his own name.

"Have to run," Harry said. "See you at dinner, Jessica? We're formal tonight."

"Yes, I'll be there."

Harry lingered a moment as Dennis unlocked his door. My eighty-two-year-old new friend winked at me — actually winked at me — and sashayed away.

I wanted to call after him, "It's not what you think, Harry," but it would have meant yelling.

Oh, well, I thought as I followed Dennis inside. *I've been on the receiving end of worse rumors.*

Chapter Fourteen

Stanton's stateroom was as neat as its occupant. A small bar had been set up on a table in front of the couch, with a variety of liquors, mixers, and a recently filled ice bucket.

"Sure you won't have a drink, Jessica?" Stanton asked as he removed his jacket and carefully hung it in the closet, assuring that it faced in the same direction as other jackets.

"Positive, but thank you."

"You won't mind if I do."

"Go right ahead."

He made himself a gin and tonic, squeezed a wedge of lime into it, and suggested that we go to the balcony. The weather had continued to improve as the day went on; the sun now shone brightly, catching the tops of small whitecaps and turning the vast ocean into a sparkling palette.

We sat in the two chairs, and Stanton

raised his glass. "To seeing you again, Jessica." I raised my fist and touched it to the rim of his glass.

"So," I said, "why does having me aboard make your life difficult, as you put it?"

He sighed, sipped from his drink, and placed it on the table. "The truth is, Jessica, you were right when you said I'm not listed on the passenger manifest. I'm using a different name."

I'd already come to that conclusion.

"Obviously you aren't taking this crossing for pleasure," I said.

"You are right, dear lady. I am on assignment."

"For whom?"

"Consolidated Casualty, of course. They couldn't do without me. After my sojourn as security officer on that bloody cruise ship in the Caribbean — God, what a slipshod operation that was — I went back to San Francisco and allowed them to entice me back to work. I struck a hard bargain, but they bought it."

"Am I right in assuming that Consolidated Casualty is the company that insured the Heart of India diamond, and that's the reason you're on this crossing?"

"A fair assumption, and a partially correct one. Consolidated is one of two insurers of that particular rock."

"There's another?"

"Consolidated likes to share the risk with items of that value. They're coinsurers with Kensington Limited, a British firm."

"Kensington?" I said. "I've met a Richard Kensington on the ship, at dinner. Do you think he might be connected with the Kensington insurance company?"

"Could be. What did he say he does for a living?"

"Something about working alone."

"Conveniently vague, wouldn't you say? I'll check it out. Richard, you say?" He wrote the name on a pad. "I wasn't informed that Kensington was sending anyone. Did he say anything about the theft?"

"No. He says he's on his honeymoon. Or rather his wife, Marcia, said so."

"Interesting."

"Mind another question?" I asked.

"Go ahead."

"What's led you to believe that the diamond might be on this ship?"

"I didn't say that, did I?"

I cocked my head at him, and raised my eyebrows, saying nothing.

He coughed and took another sip before answering. "Well, I can't be specific, of course, but sources we've developed in

180

London have led us to that conclusion."

George hadn't mentioned that officials suspected someone was bringing the gem on board. I wondered if he knew, or if he thought he was protecting me by withholding that piece of information. Should I mention my friendship with Inspector Sutherland? No, George wouldn't appreciate that. I did, however, ask, "Dennis, just out of curiosity, do your 'sources' include Scotland Yard?"

His simple nod affirmed it, but he added, "Interpol, too. I won't go into detail, but you should know that there is a possible terrorist link to the theft."

"Yes, I've heard something about that."

"It was in the papers, of course, but purely as speculation. Our boys say if there's any truth to the rumor, we'll have a battle royal on our hands to make certain we don't pay off on the policy. The governments — yours and mine — are very interested in the outcome."

I looked away from him and took in the beginning of a magnificent sunset over the ocean. It was all so peaceful out there. But on the ship, "peace" obviously wasn't in the vocabulary of some people.

"Dennis," I said, "if Consolidated has to distribute the proceeds from the policy on the diamond, along with this other firm, Kensington, who gets the money? Mr. Yang didn't have any immediate family, as I understand it."

"That's right," Dennis confirmed. "But the Heart of India was owned not by Yang himself. It was an asset of one of his many corporations."

"Which means that any business partners he had in this corporation would benefit. Did he have any?"

"Partners, you mean?"

I nodded. I suspected that Kim Chin-Hwa was a likely partner in the ownership of the Heart of India, although he had never said so, and in fact had gone out of his way to hint that the diamond was Yang's alone. But I hoped Dennis would provide additional information if he thought that I was in the dark.

"Many of his corporate entities had multiple partners," Dennis confirmed, "but there was only one other than Yang in the corporate name that purchased the diamond."

All right, Jessica, I told myself, *stop playing games.*

"Kim Chin-Hwa," I said flatly.

Dennis sat back, eyes wide. I hoped he wasn't acting. "How do *you* know about him?" he asked, shooting me an ironic look

182

and taking a final sip of his drink.

"I've met him. He was at a dinner party I attended in London at the home of my British publisher. I assume you know he's on board the ship. In fact, his cabin is next to mine. We've spent quite a bit of time together. We've played bridge, and I've danced with him."

"I think I need another drink," Dennis said, disappearing into the cabin and returning with his refill.

When he'd taken his seat again, he said, "Why am I surprised that you're way ahead of me, Jessica?"

"Pure coincidence, Dennis; several in fact. A coincidence that I've ended up on the *Queen Mary Two* with an alleged jewel thief and possible murderer. And, of course, another coincidence that I've met up with you."

"It's obvious, then, why I'm here."

"To try to recover the Heart of India from Kim Chin-Hwa — provided he's the one who stole it, had his partner killed, and has brought it with him on this trip. That seems to me like a long shot, Dennis."

"A chance worth taking. If it doesn't pay off, I'll continue the investigation elsewhere. But for now, I'm focused on this ship and Mr. Kim."

"Then you must have seen me with Mr. Kim."

"Well, I may have spotted you from afar. Since you seem to have befriended him, Jessica, perhaps you wouldn't mind sharing with me what you've learned from your relationship with Kim."

"I'd hardly call it a relationship, Dennis. Because we were at the same dinner party prior to the crossing, we naturally touched base again once we were on board. That was the first night. Actually, his demeanor toward me has changed since then. He questioned whether I was doing research for a new novel. I assured him I wasn't, but he made it clear that he would not be happy if I was. He also seems to have decided to lower his profile on the ship. I haven't seen much of him lately."

"A suggestion of guilt, I'd say."

"I wouldn't take it as that at all." I looked at my watch. There wasn't a lot of time before dinner and I needed to change into formal clothes. "Dennis, I appreciate you being forthright with me about why you're on board," I said, standing and stepping through the door into the cabin.

Dennis followed.

"I don't mean to question your methods," I said, "but how does taking your meals in your cabin further your investigation? I'd think you'd be doing everything you can to get close to Kim."

He laughed away my comment. "I haven't been a total recluse, Jessica. In fact, I've spent some time with Kim's mistress. I assume you know her, too."

"Betty LeClair."

"Right. Beautiful creature."

"Yes, she is beautiful."

"We share an appreciation for art. She purchased two lovely paintings at today's auction."

"And did you learn anything apart from the fact that she likes art?" I asked.

"Well, she's partial to expensive clothing and perfume. No question about that. Shalini perfume, if my nose serves me right, and Jacques Vert dresses."

"Important information."

I went to the door and was about to open it when I had an idea. "Why don't you break your pattern and join us for dinner tonight?"

"Couldn't possibly, Jessica."

"Kim and his party will probably be there," I said. "We don't sit together, but his table is close by. I think that you'll find the others at my table interesting. The gentleman we bumped into in the hallway is a former merchant marine captain, a lovely, entertaining man. There's an antiques dealer from Dublin, Wendell Jones. And Wendell has brought two women to the table. One is a jewelry designer, Jennifer Kahn. Her assistant is Kiki Largent. I really think that you'd —"

His expression went from surprise, to shock, back to surprise, and then to a bright smile.

"I'd be delighted to join you," he said. "What time?"

"We generally are seated at about seven. Drinks in the lounge at six, six fifteen? Oh, Dennis, what name are you using this time?"

"William MacForester. I'm in real estate in San Francisco. You can call me Bill. Can't wait to dine with you and your friends this evening, Jessica. I am so pleased we've joined up again."

Joined?

CHAPTER FIFTEEN

My time spent with Dennis Stanton raised a number of questions that I chewed on while dressing for dinner.

His surprise that someone from Kensington, the British insurer, might be on board didn't make sense to me. Dennis was working for Consolidated Casualty, which had partnered with Kensington Limited to insure the Heart of India. Surely they'd be working closely together to locate the missing gem and avoid having to pay the beneficiary of the policies, Walter Soon Yang's company, in which Kim Chin-Hwa was now the sole surviving partner. And if they were not cooperating, why not?

Too, what was behind Stanton's sudden enthusiasm for my dinner invitation? It was after I'd named those who'd be at our table that he'd changed his mind and agreed to join us. Whose name had triggered his abrupt turnaround?

I had almost forgotten about the young couple who'd shared our table that first night at sea. Aside from when I'd seen them engage in horseplay on the deck, and noticed that they now sat at a table for two, Richard Kensington and his wife, Marcia, had slipped my mind. But he shared the same name as the British insurance firm that had coinsured the Heart of India. Of course, the similarity in names could easily have been coincidental. I assumed that "Kensington" was a relatively common name in Great Britain. But that didn't mean that it *was* coincidental. Was there a link between the sour young man and the coinsurer of the Heart of India? It was too providential to simply disavow the possibility that his presence on board was connected to the theft. Were those young people really on their honeymoon? I had no tangible reason to doubt it, but made a mental note to ask some questions should the opportunity arise.

Rupesh was in the hallway when I exited my cabin dressed in a long black gown with a beaded bodice.

"Good evening, madam," he said. "You are off to the formal dinner, I see."

"Good evening, Rupesh. You work long hours, *I* see."

"Very long hours, madam. It is expected of room stewards."

"I hope you've found time to contact your mother back in India."

"Oh, yes, I did, madam. I wrote and told her that a lovely lady on the ship had reminded me to do so, and mentioned that you and Maniram live in the same town."

"Good," I said, laughing. "I trust it's the first of many letters to her."

As I walked away and set out on the long trek to the Princess Grill, I thought about Rupesh. He was an excellent steward, of course, but I wondered why he'd wanted the job in the first place. According to his cousin Maniram, he had a college degree and was skilled in computers and had taught school, among other activities. Of course, Maniram had also said that Rupesh was a free spirit, an adventurer who, it was clear to see, had trouble sticking with any career for very long. Some people have a different work ethic. They can't adjust to a nine-to-five job. Either they need constant change or they don't like having a boss or they simply want to know what else is out there. Signing on to work on the *Queen Mary 2* probably supported Rupesh's wanderlust, a chance to see the world and put away some money. I admired him for that.

In my estimation, too many young people fail to take advantage of the opportunity to travel, free of family responsibilities, to learn about new cultures and broaden their view of the world and their place in it. Chances were that Rupesh would honor whatever employment contract he'd signed and then move on to another adventure, another life-enhancing experience.

I met Dennis Stanton exiting the elevator, and we walked together into the lounge, where Harry Flynn, Michael Haggerty, Jennifer Kahn, and Kiki Largent had gathered at the bar. I looked around for Mr. Kim and his party, but they either hadn't arrived yet or had enjoyed drinks earlier and were already in the dining room. I made the introductions and was proud of myself when I managed to introduce Dennis Stanton as William — "call me Bill" — MacForester to "antiques dealer" Wendell Jones without the slightest hitch in my voice.

"Delighted to have another join our party," said Harry, who wore his double-breasted white tux jacket, a frilly pale blue tuxedo shirt, and a dark blue bow tie and cummerbund with tiny white stars on them. He stood out from the other men, who were dressed in black tuxedos and more conservative accessories. Jennifer, too, stood out in yet another shimmering designer gown, this one of pale pink satin, and her fingers and neck were adorned with obviously expensive jewelry. Kiki's black "uniform" was identical to what she'd worn the previous evening, the only change being a heavy gold necklace replacing her seashells, and gold earrings in the shape of fish. My gown for this evening fell in between Jennifer's and Kiki's in terms of formal wear, and my jewelry, while pieces I love, was not flamboyant enough to draw attention.

"We started the party without you," Jennifer said. "You'll have to catch up."

I accepted Harry's offer of a sidecar, a refreshing drink that Seth had introduced me to back home.

"That's quite a lovely brooch you're wearing," Dennis said to Jennifer, leaning in so close to observe the pin that his nose was dangerously near her décolletage.

"It's one of my more popular designs," she said of the diamond cat's head with yellow eyes. "The eyes are a kind of chrysoberyl called cymophane," she said, smiling down at Dennis as he raised his head. "I liked the synchrony of using cat's-eye gemstones for the cat's eyes. Amusing, don't you think?"

"I do," Dennis said, touching the long earrings she wore.

"Jennifer designs all her own jewelry," Michael said, scowling.

"What a talent, and so beautiful, too," Dennis said, holding her gaze. He placed his hand on Jennifer's bare arm. "Where are you from? I hope it's somewhere near the West Coast of the U.S."

"How did you know?" she replied, clearly charmed. "My family moved to San Francisco when I was ten, but I live in London now."

"My two favorite places in the world," Dennis said. "My stomping grounds are the city by the bay, San Francisco." He broke into a few bars of Tony Bennett's great hit "I Left My Heart in San Francisco." Haggerty, who sat on the other side of Jennifer, watched Stanton closely. His scowl deepened.

"How long have you lived in London?" I asked Jennifer.

"Oh, for many years," she replied, her speech taking on a hint of a British accent I hadn't noticed before. "I've even begun to talk like a limey."

"I hardly think the term 'limey' applies to this lovely lady," Harry Flynn said. "It's actually American slang for British sailors. Know where it came from?"

"Probably had something to do with limes," Kiki mumbled.

"You are exactly right," said Harry.

"Another time, Harry," Haggerty said. "I think we're ready to go into the dining room."

"Oh, of course," Harry replied, looking around as the dining room captain came to lead us to our table.

"I agree with you," Stanton said to Harry, clapping the older man's shoulder with one hand, and taking Jennifer's arm with the other. "This lady is no common sailor."

We followed the captain through the lounge, but paused to allow Betty and Kim's two bodyguards to pass us on their way to the grill. Dennis waved hello to her. The friendly gesture was met with a blank look, Betty's eyes skimming over our convivial group without comment or even recognition. I looked at Dennis for a reaction. He shrugged and smiled.

We fell in behind and took our table. Harry and Jennifer had many questions for Dennis — "Bill" MacForester, as far as they were concerned — about San Francisco and his world travels, and he handled them with aplomb. Because he was the new face, most of the interest was trained on him, much to Haggerty's obvious chagrin. His witty repartee steeped in an Irish brogue was absent, his expressive, animated face a more somber mask. It was evident to me that the root of his discontent was the attention paid to Jennifer Kahn by Dennis. *Michael must have developed a real crush on Jennifer,* I thought, *and doesn't appreciate another alpha male horning in on his territory.* I silently prayed that an ugly scene wouldn't develop between them.

We left the grill at the same time as Betty and her protectors. I asked as we passed each other, "Is Mr. Kim not feeling well?"

"That's right," she said. "He's not feeling well."

End of conversation.

Harry's suggestion that we all repair to the Queens Room after dinner for some libations and a little dancing was welcomed. It was filling up when we arrived, but we found a table large enough to accommodate our group. Two dozen couples whirled around the dance floor, including women who danced with the ship's gentlemen hosts. Betty and her two muscular escorts were nowhere to be seen, and I wondered what was ailing Mr. Kim. I didn't dwell on it, however, because before I knew it, Harry had led me to the floor, where we enjoyed dancing to the band's rendition of "Where or When," followed by "All the Things You Are." Kiki, who had made it clear from the first night that she wasn't interested in dancing, refused all invitations, but Jennifer couldn't seem to get enough of it. She was happy to let Dennis monopolize her time, laughing loudly at whatever he said, leaving a grouchy Haggerty sitting at the table with Kiki, his mood becoming darker as the hours passed. I was pleased that when Harry and I returned to the table, Dennis had escorted Jennifer there, too. Michael immediately got to his feet and brought her back to the dance floor, but his petulance did little to charm her.

I was aware that I was in a strange, somewhat uncomfortable position. I knew both Michael and Dennis, but both were operating under assumed names. I hadn't let on that I knew them well; as far as the others were concerned, I had no former connection with Dennis. Dennis told the group that we'd met during a friendly game of darts in the pub, and that I'd invited him to join our dinner table. Haggerty stuck with his cover as a Dublin antiques dealer, which Dennis never questioned, nor had anyone else. I felt very much the keeper of secrets. Harry Flynn was the only man who was who he said he was.

It was a pleasant few hours in the magnificent Queens Room. The problem, at least from my perspective, was that neither Haggerty nor Stanton was in a position to further his respective investigation. Both men had identified Kim Chin-Hwa as the prime suspect in the theft of the Heart of India, but he was nowhere to be found that evening.

Our little group started to disband when Harry announced that he was going to the casino to enjoy another toss of the dice. The rest of us declined to join him. He wished everyone a pleasant rest of the evening, kissed me, Jennifer, and Kiki on the cheek, and strode off, whistling "Ain't She Sweet" along with the orchestra.

The question of whether Michael or Dennis would get to extend the evening with Jennifer was answered when Michael announced he was tired and going to bed. Dennis suggested to Jennifer — pointedly leaving Kiki out of his invitation — that she join him in the disco. She thanked him but said she, too, was tired and needed a good night's sleep.

"I can't thank you enough for including me this evening, Jessica," Dennis said as we watched them leave the room.

"You seemed to be enjoying yourself," I said.

"Oh, the evening provided more than simple enjoyment, dear lady, thanks to you."

"I'm pleased to hear that, Dennis, and I can imagine why. You seem taken with Ms. Kahn."

"A lovely creature."

"I saw her jewelry was of interest to you; not surprising, considering all the gems you've dealt with in your — in your career."

"Don't be reticent, Jessica. When we're alone, you may feel free to refer to my previous wayward past. I have no regrets about having been a jewel thief. It's led to a rather interesting life on the right side of the law."

"Well," I said, "I'm just glad that you and Jennifer hit it off so well."

"Much to Mr. Jones's displeasure."

For a moment, I didn't recognize the name. "Oh, yes, Wendell," I said, recovering. "He seems to be taken with her, too. Will I be seeing any more of you now that you and Jennifer have — how shall I say it? — have *found* each other?"

I said it in jest, but his reply was anything but joking.

"My interest in her, Jessica, is purely professional."

197

My face expressed my surprise at the comment.

"Professional?" I said.

"Yes."

"How so?"

"The lovely lady is well-known in my professional field, so to speak."

"I hadn't realized she was such a famous jewelry designer."

"Designer? Is that what she told you?"

"Yes. Isn't she?"

"My dear, Jennifer Kahn is a rather famous — or should I say infamous? — jewel thief."

"Oh my!"

"Yes, oh my, indeed. Care for a drink?"

"If it will keep you talking."

Chapter Sixteen

"I can't believe this," Stanton said after we'd found a secluded corner of the Commodore Club.

"You took the words right out of my mouth, Dennis. You owe me a few more details."

"Jennifer Kahn is a jewel thief, and, I might add, a very successful one. I had no idea she was on the ship. Thanks to you, not only do I know it — I've had the perfect opportunity to befriend her, the pleasure of dining with her, and even enjoying a dance or two. Thank you, Jessica."

I hadn't intended to have a drink, but since I'd barely touched my sidecar in the Queens Room, I opted to order one from the waitress. Dennis bantered with her: "We're celebrating," he said. "I believe that champagne would be appropriate. Your best and two glasses."

"Cancel my sidecar," I said. "Champagne

will do just fine."

When the waitress walked away, I asked Dennis, "Why a celebration?"

"Because, dear lady, you have put me in the position of possibly killing two very large birds with the proverbial single stone."

I shook my head, confused.

"I'll try to explain," he said.

"Please do."

"But let's wait until the bubbly arrives."

The waitress delivered our champagne in an ice bucket with great flourish, deftly uncorked it, and poured the fizzy liquid into two graceful flutes. She left, and Dennis raised his flute. "To Jessica Fletcher," he said, "and to this lovely ship."

"Thank you, and now I'm eager for your explanation."

"Let me see," he said. "I'll start here. Are you aware, Jessica, that there were a number of London jewelry shop break-ins over the past few weeks?"

"Yes, I am — three, if I'm not mistaken. At least that's what I recall hearing."

"Exactly. Three. The thieves walked away with a hefty payday, gems worth millions of dollars."

Anticipating what was to come next, I said, "And you think that Ms. Kahn was behind them."

"Oh, it's not a matter of what I think," he said. "We *know* she was behind at least one of them, maybe two, and possibly all three."

"Then why hasn't she been arrested?"

"Because there's no proof — yet. She's a clever operator, has others do the actual heists, and stays very much in the background. She has an international crew of thieves working for her, and they're suspected of strikes everywhere. Paris, Rome, London, Dubai, Cairo — you name the city and chances are good that they've plied their trade there."

"And she has the perfect cover as a jewelry designer," I put in.

"Precisely. Not only does her 'work' enable her to break down the merchandise and reset it for the market, but she's expected to wear ostentatious jewelry to showcase her designs. She's been so successful lately, however, she may not have had time to remake all the pieces. We believe there are times when she simply dons one of the necklaces, pins, and bracelets taken from a recent heist, and passes it off as one of her own creations."

"Were those jewelry shops where the thefts took place insured by Consolidated Casualty?"

He took a sip of his champagne, smacked

his lips, and said, "Yes, indeed."

"But you said you're on this crossing because of the Heart of India diamond. You had no idea that she would be here?"

"Not a clue, Jessica. I was in London trying to nail down her involvement in those cases but had to abandon the investigation once I learned that Kim Chin-Hwa was about to leave London for New York. It put me in a sticky spot, deciding which one to focus on. Obviously, Kim took precedence. However, now that Jennifer Kahn is also aboard, it not only makes my job easier — it verifies to some extent what I've come to believe."

"Which is?"

"That Ms. Kahn and Mr. Kim are linked."

"Well!" I said, sitting back. "This trip gets more and more intriguing."

" 'Intrigue' is the word. You already knew that the late Walter Soon Yang was suspected of funding terrorist organizations. He got a steal on the Heart of India when certain other buyers and their representatives were unable to attend the sale. A nifty bit of maneuvering if I do say so. Yang and his investors — we know of Kim, but there may be others — were merely waiting for the diamond to increase in value before putting it back on the market. Those who'd been squeezed out of the first opportunity to buy it would likely bid up the price a considerable amount. The resulting auction would allow the sellers to net a tidy profit to share, with enough left over to pour into whatever nefarious activities they'd taken a liking to."

"Is Jennifer Kahn also suspected of aiding terrorists?"

He shrugged. "Hard to say. But she is believed to have begun fencing some of her stolen jewelry through a certain businessman in London."

"Kim Chin-Hwa?"

"We don't have names yet. But if it is Kim, that would explain her sudden presence on the ship."

"Sudden?"

"A last-minute decision on her part. She'd had plans for last weekend to visit with friends in Bath. But I'd heard she'd canceled those plans at the last minute. Now I know why. She booked passage on this ship, where Mr. Kim and party also happen to be passengers. Intriguing coincidence, wouldn't you say, Jessica?"

I sipped my champagne and gazed through the large window at the ocean illuminated by a full moon.

Had I made a mistake in accepting the offer to lecture on the *Queen Mary 2*? I certainly couldn't be accused of having instigated any of the mounting mystery that had swirled around me ever since leaving Southampton on Saturday. Nor could I have anticipated that the theft of a famous diamond in London, and the three break-ins of London jewelry shops, would have followed me on board.

All these coincidences!

I hadn't seen Michael Haggerty in years, yet there he was at the dinner party, and here he was on the ship. And Dennis Stanton, my reformed jewel thief friend, also showed up after years of no contact.

Had Kim Chin-Hwa murdered his partner, Walter Soon Yang, in order to take possession of the Heart of India? If so, had he brought it with him with the intent of selling it in New York, and using those funds to aid terrorist activities around the world?

Jennifer Kahn was the mastermind of an international jewel theft gang? Was Dennis correct in suspecting that she'd begun fencing the jewels stolen by her gang through Yang and Kim? Had she booked last-minute passage on the ship because Kim and his entourage would be on board? What would she gain by that? Was she there to keep an eye on him? I certainly hadn't witnessed any connection between them, no conversation, no meetings. Of course, it was also possible that any fencing of her stolen gems through Yang or Kim might have been executed by a middleman, and that neither Yang nor Kim knew who she was or that she was involved. I doubted that, but it was a possibility. *So many possibilities.*

But there had been that clandestine night-time exchange between an unknown person and Kahn's assistant, Kiki Largent. Whom had she met, and why?

Michael Haggerty was aboard because of allegations that Kim funded terrorists. Perhaps Uri, the Israeli intelligence agent, booked the crossing for the same reason. Aside from when I'd seen him tailing Kiki Largent, he'd been invisible. Was he working hand in hand with Haggerty? It would be just like Michael not to mention that.

Dennis intruded on my silent introspection. "Tell me more about this Kensington chap, the honeymooner," he said.

"Oh, yes. I looked for him at dinner tonight, but he and his wife weren't at their usual table. They probably decided on room service — they are on their honeymoon after all — or ate in the Kings Court." *But are they really on their honeymoon?* I silently wondered. "Frankly," I said, "I can't help but wonder whether he has some connection with the Kensington insurance firm."

"I don't blame you for wondering that, Jessica. I've been working with a British freelance agent who's been assigned to the case. I'll call or e-mail him and see what I can find out."

Without waiting to be served again, Dennis lifted the champagne bottle from the bucket and poured himself a second glass. I waved my hand over mine. I was tempted to reveal that he wasn't the only person on the crossing using an alias, and that there was another undercover agent interested in stolen jewelry — Michael Haggerty. Their motives for being passengers were different, however. Haggerty was tracking the terrorist aspect of the case, while Stanton wanted to save his insurance company a large payout. It might prove beneficial for them to join forces, or at least compare notes. But to raise that would be to expose both men for who they really were, and I'd promised each not to betray them.

"You keep drifting off to another planet," he said.

"I'm sorry. There's a lot to digest in what you've said."

"Yes. I'm sorry to burden you with all this when you were expecting simply to have a pleasant voyage. But your connections with these individuals could prove very beneficial for me, and I'm eager to hear your thoughts."

What I'd actually been thinking was how much I wished I could talk to George Sutherland. He would be able to sort it all out for me. He's one of the most clear-headed, rational, and insightful men I've ever known, and to be able to analyze the various scenarios with him would have been wonderful.

"I think a good night's sleep will aid my weary brain immensely," I said. "I'm going to go back to my cabin."

"But you've barely touched your champagne."

"It was wonderful, Dennis, but I've had enough to drink for tonight."

"Hope my laying this out hasn't upset you."

"Upset me? Not at all. But I do have some thinking to do."

"Lecturing tomorrow?"

"Yes, in the evening."

"See you at breakfast?"

"I suppose so."

"You don't mind my sharing your table again?"

"To stay close to Jennifer? Of course not. You've been a big hit with everyone."

"Except that Jones fellow."

I smiled. "I think he considers you a competitor for Jennifer's affections. He doesn't know that she steals jewels for a living."

Dennis laughed. "I promise not to disillusion him."

As I prepared to leave, I thought of one more question. "What about Jennifer's assistant?" I asked. "Do you know anything about Kiki Largent?"

Dennis's smile was rueful. "From what I hear, she's Jennifer's muscle."

"Muscle?"

"Kiki does the dirty work when someone in Jennifer's gang gets out of line. She can turn quite nasty, they say."

"That means she's probably Jennifer's bodyguard, too," I said. "If I were you, I would step carefully around that one."

"I've got a pretty good uppercut, but I've never used it on a woman."

"Let's hope you never have to."

With that last bit of scuttlebutt in mind — I thought of Harry Flynn and wondered how he'd done in the casino — I made my way back to Deck Eleven and my stateroom. When I turned the corner from the elevator lobby, I saw a pair of uniformed crew members standing in front of Kim's open door. As I passed by, I paused and peered between them. One of them politely asked me to move on, but just then my steward, Rupesh, emerged from the cabin, followed by another crewman. Although I couldn't be sure, it appeared to me as though he was being escorted from the room.

"Good evening, Rupesh," I said. "Is everything all right?"

He looked at me, said nothing, his face devoid of expression, and walked away swiftly, preceded and followed by members of the *QM2* staff.

"What's going on?" I asked the remaining crewman as he closed the door and took up his position in front of it.

He nodded curtly.

"Is something wrong in Mr. Kim's cabin?"

"No, ma'am."

"Why was my cabin steward being led away?"

"I'm not at liberty to say, ma'am."

"Has something happened to Mr. Kim or his companion?"

"There's been an accident, ma'am. That's all I know."

CHAPTER SEVENTEEN

My mind was bombarded with conflicting, confusing thoughts as I entered my cabin. An accident? Who'd been hurt? Had Rupesh suffered some sort of injury? He looked healthy enough to me, albeit grim-faced. The more I thought about it, the more it became clear that he'd been escorted from Kim's stateroom by uniformed staff the way criminals are led from a scene, although I hadn't seen any handcuffs. What had he done, or what was he accused of doing?

I thought back to seeing Betty in tears, and Rupesh telling me that something, or someone, was missing from her cabin. What was that all about? It seemed I was missing too many pieces to fit the clues together.

I opened my door a few times and saw that the crew member was still standing guard outside Kim's stateroom. I smiled at him each time but received only a blank stare in return.

I turned on the TV and flipped through the channels. A movie that held no interest for me was playing. Other channels didn't offer a respite from my cluttered mind, nor did sitting on the balcony. Rupesh had already prepared the room for the night, turning down the bedspread and placing a small square of chocolate on my pillow. He had also carefully hung my robe on a hook in the bathroom. I debated changing into my nightclothes, and decided against it. I'd been tired before, but I was now wide-awake.

I ended up pacing the room, going from the door to the balcony and back again, over and over, until I decided that I simply could not stay there any longer. I hung up my long gown, changed into a more comfortable pair of mauve slacks, simple white shirt, and sandals, grabbed my purse from where I'd dropped it on the bed, and stepped into the hallway. Another stern look from the uniform in front of Kim's door said loud and clear that to ask questions would be futile.

I set off without a destination in mind. I suppose I was hoping to run into Haggerty, or Stanton, but I didn't count on it.

Harry Flynn. Would he still be in the casino?

He was, standing at the craps table surrounded by a half dozen other players. From the pile of chips in front of him, I concluded he was having another good night. He spotted me and waved me to his side. "Now," he said into my ear, "I'll really get on a roll."

I stood next to Harry while he continued to throw the dice. Each time he did, a whoop and a holler came from others at the table. My knowledge of how craps is played is sketchy at best, but even to a novice like me it was plain that each time he rolled, the numbers on the two dice combined to match numbers on the table on which chips were piled. And each time a cheer went up, the crew chief, a tuxedoed lady flanked by two others, stacked chips in the front of the winners.

It took another three rolls before there was a collective groan, followed by applause and shouts of "Nice roll, man," and "Way to go."

Harry bade everyone farewell, tossed a handful of chips on the table as a tip for the crew, took my elbow, and headed for the cashier, where he deposited his large stack of chips. The cashier counted out bills in return: twelve hundred dollars.

"You did really well tonight," I said.

"Lady Luck was by my side in the person of Jessica Fletcher," he said. "What brings you to the casino?"

"Couldn't sleep."

"Something bothering you?"

"Actually — have you heard anything about an accident on board?"

"No. An accident with the ship?"

"I don't know."

"Let's find a quiet place to talk," he said.

We went up one deck to the Chart Room, where we found a table for two far from the jazz trio that was into its last set of the evening.

"Tell me more about this accident," he said as a waitress approached. He ordered rum, neat. I asked for a cup of chamomile tea.

"I don't know any more." I was filling him in on what I'd seen — Rupesh being taken away, the guard at Kim's door — when two couples approached us.

"Jessica Fletcher," one of the women said, "I've been dying to tell you in person how much we love your lectures, and your books, of course."

"Thank you. That's very kind of you —"

"Your talks lift the spirits," one of the men said, interrupting me. "Good thing, too, after what's happened tonight."

"I'm not sure I know what you mean," I said.

The other woman leaned close and said in a low voice, "We thought you would surely know. They say he was murdered."

"Who was murdered?" I asked.

"We don't know," her husband said. "Other people we were with said that one of the bartenders told them a body was found."

"Are you sure it was murder?" Harry asked.

The second woman shrugged. "We only know what we were told. We'll probably learn a lot more in the morning. You know how rumors fly around a ship. Well, thanks again. We love your books and we can't wait for your next lecture. Maybe you'll be able to tell us about a real live murder then."

"I wonder if they'll mention it in the *Daily Programme,*" I heard her friend say as they moved off.

"Kim," I said absently after they'd gone.

"Pardon?"

"Mr. Kim. I'm afraid he may be the victim."

"Now, now, Jessica, this is all just a rumor."

"I know," I said, "but it adds up to me. I wonder if there's someone I can speak with about it, someone in an official capacity."

"They're likely to be pretty tight-lipped, if

I know the rules of the sea," Harry said.

Harry's drink and my tea were delivered. "Ah," Harry said, "just what the doctor ordered, a taste of Nelson's blood." He took a long sip and coughed.

"Nelson's blood?"

He cleared his throat. "When Admiral Lord Nelson died in the Battle of Trafalgar, the crew preserved his body in a keg of rum for the long trip back to England. You don't hear the term used anymore, not with today's younger sailors. But, of course, I'm not one of those younger types."

I sat silently, my mind racing.

"Sorry if my injecting trivia into the serious topic of murder offended you," he said.

"Oh, no, that's all right," I said, absently stirring my tea to cool it. "I wonder if the staff captain would be forth-coming with me if I tell him that I'm a friend of the family. Rupesh, my cabin steward, has cousins in Cabot Cove."

"Worth a try, I suppose. I'll come with you."

"No need to do that, Harry."

"Nonsense." He finished his rum, waved over the waitress, signed the tab with his room number, and we left the Chart Room and headed down to the purser's office. I had no idea where the staff officer's base of operation was, but hoped that the purser would be able, and willing, to tell me.

There was no one in line that time of night, and a lovely young lady greeted me by name and asked if she could help me.

"I hope so," I said. "The cousin of very dear friends of mine back home — that's Cabot Cove, Maine — is my cabin steward. I'm afraid something might have happened to him and I'd like to speak to the staff captain about it."

She pondered the request for a moment before saying, "I don't believe it's a matter for the staff captain, Mrs. Fletcher. Perhaps the hotel manager, or someone in human resources, can help you tomorrow."

"Probably so," I said, "but the staff captain had been very gracious when we met. I really would prefer a word with *him*. I won't take up too much of his time."

"Let me see if I can raise him," she said, disappearing into an area out of my view.

Harry, who stood with me, asked quietly, "Why him specifically?"

I responded in an equally low voice. "I have a suspicion that my cabin steward's troubles are more of a criminal nature, and it's the staff captain who oversees the security force on board. When a crime occurs at sea, they act as a police force until reaching port."

Harry didn't respond. As a former seaman, a captain, himself, he'd likely known the answer, but I could see that he was mulling over what I'd said.

The crew member returned and said, "He's tied up right now, but said he'd be happy to meet with you in a half hour in the officers' wardroom." She gave me directions, and Harry and I went to find it. When we reached the wardroom, a crew member asked us to wait in a small anteroom until the staff captain was available. "He's in a meeting at the moment," the young officer said in a clipped British accent.

We took chairs and waited in silence until Harry said, "Perhaps I should leave. He might not appreciate two people taking up his valuable time, double-teaming him, so to speak."

"I don't think that would be a problem, but it's late, I know. You probably want to get back to your cabin. I don't mind waiting alone."

"No, no. I just thought you might want to do this by yourself. I'm happy to stay. Kind of curious to know what's happened."

"And I'm happy for the company, but I have to tell you I'm not certain he'll talk to me at all. We may be on a fool's errand."

Twenty minutes later, a female officer in her sparkling white uniform came from the wardroom. "The staff captain is still occupied," she said, and left the area.

A minute later, the door opened wide. I expected to see the staff captain emerge.

It wasn't the staff captain.

It was Michael Haggerty!

Chapter Eighteen

"Hello, Wendell," Harry Flynn said cheerily. "What are you doing here?"

An officer tapped Haggerty on the shoulder. "Michael, we need to see you again."

"Give me a minute," Haggerty replied.

"Michael?" Harry said.

Haggerty's raised hand put a stop to the words. He used his index finger to motion for me to follow him from the area.

"Maybe I should leave," Harry said.

"You don't have to," I said. "I'll be back in a moment."

I followed Haggerty to the empty hallway leading to the officers' wardroom.

"What's going on?" I asked in a whisper.

"I don't have time to go into every aspect of it, Jessica, but there's been a murder."

"Kim Chin-Hwa."

"Why do you say that?"

"News of a dead body being found is already making the rounds of the ship, Michael. Passengers are talking about it. There's a guard outside Kim's stateroom, and my cabin steward was led away by security. It *was* Kim Chin-Hwa, wasn't it?"

He nodded.

"But why are *you* involved? Does the staff captain know your true identity?"

"Yes. The top officers know why I'm on board. I'll be lending a hand in the investigation, with their full backing, of course. What's important is that the investigation be done quietly, no fanfare. The ship's crew doesn't want this to impact other passengers. Their first obligation is to them, and they're deadly serious about it."

"How was Kim killed?"

"Look, I need to go back inside. Give me thirty minutes, an hour tops, and I'll come to your stateroom."

"No, better I come to yours. There's too much activity on my deck."

He agreed and gave me his cabin number.

I returned to the anteroom to find Harry had gone. I couldn't blame him. He'd sensed that something strange was underfoot and he evidently didn't want to get in the way.

But get in the way of *what*?

I didn't have any role in the investigation that would ensue, at least not an official one. Haggerty obviously felt it appropriate to clue me in on what was occurring, and I appreciated that. As much as I never intended to become involved in jewelry thefts, murder, and terrorist funding, the unfortunate fact was that I'd ended up smack-dab in the middle of it, which generated not only apprehension but also a parallel rush of adrenaline.

Was it too late to call Dennis Stanton on the chance that he had information about Kim's murder? He certainly would be vitally interested in it. Kim was his chief suspect in the theft of the Heart of India, and his murder would necessitate a shift in the direction of Dennis's inquiry.

I had a little time to kill before meeting with Haggerty. I considered going to my cabin, but by the time I got there, I'd have to leave again. I was, of course, concerned about Rupesh and had hoped to learn something about him from the staff captain. But that hadn't happened, and I felt it would be inappropriate to continue to pursue the busy officer. He obviously had enough on his hands at that moment.

The casino! It would still be open, and maybe Harry had gone there. I could apologize for having abandoned him — again.

He wasn't there, but a parade of well-dressed, happy people — probably coming from the Royal Court Theatre — were enjoying another formal evening on the ship. Apparently not everyone had heard the rumor that someone died on the ship, given the cheery demeanor of the men and women, and a few children, who strolled by, chatting, laughing, reveling in the floating palace that was the *Queen Mary 2.*

It was time to meet Haggerty at his cabin. As I headed for the elevator, I saw him in the distance accompanied by another man. I walked quickly in his direction but couldn't get there fast enough before they stepped on an elevator and the doors closed. But I'd gotten close enough to see the person with him. It was Rupesh, my cabin steward.

I'd almost called out Michael's name but held back, not knowing whether he still used the Wendell Jones alias when not conferring with the ship's staff. Besides, my mind was now focused on Rupesh's reemergence and the circumstances surrounding it. I was certain that it was no coincidence that he and Haggerty ended up together. They'd walked side by side to the bank of elevators. I would ask Haggerty in a few minutes, assuming of course that he was on his way to his stateroom. Maybe Rupesh would be there, too.

I took my time going to Haggerty's deck, walked slowly down the long hallway, reached his door, and knocked. Haggerty answered. "Good timing," he said. "I just got here myself. Come in."

I looked past him and saw that no one else was there. The TV was on, tuned to the ship's twenty-four-hour-a-day channel. A video of my second lecture filled the screen.

"You look good," Haggerty said, nodding at the TV.

"Thank you, but I'd really prefer that you turn it off so we can talk."

He shrugged and did as I asked. The room was now bathed in silence, the only sound coming through his open glass doors to the balcony. The liner's thirty-knot-an-hour move through the Atlantic created a soothing "white sound."

"I have some champagne my steward delivered to me."

"No thanks, but you go ahead."

He carefully hung up his tux jacket, and shed his tie and cummerbund, dropping them on the desk atop some papers, then pulled the champagne from a bucket of ice and water. "Just let me get a towel," he said, carrying the dripping bottle to the bathroom.

"I just saw you get on the elevator in the Grand Lobby with my cabin steward, Rupesh," I said loud enough for him to hear me. I brushed aside his cummerbund to see what was beneath it.

"You did?"

I heard a pop, and turned as he came back with the bottle, now foaming. "Yes," I said. "The last time I'd seen him, he was being led away from Kim Chin-Hwa's stateroom. Now he shows up with you. What's going on?"

"Sit down, Jessica," he said, indicating the couch. Michael poured himself a flute of the bubbly wine and took the chair across the cocktail table from me. "You're very observant," he said.

"Is that bad?"

"No, not at all. I mean it as a compliment."

"Well?"

"Well *what*?"

"Tell me about Rupesh. Is he in trouble?"

"Not that I know of."

"Oh, come on, Michael, you're fudging. Why was he with *you* tonight?"

"That question's off-limits, Jessica."

"I don't accept that, Michael. You invited me here, supposedly to fill me in on what's been going on. The man that you suspect stole a precious blue diamond in London has been murdered. My cabin steward — who, by the way, happens to be a cousin of friends back in Maine — is taken away like a criminal, and then shows up with you. You meet with the staff captain, obviously about the murder, and tell me that the top-level staff members know that you work for British intelligence. You end up flirting with an international jewel thief and —"

"I beg your pardon," he said, raising both hands. "Say that again."

I hadn't meant to mention Jennifer Kahn. It just came out. But I was instantly glad it had. I'd reached a point where I wanted as much information as Haggerty possessed. Maybe by sharing something with him that he didn't know — or so I believed — it would grease the skids. But I wouldn't cite Dennis Stanton as my source. That wouldn't have been fair unless Dennis gave me permission.

"All right," I said. I leaned closer to Michael and said, "Jennifer Kahn is reputed to be one of the world's most successful jewel thieves. She runs a gang that steals gems from countries around the globe — England, France, Egypt, Hungary, Canada — you name it."

"That's absurd," he said. "Your fertile

imagination has run away with you."

"Not so, Michael. Jennifer may have been behind those three break-ins in London last week. It's not my imagination; it's what the authorities believe."

"Who told you this?"

"I can't say at the moment."

He guffawed. "You want me to tell you everything, but you clam up. This isn't a one-way street, Jessica."

"Nor do I intend it to be. I'll tell you my source as soon as he gives me permission."

"Aha," Haggerty said, snapping his fingers. "It's that older guy, Harry. Right? He's full of stories."

"I'll tell you when I think it's the right time. Meanwhile, I suggest that you take seriously what I've just said. At least consider it a possibility."

Haggerty shook his head. "A jewel thief?" he said, more to himself than to me. "That ravishing creature steals jewels for a living?" He shook his head again, more vigorously this time. "Can't be, Jessica. She *designs* jewelry. She doesn't *steal* it. You've spent time with her. Be serious. I can't believe that someone with your intelligence and insight into people could buy such rubbish."

I was tempted to counter with, "And someone with all your worldly smarts shouldn't dismiss it out of hand." I didn't. Instead, I said, "Check with, well, whoever it is you check with. In the meantime, all I ask is that you consider the possibility in relation to your investigation into the Heart of India case. I think you know me well enough that I don't blithely toss around accusations about people. All I can say is that my source is credible. Now, what about Kim Chin-Hwa? How was he killed?"

"A knife in the chest."

"Where did it happen?"

"The Lookout on Deck Thirteen, at the front of the ship. He was found in one of two small whirlpool baths up there. At least whoever did it had the sensitivity to not mess up one of the inside rooms."

"Who found the body?" I asked.

"His lady friend, Betty."

"Who just happened to be up on an outside deck in the dark of night and looked in a whirlpool bath?"

"I'm simply giving you what I know. There'll be a lot more information once the security staff — which, by the way, is top-notch — and I have a chance to interview everyone connected with Kim. That process will start in the morning. In the meantime, I suggest you get some sleep. You have a lecture tomorrow?"

"Yes. You won't tell me anything about my cabin steward?"

Haggerty gave me one of his self-satisfied smiles that I'd seen him use many times before when he was holding his cards close to his vest. "Forget about him," he said. "I'll see you at breakfast."

Our little confab was over. I thanked him for what information he had shared and went to the door.

"A word of advice?" he said.

"What's that?"

"Maybe you'd better keep your best jewelry in your safe for the duration of the crossing, especially when Jennifer is around."

"Very funny, Michael."

"Yes, it is, isn't it? Very funny. Sleep tight."

CHAPTER NINETEEN

Haggerty had suggested that we get some sleep, but it seemed that was out of the question. I was "wired," as some term it, and felt a need to keep moving. I wasn't sure where I wanted to go, but knew that retiring to my cabin for the night wasn't the answer.

I decided to go to the Queens Room to see if I could find Stanton, Jennifer, Kiki, or Harry. Passengers had enjoyed their formal dinners and after-dinner entertainment, and most were probably getting ready for bed. Although from the look of things in the Queens Room, plenty of them had decided to extend the evening — but not the quartet I was looking for.

As I gazed around the regal room in which dozens of couples swayed on the dance floor, the immense size of the ship hit home. Looking for someone on board was a daunting challenge. There were thirteen floors, each the length of four city blocks in Manhattan, and literally dozens of public rooms, bars, shops, restaurants, meeting rooms, exercise facilities, including those outdoors on the decks, hundreds of places for people to seclude themselves, including, of course, all the staterooms. Finding a specific person was akin to searching for that elusive needle in a haystack, albeit a haystack in the middle of the Atlantic Ocean.

I decided that I was getting nowhere, conflicting ideas pulling me in too many directions. What I needed was some fresh air.

I went to Deck Seven and fought the wind to open one of the doors leading out to the promenade that circled the ship. Hit with a cold gust, I briefly reconsidered my action, but the chilly air would clear my mind and that was exactly what I needed. The moon was hidden behind some clouds, but most of the sky was clear, promising a beautiful day to come in not too many hours. I marched off in the direction of the bow and realized that since coming aboard I had been so involved with the case, I had neglected to enjoy a brisk constitutional on the deck, an exercise I had faithfully undertaken on my *QE2* trips, where five circuits equaled a mile. Because the *QM2* was significantly larger, it would take only three times around to achieve the same distance, a sign informed me.

I saw a few other people battling the breeze with me, their bodies bent forward in the face of the wind, working to keep from being pushed into the railing, the only structure separating us from the churning waters below. We gained a moment's respite in the shelter of the bow's covered walk before taking up the fight again — this time with the wind at our backs — as we headed toward the stern.

I watched as the other intrepid walkers hauled open the heavy doors and retreated inside, one by one, until I was the only one on deck. As I walked, I told myself that I had no reason to be concerned about my safety. But being out in the elements with no other passengers in sight created a certain apprehension, and I frequently stole a glance over my shoulder to make sure I was still alone. I justified my heightened awareness. After all, there had been a murder that night; a man I'd gotten to know to some extent, and had even danced with, had been killed, a knife rammed into his chest.

Envisioning that gruesome scene sent a chill up my spine that had nothing to do with the bracing air.

I reached the bow again, circumvented it, and was halfway back on the opposite side of the ship when I was surprised by a solitary figure sitting against the side of the ship in an alcove. Although the ship's lights illuminated portions of the deck, the hooded person was in the shadows, arms crossed. It took me a moment before I recognized who it was — the honeymooner Marcia Kensington.

Should I intrude on her private thoughts? I debated only for a few seconds before approaching.

"Marcia?" I called out. "Are you okay?"

My unexpected words caused her to flinch and to gasp.

"I didn't mean to startle you," I said, coming to where she sat on a large wooden box the crew used for storage.

"I just didn't know you were there," she said, pushing the hood back to get a better look at me.

"I'm Jessica Fletcher," I said. "We met that first night at dinner in the Princess Grill."

"I remember."

"Getting some fresh air?" I asked, trying to make conversation.

She nodded and stared straight ahead

toward the sea. The wind whipped strands of hair across her eyes, which she brushed away impatiently.

"It's breezy tonight, isn't it?" I said, taking a deep, prolonged breath.

"Yes."

Then, without warning, she began to sob, the binoculars around her neck bouncing on her lap with each heave.

I took a seat beside her and put my arm around her shoulders. "What's wrong?" I asked. "Is there anything I can do?"

When she didn't answer, I said, "A spat with your husband? Those things happen now and then."

"We're not . . . he's not —"

I waited.

"He's not my husband," she said, and her sobbing intensified.

"Oh," I said. "I thought you said —"

She turned to face me. "It's all a lie," she said.

More silence ensued before she added, "He wanted us to say we were married."

I tried to imagine why he would have done that, unless, perhaps, he was protecting her reputation, wanting people, especially older ones, not to view her with disdain for traveling with him before they got married.

"I don't know about your relationship," I

233

said, "but I can understand his — his name is Richard, right? His wanting to — oh, how can I put it? — not wanting people to think unkindly about the two of you sharing a cabin and —"

She faced me again. Her tears had subsided. The pretty face that had been softened by the tears was now hard.

"You don't know what you're talking about," she said.

"That wouldn't be the first time," I said. "If you'd rather not discuss it, I certainly understand."

"I didn't want to do it," she said. "It was wrong."

"What was wrong?"

"Pretending we were married."

"Oh," I said, injecting a laugh to make light of it. "Saying that you were a married couple isn't the worst thing in the world."

But saying they were on their honeymoon *did* strike me as an unnecessary addition to the lie.

"I'm sorry," she said.

"Nothing to be sorry about. Where is Richard now?"

"I don't know. He was in a bad mood."

From my limited observation of him he seemed always to be in a bad mood.

"Look!" She jumped up and ran to the rail.

The moon had slipped from behind a cloud, and a pair of dolphins had surfaced, swimming in the reflection, the moon's rays catching their silvery shapes as they dove and surfaced, keeping pace with the ship.

"How beautiful," I said, coming to lean on the rail next to her.

"I was hoping to see dolphins or whales," Marcia said absently.

"Well, now you have," I said, "and so have I."

A small smile played on her lips and she wiped the tears from her cheeks.

I breathed in the salty air and made a decision. "Marcia, I'd like to ask you a question."

She nodded.

"I assume you've heard of the theft of a precious blue diamond called the Heart of India. It happened in London last week."

Because our sides touched, I felt her stiffen.

"There's a British insurance company, one of two companies that insured that diamond, a firm called Kensington. Does Richard have anything to do with that firm?"

She said nothing.

"You may have heard that there's been a

death aboard this evening. It appears that it was murder."

"It's terrible," she said. "I know who it was. That Chinese man."

"Korean. Mr. Kim Chin-Hwa. He was a business partner of the man who owned the Heart of India, the one who was killed during the robbery."

She looked up at me. "Why are you talking about those things with me?"

"I suppose because I'm interested in seeing murderers brought to justice. I thought that maybe Richard was on the ship on behalf of the insurance firm that shares his name. If so, he might have something to offer the authorities who are investigating."

"Why would he?" she snapped. "And what do you have to do with this?"

"I don't mean to upset you any more than you already are, Marcia, but I'm afraid that I've been drawn into the nasty things that have been going on."

"Richard doesn't know anything!"

I read her emphatic denial to mean that he most certainly did.

I expected her to excuse herself and leave. But as much as she appeared to be annoyed with the topics I'd raised, she simultaneously seemed to want to continue the conversation, and I was willing to accommodate.

After an awkward lull, she said, "You don't know how it is."

"How *what* is, Marcia?"

"How —" She turned and leaned her back against the railing. "Richard will be furious if he finds me talking about this to a stranger."

"I'd like to think I'm not a stranger," I said. "We are, after all, both passengers on this lovely ocean liner, and we did have dinner together one night. *And* a murder of one of our fellow passengers has been committed. I think we all have a stake in seeing justice done."

"You seem like a nice person," she said.

"I try to be."

She wrapped her arms about herself and shivered.

"Cold?"

"Afraid."

"Afraid of what?"

"I —"

We never saw him coming until he was upon us. Richard Kensington grabbed Marcia's elbow and spun her around.

"What are you doing out here?" he demanded.

"I was — I was getting some air."

"I've been looking all over the damn ship

237

for you." He put out his hand.

"I don't want to go," she said.

"You're coming with me, Marcia." He yanked her arm, but she resisted, grabbing hold of the rail.

"You're hurting her," I said.

"You stay out of it," he snarled.

"No, I will *not* stay out of it. You have no right to force her to come with you."

He let go of her and brought his face inches from mine. "You watch yourself, lady. You mind your own business."

"Abusing a woman is everyone's business, even if she is your — your girlfriend."

"What have you been telling her?" he demanded of Marcia.

"Nothing, Richard, I swear it."

He pulled her away from me and dragged her down the deck toward a door. I watched as he flung it open, pushed her through, and followed her inside.

What a volatile young man, I thought. She'd best think twice about marrying him, if that was ever in the cards to begin with.

My initial reasoning why they claimed they were married no longer satisfied me. There had to be more to it than that, particularly since he'd erupted over her having admitted to me that they weren't married. This wasn't a matter of wanting to establish propriety. He wasn't concerned about what others might think of their living arrangement, certainly not in this day and age, where cohabitation before marriage is hardly unique.

But why was he so angry? Why the big fuss over something most people would ignore?

Did it have to do with the British company whose name was the same as his? I couldn't see any clear connection at that juncture, but my instincts told me that there had to be a link.

As I returned inside the ship, I said a silent prayer that his temper tantrum didn't result in injury to Marcia. She was frightened and vulnerable, something I hated to see in any young woman.

I rang for the elevator, and when the door opened, I came face-to-face with Harry Flynn.

"Fancy meeting you here," he said, chuckling. "I'm just on my way to Churchill's Cigar Lounge."

"I didn't realize that you smoked cigars."

"Only occasionally," he said. "I hope the smell doesn't put you off."

"It's okay," I said. "My late husband, Frank, was a pipe smoker."

"I've enjoyed pipes, too, although I never did get the hang of all the rigmarole that goes with it. Why don't you come with me? You look like you could use a friendly ear."

I debated for only a moment before agreeing.

In Churchill's we sank down into two overstuffed leather chairs as Harry fired up the biggest cigar I'd ever seen. He puffed contentedly for a moment, then leaned over, careful to hold the cigar away from me at arm's length. "What have you learned about the murder?"

"Not very much. Have you seen Betty Le-Clair, Mr. Kim's friend?"

"Can't say that I have. It *was* Kim who was killed?"

"Yes."

"And what about Mr. Jones?" he asked. "Why did that officer call him Michael?"

I sighed and pressed my lips together. Now that Haggerty had come out of the closet, as it were, I saw no reason to not speak freely of him. "It's a long story, Harry. Michael — his real name is Michael Haggerty — is a retired member of British MI6, the intelligence agency. Actually, he's come out of retirement because of the diamond theft and murder in London last week, something to do with money from jewelry thefts being funneled to terrorist groups."

"My goodness," he said, sitting back and

drawing on his cigar, "I had no idea that I've been sharing the dinner table with someone that important."

I smiled. Haggerty would have been pleased to hear that said of him. "He's involved in the shipboard investigation of Mr. Kim's murder," I said.

"A good thing someone with his credentials is on board, isn't it?"

"I suppose it is. He's very good at what he does. Have you picked up any scuttlebutt around the ship about the murder?"

"A few people have mentioned it. One woman was quite upset at the news. I suppose you can't blame her being concerned that a killer is aboard. Interesting term, 'scuttlebutt.' Do you know the origins of it?"

"As a matter of fact, I do," I said, "compliments of Harry Flynn."

He laughed. "I sometimes forget what stories I've told," he said. "Sorry. It comes with age."

We fell into a comfortable silence, Harry puffing away on his cigar, me engrossed in myriad thoughts pulsating in my brain. I looked into the Commodore Club through the glass doors and saw Dennis Stanton walk by. I sat up abruptly.

"Oh, there's, um, Bill," I said.

"Why don't you go have a talk with him while I finish my cigar?" Harry said.

"Are you sure, Harry? You don't mind?"

"Not at all. Go! I'll come find you when I'm done."

"Thanks."

He started to get up, but I placed my hand on his arm. "No need," I said. "See you in a few minutes."

I entered the club and saw that Stanton had joined Jennifer Kahn and Kiki Largent at a far window. I glanced back to see that Harry seemed content to be working on his cigar, and judging from the size of it, he'd be there a while.

"Mind if I sit with you?" I asked the three-some.

Stanton looked up. "Please do," he said. Kiki's expression said that she wasn't happy about my intrusion. Jennifer smiled and gave me a cheery hello, but added that they were about to leave.

"Terrible what happened tonight, isn't it?" she said.

"The death of Mr. Kim?" I said, not sure if she knew it was a murder.

"Oh, is that who it was? We heard a rumor that someone drowned in a whirlpool. Yes, it is terrible," Jennifer agreed. "He seemed like a nice man, although I barely met him."

"Did you know that he was the partner of the man who was killed in London last week during the theft of the Heart of India?"

"No!" Jennifer said, coming forward in her chair for emphasis.

"You didn't know about that?" I said.

"About the theft and murder?" Jennifer replied. "Of course I knew about that. You couldn't escape it. It was all over the news, not to mention talked about endlessly by everyone in the industry. But I had no idea Mr. Kim was involved in that case. He was a partner of the slain man, you say? That means — well, that certainly points to there being some connection, wouldn't you say?"

"I'd say that's a good possibility," I agreed.

"Have they ever determined who stole that diamond and killed the owner?" she asked.

"Not that I'm aware of."

Stanton, who'd said nothing during this exchange, shifted in his chair, ran his thumb and index finger down the razor-sharp crease in his slacks, and commented, "I read somewhere that there could be a link between that robbery and the rash of heists that took place in London around the same time." He directed the comment specifically at Jennifer, who stared blankly at him.

"I mean," Stanton said, "it's what I've

read. You're a jewelry designer, Jennifer. What's your take on all these robberies and murders that have taken place?"

She sat back and smiled. "I design jewelry," she said. "As far as I know, every gem I've handled has come from legitimate sources. I really know nothing about the underworld of jewel thieves." She looked at me. "It's pretty ironic that Mr. Kim was killed, considering he had those two large men with him," she said. "I assumed they were his bodyguards."

She looked at Kiki, who shrugged. "Let's go," she said to Jennifer.

Just then, Michael Haggerty walked into the club. He spotted us, hesitated, and came to where we sat.

"Hello," I said. "I thought you were retiring for the night."

Haggerty plopped down and released a rush of air from his mouth. "Cozy little group," he said.

"Having a good evening, Wendell?" Stanton asked.

Haggerty looked at me before responding. "I'm not sure I'd call it that," he said. "It looks like you've been busy."

Stanton looked at him quizzically.

Haggerty ignored him and said to Jennifer, "Getting tips on San Francisco real estate?"

"I'm not sure what you mean," she said.

"Forget it," Haggerty said, giving Stanton a mean look.

"I'm leaving," Kiki said.

"I think I'd better leave with you," Jennifer said.

"Don't leave on my account," Haggerty said. "I'm sure that you and your real estate adviser have more to talk about."

"What's this all about?" Stanton asked.

I knew what was behind Michael's foul mood. There was little doubt that he'd developed strong feelings for Jennifer Kahn, and viewed Stanton as a rival for her affections. And my revelation about her true nature apparently hadn't sat well.

Haggerty looked at me. "Maybe you should tell Jennifer what you told me, Jessica."

"Perhaps you have something to tell Jennifer yourself," I replied.

I certainly wasn't about to get into a discussion about Jennifer being an international jewel thief. And it was doubtful Haggerty had confessed his true identity to the object of his fascination. I couldn't envision her sitting quietly in the company of an intelligence agent for MI6 who'd come out of retirement to track down jewel thieves and their possible connection to terrorist-group funding. Surely she would have said something. But I didn't know for certain. Now that the ship's staff knew who Michael was and had enlisted his help in the murder investigation, he should come clean to his companions. But that was his decision.

"I think I'm going to get a cup of tea," I said. "Anyone else?"

Everyone declined. I went to the bar to see if the staff would make me a cup of tea, and was delighted to be given a choice of several varieties. I chose chamomile, hoping that at least a few hours' sleep would be afforded to me before the night had fled altogether.

Jennifer and Kiki had left, passing Harry Flynn on their way out. Haggerty and Stanton sat alone, glaring at each other.

"I hope it wasn't something I said," Harry joked as he joined me at the bar, and ordered a Cognac. "Those ladies seemed to be in a rush to leave."

I smiled. "I'm sure not. It's late. They probably want to get some sleep, as all smart people should."

When Harry and I arrived back at the table, Stanton and Haggerty were in a spirited discussion.

"I can't believe this, Jessica," Stanton said. "Why didn't you tell me that Wendell Jones here isn't Wendell Jones, that he's Michael Haggerty from British intelligence?"

"I wasn't supposed to tell anyone," I said, shooting Michael a look. "I've only just told Harry, but that was because he overheard the staff officer call Michael by his right name."

"I'm sure everyone appreciates that you're here to find the murderer," Harry said.

Haggerty seemed unsure of what to do or say. Since he'd revealed to Stanton his real name and profession, I looked at Stanton to see whether he'd reciprocate. He hadn't yet, because Haggerty referred to him as "Bill."

"Mind a question?" Harry asked Haggerty.

"Shoot."

"I realize that this is none of my business, but I wondered whether you'd considered the possibility that Mr. Kim was killed by someone in his party."

"Every possibility's on the table, Harry."

"Those two large men who've been accompanying him," Harry said. "I heard one of them in the gym say to the other that he wouldn't mind seeing 'the boss' — that's how he referred to him — wouldn't mind seeing 'the boss' get it 'the way Yang did.'

That's exactly what he said."

"You heard him say that?" Haggerty asked.

"Yes, I did."

"Interesting," said Haggerty.

"Of course," Harry said, "as Jessica pointed out to me when I told her this, it was probably only idle talk, you know, the way people say they would like to see their boss killed. I've heard my share of that sort of talk when I was captaining freighters. Sailors can be a disagreeable lot — never satisfied, it seems. If they meant it every time they said they'd like to kill me, I'd have been gone long ago."

"Does anyone know much about Kiki Largent?" I asked no one in particular.

"Why do you ask?" Haggerty said rather abruptly, as though annoyed at my question.

"I just wondered," I said. "She seems — well, she seems somewhat mysterious, doesn't say much, stays close to Jennifer's side." I was thinking, of course, of having seen her rendezvous with someone on the deck during the storm. I'd told Haggerty about that incident, but he seemed uninterested.

"Forget about her," Haggerty said. "She and Jennifer aren't on my radar."

I took a sip of my tea to shield my smile.

No doubt about it, Michael Haggerty had fallen for Jennifer Kahn. That he would allow his emotions to override his investigative efforts surprised me.

Harry checked his watch. "If you'll excuse me," he said, "I'd like to get in a last few minutes at the casino. I feel lucky."

It was tempting to suggest that he keep his winnings from previous forays to the craps table and not risk giving it all back, but who was I to throw cold water on the man's pleasure? I wished him luck. He reached for Haggerty's hand and said, "It's a distinct pleasure to shake hands with a man like you, Mr. . . ."

"Haggerty."

"Yes, Mr. Haggerty, *Agent* Haggerty."

Harry saluted Stanton and me, and walked off in his usual jaunty style.

"I have to go, too," Haggerty said, standing. "See you both at breakfast."

"Before you go," Stanton said, raising a finger. "In the interests of fair play and all that, there's something I should tell you. I'm not who I said I was either."

Haggerty frowned.

"Name's Dennis Stanton. I'm a private investigator for a large insurance company in San Francisco that is a coinsurer of the Heart of India diamond."

Haggerty looked at me as though expecting verification.

I nodded. "Yes, I knew who Dennis was," I said. "We'd met years ago."

"Why didn't you tell me?" Haggerty asked.

"I don't breach someone's cover when they ask me not to say anything. Besides, there was no need to, Michael. But now that you know, the two of you working together might make some headway."

"I, ah — I'll have to think about that," Haggerty said.

He walked away and exited the club.

Stanton changed chairs so that he sat close to me. "Why didn't you tell me who this guy really is?" he asked.

"It wasn't my place to do that, Dennis."

"Did you clue him in about Jennifer Kahn?"

"That she's a jewel thief? I told him that someone alleges that she is."

"And?"

"He didn't believe me. You might have noticed that he's smitten with her."

"Yes, I picked up on that. Did you say that you got your information from me?"

"Of course not. But since he knows who you are, I imagine he'll figure out where I got the information. I suggest you tell him yourself. Maybe he'll believe it coming from you."

"I will. I want to stay close to him, Jessica, now that I've learned that he's involved in the investigation of Kim's murder. You might want to know that I've been back and forth with London and San Francisco today via a couple of e-mails and a phone call. I made some queries about this guy Richard Kensington. Listen to this, Jessica." He unfolded a sheet of paper he'd drawn from his pocket. "Richard Kensington is the only son of Kensington's founder and chairman. The son and the old man have been on the outs for a long time. According to my source in California, the kid doesn't work for the firm any longer."

"And he's not married and on his honeymoon," I put in.

"How'd you find that out?"

"A conversation I had this evening with the young woman traveling with him. Her name is Marcia."

"What's he up to?" Stanton asked. "Why the lie?"

"Beats me, Dennis, but I suspect they know something about the Heart of India. She became very defensive when I raised the topic."

Stanton digested this before asking, "What

251

about Kim's lady friend, Betty LeClair?"

"I haven't seen her. I meant to ask Michael if he had, but it slipped my mind."

"Damn!" Stanton muttered. "We've only got two more days at sea. Kensington has investigators working the case in London. They don't think the diamond is on this ship. Neither does my home office. They're really putting the pressure on me. They think I'm wasting my time making this crossing. I'd really love to prove them wrong."

"Well," I said, unsuccessfully stifling a yawn, "there's obviously a lot to be accomplished in two days. I'm going to my cabin."

We promised to meet for breakfast, although I had no illusions of how I'd feel having to get up in time. I headed for my stateroom and hopefully a good night's sleep, as abbreviated as it would be. I was halfway down the corridor from my stateroom when I noticed, far ahead, that the security officer was still posted outside Kim's door. As I watched, another man stepped into the hallway. He'd come from Kim's cabin, and there was no mistaking who he was, not with his size. It was Uri. He didn't see me and walked in the other direction. I picked up the pace, but he'd already disappeared around the corner in the direction of the elevators and staircase.

Frustrated — I'd intended to confront him — I fumbled for my key in my pocket and had just inserted it when I heard a door open behind me.

I whirled.

It was Rupesh.

CHAPTER TWENTY

I drew a deep breath and smiled. "I'm relieved to see you," I said.

"Good evening, madam."

"I was worried about you. I saw you leave with the security men and —"

He raised a finger to silence me and glanced at the guard, who seemed disinterested in our conversation.

"Come in. I was intending to call you," I said, adding for the guard's benefit, "There's something wrong with my TV."

Rupesh extended his arm, and I preceded him into my stateroom, stopping only to pluck a message from my mail basket as I passed by. I glanced at the envelope. MRS. FLETCHER was typed on the front. The lettering looked the same as the previous message I'd received.

I turned and held up the envelope for Rupesh to see. "Do you know who delivered this, Rupesh?"

"No, madam," he said, allowing the door to close behind him.

I opened it. The typewritten message was: "LIFE WAS MEANT TO BE LIVED, AND CURIOSITY MUST BE KEPT ALIVE." ELEANOR ROOSEVELT.

He must have seen the concern on my face. "Is something wrong, madam?"

"No, nothing wrong, Rupesh."

I swung around the desk chair so that it faced the small couch, and sat in the chair. Rupesh perched on the couch's arm.

"When we first met, I said that I'd like to find time for us to have a chat. Is this a good time for you? I know it's late and —"

"No, it is not too late, Mrs. Fletcher. I would like very much to speak with you."

It was the first time that he'd used my name.

"I have many questions, Rupesh."

"I understand."

"You know about the murder of Mr. Kim tonight."

"Yes. I was informed."

"I have a feeling that you know more about it than having simply been 'informed.'"

When he didn't respond, I added, "And I also suspect that what you know might have come from a friend of mine, Wendell Jones, although that's not his real name."

"I know Mr. Jones's real name, Mrs. Fletcher."

"I suppose you do," I said. "I saw you with him earlier this evening."

"Mrs. Fletcher, I mustn't stay long, but there is something I need to say to you."

"Go ahead."

"I'm not at liberty to divulge how I know certain things, but it is enough for you to know that there are bad people on the ship, very cruel people."

He had my full attention.

"Mr. Jones — Mr. Haggerty works for the British intelligence agency MI6. He is on the ship because of these people."

My immediate reaction was surprise that this room steward would so blithely reveal to me that Haggerty was an intelligence agent. But he quickly explained. "Agent Haggerty has told me that you and he have worked closely together in the past, and that I am to trust you."

"He told you that?"

"Yes, madam."

"I suppose I should be flattered but —"

"At first I suspected you might have been the one to kill Mr. Kim."

"Me?!"

He nodded. "You were very interested in

Mr. Kim's cabin and its contents. You asked me to tell you if he had a computer and printer."

"Oh, yes, but that was because —"

"However, Agent Haggerty also told me that you have certain — how shall I say it? — that you have certain ideas about some of these people, certain insights."

Why Haggerty would have said that was but one of many questions I had at the moment, the most pressing of which was why he would be sharing things with Rupesh. Had this young man come upon some information that was helpful to Michael in the investigation? As a room steward, he would be privy to what went on in his area of responsibility, including passengers Kim Chin-Hwa and Betty LeClair. If that was the case, I was naturally curious to see what it was.

I asked again about the scene in which Betty was crying in her cabin. Rupesh had said it had to do with something, or someone, missing.

"The lady claimed that someone had entered her cabin without her permission and taken some papers."

"What sort of papers?"

"That I do not know."

"Rupesh," I said, "when I approached my

cabin a few minutes ago, I saw a man leaving Mr. Kim's stateroom. He was a heavyset man with a beard. He wears a skullcap."

Rupesh paused before answering. "That man is working with Mr. Haggerty."

"Have you met him?"

"Yes, Mrs. Fletcher."

"He's another intelligence agent?"

"I am not at liberty to speculate on that."

I didn't press. I didn't have to. I already knew that his name was Uri — at least that's what Haggerty had told me — and that he worked for Israeli intelligence.

"I appreciate your candor with me, Rupesh," I said, "but I'm afraid I don't understand your involvement with Agent Haggerty, or with this other man, whose name, by the way, is Uri."

"Then you know him."

"I only know *of* him."

He got up, went to the glass doors, and stood looking out for what seemed a long time. When he turned to me, he smiled. "There are things I cannot share with you at this moment, Mrs. Fletcher, but I hope to soon. In the meantime, I must go. I have final chores before going to my cabin for some rest."

"Of course," I said as I walked him to the

door. "Is Ms. LeClair next door in her cabin?"

"I don't believe so."

"Where is she?"

"With the staff captain and his security officers. They are questioning her. She will not be returning to her stateroom."

"Where will she go?"

"I don't know, Mrs. Fletcher."

"Is Agent Haggerty with them?"

"I believe so, but I cannot be certain. I must go, Mrs. Fletcher. I hope you have a restful sleep."

He was no sooner gone than my phone rang. "Jessica? It's Michael. Hope I didn't wake you."

"No such luck."

"Beg pardon?"

"No, as a matter of fact you didn't wake me. I was just having a conversation with my cabin steward, Rupesh. I understand you've been talking with him."

"I'd like you to come to the officers' wardroom."

"Now?"

"I'd really appreciate it, Jessica. But if you'd rather not, I —"

"No, I'll be there. Give me fifteen minutes."

Any thoughts of enjoying even a few

hours' sleep were rapidly dissipating. I freshened up and headed out again. I could easily have begged off, but the lure of adding to what I'd learned so far about the Heart of India diamond, jewel theft in general, and the murder of Kim Chin-Hwa was too compelling. The old adage "In for a penny, in for a pound" came and went as I walked the length of the hallway and eventually arrived at the wardroom, where the staff captain, Michael Haggerty, and the Israeli intelligence agent Uri were seated around a conference table. The captain and Uri stood as I entered, and Haggerty raised himself but settled back down immediately.

"Thank you for coming," the staff captain said. "Please, have a seat."

Haggerty got right to the point. "I think you know everyone here," he said.

"I'm afraid that's not true," I said, gesturing at Uri. "I've only *seen* this gentleman, but we've never been introduced."

Uri reached across the table with a large hand and said, "Uri Peretz, Mrs. Fletcher. I work for Mossad."

"It's about time we've met," I said lightly. "I kept seeing you, in London and here on the ship, but never really knew who you were."

"Well," he said in a deep voice, "now you

do, and it is my pleasure. My mother is a big fan of your murder mysteries. She reads the Hebrew editions. She will be excited to learn I have met the great Jessica Fletcher. Perhaps now she will think better of her son and not complain so much that I don't visit her enough."

I smiled. "Thank you. Do you mind my asking why you chose to follow *me* the day after Michael and I had dinner?"

His laugh was low and guttural. "Standard procedure, Mrs. Fletcher. When I saw that Michael was with an attractive woman, I was compelled to find out who she was. I must admit that when I discovered that you were such a famous woman, I was taken somewhat aback."

"Surely once you knew who I was, your interest in me should have ended."

"Not quite that simple, Mrs. Fletcher. It became obvious to me that your involvement with Michael had nothing to do with writing books. You're working together."

"That's hardly the case, Mr. Peretz."

"But here you are, part of the *team*." He turned to Haggerty. "Please proceed, Michael."

"Could we have Ms. LeClair rejoin us," Haggerty said to the staff captain.

He left the room, returning seconds later

with Betty. She looked at me with red, puffy eyes and took a chair next to Haggerty.

"The reason I asked you to come here, Jessica, is Ms. LeClair. As you know, she's occupied the cabin next to yours since we left Southampton, and you're also aware of the murder of her companion tonight, Mr. Kim."

"Unfortunately, yes." I turned to Betty and said, "I'm so sorry, Betty."

"Thank you," she managed in a barely audible voice.

Haggerty continued. "Ms. LeClair is the one who discovered the body. Naturally, she's the first person we wanted to talk to. This has been extremely upsetting for her, as you can imagine. We're done with our questioning and are satisfied that she's told us everything she knows."

"I swear it," she said, her voice stronger.

I had many questions for her, but assumed they'd already been posed by the others.

"I'll get right to the point, Jessica. Besides being understandably upset by what's happened this evening, she's also concerned for her safety. Obviously, she can't return to her cabin for a number of reasons. I'm informed that there is one vacant suite on the ship for Ms. LeClair to use for the duration of the crossing. Her belongings have already been moved."

I said, "I think your decision is a wise one, Betty."

"I couldn't possibly go back to that cabin where —" She sniffled and dabbed at her eyes with her handkerchief.

"The reason I've asked you here this evening," Michael said to me, "is to ask a favor. I've suggested that you accompany Ms. LeClair to the suite and help her get settled, you know, engage in some girl talk, make her feel comfortable."

Had I conjured a dozen reasons why Haggerty had asked me to join them, this wouldn't have made the list.

"Will you, Mrs. Fletcher?" the staff captain asked.

"Is this appropriate?" I asked. "I would have thought that you'd want a member of the crew to do this."

"We discussed various options with Ms. LeClair," the staff captain said, "and your name came up. She prefers that it be you. Besides, our female crew members of a certain rank are extremely busy with other duties."

I looked across the table at Haggerty. A tiny smile was on his lips, and his raised eyebrows called for an answer. Betty LeClair's expression was also a question mark.

Uri Peretz grunted and looked down at his lap.

"Well, of course, if I'm needed," I said.

"Splendid," Haggerty said, slapping his palms together. "Thank you, Jessica. I knew you'd come through."

"Thank you so much," Betty said. "I didn't want a stranger with me tonight. I don't intend to be a bother. It's just that —" She stopped and blinked back tears.

"Don't think a moment about it. I'm happy to help," I said. "You've been through a terrible ordeal."

The staff captain escorted Betty from the room, and Uri excused himself, saying he had things to do elsewhere, which left Haggerty and me alone.

"Michael, why do I have the feeling that your reason for arranging this is about more than simply providing Ms. LeClair female company?"

He clasped his hand to his chest. "You really know how to hurt a man, Jessica."

I waited for a better answer.

"All right," he finally said, "having you close to her could reap rewards in the investigation."

"Really?" I said. "I had the impression that you'd ruled her out as a suspect in Mr. Kim's murder."

He winced. "Not exactly," he said.

"Then —"

He lowered his head and looked up at me from under his eyebrows.

"Then she might be a cold-blooded murderer," I said.

"Let's hope not," he said, brightening and standing. "You're a trouper, Jessica Fletcher. It was my lucky day when I ran across you on that steamy Caribbean island years ago. We didn't get anywhere with our questioning of her, but you might."

"With some 'girl talk.' "

"Exactly."

"I'll do my best, assuming I survive the night."

CHAPTER TWENTY-ONE

A ship's officer accompanied me to Betty's new quarters, a lovely duplex suite. I tried to put her at ease in our first few minutes together, and she seemed eager to do the same for me. I wasn't sure how to initiate a conversation that wouldn't further upset her. After all, she'd just discovered the body of her companion, presumably her lover, the victim of a vicious knife attack, and endured questioning that was undoubtedly strenuous and possibly accusatory.

I suggested that we call room service for tea and an assortment of sweets for us to share. She liked that idea, and I placed the order. Ten minutes later a sharp knock at the door announced that it had arrived. I opened the door, expecting to greet someone from room service. Instead, to my surprise, Rupesh stood behind a rolling service cart.

"You work room service, too?" I said.

"No, ma'am, but because I'd been Ms. LeClair's room steward before, it was felt that she would be more at ease with me. I've been assigned here for the duration of the crossing."

What he said made sense, of course, but something inside me felt at odds with that explanation.

He rolled in the cart, arranged the pastries and tea service along with napkins and utensils, and quickly left.

"He's a nice young man," Betty said when she emerged from the bathroom. She'd freshened up, having skillfully applied a modicum of makeup and dabbed on a strong and distinctive perfume — Shalini, Dennis Stanton had said.

"Very nice," I agreed. "He has family living in my town in Maine."

"I would like to know more about Maine, Mrs. Fletcher."

"And I'll be happy to tell you all about it, provided you call me Jessica."

As we sipped our tea, I told her about Cabot Cove and my friends there. She listened politely, although I sensed that her attention was elsewhere for much of the time. I couldn't blame her. She had a lot on her mind at that moment, and I tried to catch an appropriate time to turn the conversation in her direction. That break occurred when she compared Cabot Cove to Paris. "I don't know if I could ever be happy living in a small town," she said. "I've spent my whole life in large cities."

"It must have been exciting being a model in Paris," I said.

"It had its moments."

"Oh," I said through a laugh, "I forgot what you'd said at Tom Craig's dinner party. You found it boring."

She managed the first smile since we'd sat down.

"I'm sure you're tired from everything you've been through tonight. If you want to go to bed, please just tell me to go."

"Oh, no, Jessica. I could never sleep." She shivered at the thought. "Besides, I enjoy talking with you. I like it that you don't seem to be judgmental."

"I try not to be."

She looked down, deep in thought. When she looked up, she said matter-of-factly, "I'm afraid I've made many mistakes in my life."

"We're all guilty of that from time to time," I said.

"No, I mean serious mistakes, becoming involved with the wrong people and for the wrong reasons."

Her comment was both interesting and provocative. George Sutherland had told me that she'd become a "party girl" after her modeling career had ended, using her natural beauty to attract wealthy older men. Was that what she was referring to, that unsavory aspect of her life? Was Kim Chin-Hwa one of those "wrong people"?

I didn't have to encourage her to continue.

"I feel terrible for Kim," she said, "the horrible way he died."

"How did you happen to find him?"

"I'd rather not talk about it, if you don't mind. It was just too horrible." She shivered again. "Sometimes I wonder if there is a God."

"Why do you say that, Betty? Surely no God would want to see anyone brutally murdered."

She nibbled on a pastry and put it down. "It's just that — it's just that he wasn't the nicest of men."

"I'm listening."

"He was Walter Yang's partner. But you knew that."

"Yes, of course. He spoke openly about the relationship at the dinner party."

"They weren't really friends. Kim lied. He was planning to end their business relationship before Walter died."

"I wasn't aware of that. Yet, it's my understanding that Kim might have been the beneficiary of the insurance on the Heart of India."

She exhibited a sardonic smile. "He was expecting a big windfall. It softened the 'blow of losing Walter.' "

"But you say he was going to end the partnership."

"When Walter conveniently died."

"I'm sorry, Betty. I'm not following."

She said nothing, nor did she have to. I decided to be direct. "Are you saying that Kim killed his partner?"

I wasn't sure whether the crying that ensued was legitimate or not. "It's terrible for me to say such a thing," she said, tears streaming down her cheeks.

"Not if it's true," I said. I waited a decent interval before adding, "Is it?"

She didn't look at me as she said, "I am afraid it is, Jessica." She used a lace-trimmed handkerchief to dab her cheeks. I don't know why it occurred to me, but I realized I hadn't seen a woman use a handkerchief in a long time. I carry packets of tissues. Most of my handkerchiefs were gifts from students or more likely their mothers. I had them carefully folded away in my bureau drawer with scented sachets. *I should make an effort to use them,* I thought, watching Betty deftly wipe under her eyes without disturbing her flawless makeup. She was a very studied young woman; every part of her dress and demeanor had been thought out. I wondered how much of her story followed the same pattern.

"Are you sure Kim killed Yang?" I said.

"I am," she replied. "I don't mean to shock you."

"You're not shocking me, Betty. Are you also saying that Kim stole the Heart of India from Mr. Yang?"

She'd sat there with her head hung low, avoiding direct eye contact. Now she looked up and shrugged. "What other answer could there be?"

I let her accusation sink in as I poured more tea.

"I'm sorry, Jessica," she said.

I waved away her apology. "Can you prove it?" I asked.

"Prove it? No. I only know that Kim hated Yang, hated him for a long time. He accused Walter of stealing funds from the partnership to support his political cronies, a bunch of thugs. It became very nasty after a while. I heard Kim threaten to kill Walter more than once, but I never thought he'd really do it till it happened. I've been so afraid

271

ever since. I knew something terrible would happen." Tears rose in her eyes again, but she blinked them back.

I thought back to our first meeting at Tom Craig's. Had she seemed nervous or uncomfortable in Kim's presence? If she had been afraid, she'd hidden her emotions well. The only time I hadn't seen her perfectly composed was when she left Kim's stateroom in a fury or when she barked at his bodyguard at dinner one night. Apparently anger and annoyance were emotions she felt free to exhibit. But here was a new Betty, morose and vulnerable. Was she genuine? She had been a high-fashion model. Successful models need to be able to express myriad emotions. Was this just a very good actress before me?

"What about the diamond?" I asked. "Did Kim bring it on board with him?"

"No, I don't think so. I never saw it, although he talked about it."

"Talked about having it?"

"No. But he was jealous of Walter for having bought it."

I sat back and rubbed my forehead. The last thing I'd expected was this accusation from her. Had she said the same thing to Haggerty and the staff captain during their questioning of her? I doubted it. If she had,

Haggerty would certainly have filled me in before asking me to accompany her to her stateroom.

I also thought about Kim Chin-Hwa. He was a small man with delicate features and almost feminine hands. George had said that Yang was strangled and beaten. By Kim Chin-Hwa? Impossible! Which didn't mean, of course, that he hadn't enlisted others to do his killing for him. George had said as much when we'd met for breakfast in London.

Naturally I also wondered why Betty had chosen to tell *me* of her suspicions. Did she expect me to pass along the information to Haggerty and the ship's security staff?

"You were just with officials investigating Kim's murder," I said. "Did you tell them about your suspicions regarding Yang's death?"

"No," she replied. "It doesn't have anything to do with this — does it?"

"I don't know," I said, "but those charged with investigating what happened to Kim certainly should be made aware."

"You can do that if you wish, Jessica."

"I think it would be more appropriate coming from you."

I knew that I would relay the information, of course, at the first possible moment. But it occurred to me that she'd accused Kim of murder only *after* he'd died. He was no longer able to defend himself against such a scurrilous charge. George Sutherland had questioned Betty following Yang's murder and she hadn't accused Kim of anything. Was it because he was still alive at that juncture? Had she really been afraid to come forward, or had she deliberately waited until he was dead to point a finger at him?

All of which led to yet another question, the most important one of all: Had Betty LeClair murdered Kim Chin-Hwa?

"I'm afraid I am tired now, Jessica," she said, standing and stretching. "Would you mind terribly if I went to bed?"

"Of course not," I said. "Frankly, the thought of getting into bed is appealing to me, too. I assume that you won't be coming to the dining room for meals."

"Mr. Haggerty wants me to take my meals in the cabin."

"That's good advice. Good night, Betty. I'll check in on you in the morning."

CHAPTER TWENTY-TWO

Fourth Day at Sea

As fatigued as I was after returning from Betty's suite, I had trouble falling asleep. Our conversation had taken a dramatic turn from what I'd expected and had left me with a brain that was active in every lobe, firecrackers going off one after the other. The harder I tried to shut it down, the worse it became, and it wasn't until the sky was lightening that sleep finally put a stop to it.

My rest didn't last long, however. The phone rang, jarring me awake at what seemed to my exhausted body to be only moments later.

"Were you sleeping?" Haggerty asked.

"Yes."

"Sorry about that. How did it go last night with Ms. LeClair?"

"How did it go? It went — why don't we talk about it over breakfast. Give me an hour?"

"Okay. They'll still be serving then. What about your buddy Stanton, or whatever his name is?"

"I haven't heard from him."

"Give him a call and tell him to join us for breakfast."

"I'll call and *ask* if he wants to do that."

"Whatever you say, Jessica."

After showering and dressing, I put on a lightweight jacket with a hood and took a few minutes to sit on my balcony before heading for breakfast. I was still tired; I could have used a few more hours of sleep. I was also feeling out of sorts. The crossing on this lovely ship had turned into a stressful experience, becoming more so every day.

The weather was superb, a crystal clear blue sky, with abundant sunshine and a temperate breeze. The ship continued its relentless journey through the Atlantic, a luxurious and technological marvel plying the waters for six days between England and New York, where wind-powered schooners once took weeks, if not months. I looked out over the vast stretch of ocean and thought of those who'd crossed it centuries ago, brave men and women without the benefit of today's technological marvels — sonar, radar, positioning devices, communications satellites, and all the other equipment that makes crossing oceans routine and safe. No matter where we were at that moment, I could be in touch with anyone in the world by picking up my cabin telephone, or logging on to a computer to send an e-mail. That train of thought led me to realize that I hadn't checked my e-mail since leaving Southampton, nor had I spoken with anyone ashore.

I returned into my cabin, picked up the phone, and placed a call through the ship's operator to George Sutherland's cell phone. I had no idea where he was at that moment but hoped that he'd be available to take the call. He was.

"George. It's Jessica."

"I was hoping to hear from you," he said. "It was on my agenda to try you later today."

"There's been a murder."

"So I've been informed. That fellow Kim. The Yard received the news from MI6. They have an agent on the ship."

"His name is Michael Haggerty. I knew he was going to be aboard."

"Oh? You never said anything."

"We go back a long way." I explained how I knew Haggerty, and went on to tell George about Dennis Stanton and his unexpected appearance on the *Queen Mary 2*.

"It looks as though you're up to your

lovely neck in murder — again."

"You sound like Seth Hazlitt."

"Just a statement of facts, Jessica."

"Unfortunately that's true," I said. "Listen, George, I have a question for you. You said at breakfast that one of your female officers detected the aroma of heavy perfume in the room where Mr. Yang was murdered."

"That's right, but it didn't take a woman to come to that conclusion. I was aware of it, too."

"By any chance, have your lab people identified the maker of the perfume?"

"As a matter of fact, they did. We captured an air sample, as well as a pillow on the sofa that seemed to be impregnated with the scent."

"Do you remember the name of it?" I asked.

"I don't have the result in front of me, but I can get it quickly. Care to hold or shall I get back to you?"

I knew that ship-to-shore phone calls were expensive, but I wasn't about to lose him. "I'll hold," I said, checking my watch. I was running late for breakfast with Haggerty, and hadn't called Dennis Stanton.

George came back on the line shortly. "I called the lab. It's a French perfume called

Shalini." He spelled it for me. "Quite dear, as I'm told."

"Thank you, George."

"Why are you interested in that?"

"Just trying to tie up loose ends. When you interviewed Betty LeClair, Kim's mistress, were you aware of that same perfume scent?"

"No, can't say that I was. But now that I think of it, she was in the shower when we arrived. Had to sit on our hands for an hour until the lady presented herself. If she wore any scent, it was lavender soap. I take it you've been exposed to a stronger perfume on her person recently."

"That's right."

"I understand that she was the one who discovered Kim's body."

"That's what she told the authorities on board."

"Makes her a prime suspect."

"Along with anyone and everyone who traveled with Kim, including his two burly bodyguards."

"And others, of course. The murderer doesn't necessarily have to come from the passenger ranks. It could have been a crew member."

I recounted for him what Betty LeClair had told me.

He laughed. "You're quite the interrogator, Jessica. She never offered that scenario to me."

I proffered my thesis that she might have waited until Kim was dead before making such a charge.

"A motive for having killed him," he said.

"I'm thinking the same thing."

George paused, and I could almost see his mind working. "What about the missing diamond?" he asked.

"No sign of it. Ms. LeClair says she's never seen it. There are a couple of interesting women on board, George, a Jennifer Kahn and Kiki Largent."

"Ah, that's where Jennifer Kahn is," he said, excitement evident in his voice.

"So you've heard of her."

"Every law enforcement agency has heard of her, Jessica. She's reputed to have been involved in jewelry thefts around the globe, although no one has ever come up with even a modicum of evidence to link her to those thefts. We're working on the assumption that she was behind the three London jewelry store heists last week. We had her under surveillance, but she slipped away from us. I'll say this for Jennifer Kahn. She's as elusive and clever a thief as I've ever seen."

"Is she capable of murder, George?"

"She's never been linked to one. Are you thinking of Kim's murder?"

"And Walter Yang."

"You say that this Agent Haggerty is taking an active part in the investigation."

"Yes, and Dennis Stanton will undoubtedly play a role, but for a much different reason."

"All I can say, Jessica, is that I'm relieved that you have two good men there alongside you. You could be in jeopardy. I don't like to think about that."

"I'll be careful, George. Where are you now?" I asked.

"At Scotland Yard."

"Can I reach you again later?"

"Always on my trusty mobile. You will take care?"

"Yes, of course. Thanks for the information. I — I really miss seeing and talking to you at a time like this."

He laughed. "*Only* at a time like this?"

"You know what I mean. I always miss seeing you, George, but murder raises the stakes."

When our conversation ended, I dialed Stanton's cabin, got no answer, so set off for the Princess Grill. I wondered whether Jennifer and Kiki would be there. Had they become aware of Haggerty's real name and true mission? If they hadn't, they would soon enough, I was sure. Too many people knew now, and the *Queen Mary*'s rumor mill was every bit as active as Cabot Cove's. It would be interesting to see their reaction when they did find out.

Haggerty and Stanton were together at the table when I arrived.

"Thought you'd forgotten us," Haggerty said.

"Sorry to be late," I said, folding my jacket over the arm of the chair. "I was on the phone with a friend in London. Have any of the others been here?"

"Flynn was finishing up breakfast when I arrived. He left."

"What about Jennifer and Kiki?"

Haggerty and Stanton looked at each other before Haggerty said, "Haven't seen them. Dennis — or rather 'Bill' — here informs me that he's the one who told you about Jennifer's reputation as an international jewel thief." He laughed. "Didn't come as a big surprise when you told me, Jessica. I'd had my suspicions all along that something wasn't quite right about her."

I was successful in suppressing a smile; the male ego at play, his need to save face.

I related my conversation with Betty Le-Clair and her accusation that Kim Chin-

Hwa might have murdered Walter Yang and stolen the Heart of India.

"Why didn't she tell *us* that when we questioned her?" Haggerty asked.

"I don't have an answer for that," I said, "unless she felt having me pass it along would carry more weight with you."

"Why would it?" Haggerty asked.

"I don't know," I said, "just a supposition. I can't help but wonder whether she's pointing a finger at him to deflect attention from herself."

Haggerty grunted.

"Do Jennifer and Kiki know who you really are and why you're on the ship?" I asked him.

"I didn't tell them," he said.

"They're bound to find out," I said.

"I'm sure you're right."

"But there's no reason for them to learn the truth about you, Dennis," I said.

He nodded. "And I'm not ready to divulge that information just yet. Let's keep it just amongst us, shall we?"

"It gives you an edge with them," I added.

"Precisely."

"Well?" I said to Haggerty. "Now that you're in charge of the investigation, what's your next move?"

"We've got Kim's two bodyguards in

temporary custody. I'm meeting them, separately of course, in an hour. Feel free to join me."

"I'd like to sit in on that," Stanton said.

Haggerty shook his head. "It's better that you stay away from the investigation, at least officially. I think that —"

The arrival of Jennifer and Kiki brought a halt to our conversation.

"Late start?" Stanton said pleasantly. "They're about to stop serving."

"I'd better put in my order," I said. To Jennifer: "A late start for me, too."

If they'd been made aware of Haggerty and his true identity, they said or did nothing to indicate it. Haggerty excused himself without saying where he was going. When he was gone, Jennifer asked whether I had another lecture to give.

"Tonight," I said as the waiter came to the table and took our orders. "I'm glad you reminded me. I'd almost forgotten. It wouldn't do to have an auditorium full of people and no speaker."

"Is there anything new about Mr. Kim?" Jennifer asked.

"Not that I know of," I said, comfortable in feigning ignorance.

"I feel sorry for his girlfriend," Jennifer said. "Imagine, expecting to have a tryst with your lover, and instead discovering his body."

I agreed.

"Where is she, by the way? Did she come in for breakfast?"

"I haven't seen her," Dennis put in.

"I've heard that they've moved her to another stateroom," I said.

"Can't blame her for not wanting to stay where she was," Jennifer said. "Gives me the creeps, thinking there might be a murderer on board. It had to have been someone in the victim's party, those two goons traveling with him, or his girlfriend."

Her comment about the "two goons" triggered a thought. If they traveled with Kim as his bodyguards, why was he alone at night on an open deck? Had his bodyguards deliberately left him alone at that fateful moment to allow his killer to strike? I thought back to Walter Yang's murder, in which the alarm system had been conveniently deactivated.

"I suggest that we put all thoughts of death behind us," Stanton said with enthusiasm. "We only have a couple of days until we reach New York and I intend to enjoy every minute. Would you ladies like to join me for a brisk walk around the deck, work off breakfast?"

"Not me," Kiki said. She said to Jennifer: "See you later."

"She certainly doesn't say much, does she?" Stanton quipped to Jennifer when Kiki walked away from the table.

Jennifer laughed. "The best kind of assistant, strong and silent," she said. "Yes, I'd enjoy a walk. What about you, Jessica?"

"I think I'll linger here a few more minutes and finish my coffee," I said. "You go ahead. I'll look for you in a little while."

Stanton tossed me a surreptitious wink as he held out Jennifer's chair and took her arm.

I poured myself a second cup, musing on Haggerty's upcoming interview. Interesting, I thought, how investigating a murder in the middle of the Atlantic Ocean differed from procedure on land, where the police would take the lead. There was no police force at sea, no detectives, no forensic technicians, no district attorney to help develop a case. The ship's sixteen-person security force was obviously top-notch when it came to securing the passengers' safety and well-being, but they lacked experience, as well as jurisdiction, when it came to murder. They certainly wanted to identify Kim's killer, if only to ensure that he or she wasn't still at large and posing a threat to other passengers. I knew that every ocean liner had a brig in which to incarcerate criminals or troublemakers. But the responsibility to question suspects had fallen to Michael Haggerty based upon his credentials as an MI6 intelligence agent. Whether *he* was up to the task was conjecture at best.

The salty air was delightfully refreshing as I stepped out onto the promenade and zipped up my jacket. The splendid weather had lured hundreds of other passengers outdoors, too, walking, jogging, leaning on railings in search of whales or dolphins, or lounging in deck chairs and soaking up the sun. Finding Jennifer Kahn and Dennis Stanton in the crowd would be a challenge, but surprisingly, I ran into Marcia Kensington.

"Good morning," I said, waving as she walked toward me.

Her face reflected her inner debate whether to keep going or stop to talk with me. She opted for the latter, although she was clearly reluctant.

"I want to apologize for the way Richard acted the other night," she said.

"You don't need to apologize," I said.

"Yes, I do. Richard can be — well, he can be difficult at times."

"He did seem angry that you were speaking with me. I was a bit taken aback when he warned me to mind my own business. All we were doing was having a conversation."

"I know," she said. "I'm sure he's sorry he spoke so rudely."

"Yes, I'm sure he is, too." I pointed to the large pair of binoculars hanging from a strap around her neck. "Whale watching again?" I said.

She looked down at the binoculars and nodded. "Maybe I'll get lucky."

"I hope you do. I'm glad to see you in a happier mood. Maybe we'll have time to chat again before we reach New York."

She walked away, looking back at me a few times, a pained smile on her pretty face. Was Richard Kensington on board because of the Heart of India? Was he on the *Queen Mary 2* in some official capacity for the insurance company, working undercover the way Dennis Stanton was? Was that why he had Marcia lie about being on their honeymoon? And why he'd gotten so angry when he thought she'd broken their cover?

I had so many questions, so few answers.

The interview with Kim's two bodyguards was conducted in the wardroom. I joined Haggerty and Uri Peretz at the table as the first one was brought in. He wasn't very talkative, claiming limited understanding of the language, when I knew from Harry Flynn having overheard the two bodyguards that they both spoke English very well. His responses to Haggerty's questions were more grunts than words, although I had the feeling that his performance was just that, a performance. It was effective, however, and after a frustrating half hour he was dismissed with the admonition that he was likely to be questioned again.

His colleague, equally large in stature, was a different matter. Unlike his predecessor, of whose testimony he was unaware, this man was neither arrogant nor evasive. In fact, he seemed anxious to respond to Haggerty's questions.

"Do you have any idea why your boss went up alone to Deck Thirteen?" he was asked.

"Yes," he replied. "Kim and Betty had been fighting. He said he was going to get some air and cool off."

"What was the fight about?" Uri asked. That the bearish Israeli intelligence agent was there surprised me, although I assumed that Haggerty wanted another presence to add weight to the interrogation; in Uri's case, "weight" could be taken literally.

"I really don't know," the bodyguard said.

"You never overhead anything they said?"

He shook his head. "It was more attitude than anything else. They used to be fine together. It was just bad in the past week or so. They barely talked after the first night on the ship unless it was an argument, but it was over stupid stuff, like where he put something or why she kept him waiting."

"How long had you worked for Mr. Kim?"

"Two years."

"Did you know his partner, Walter Yang?"

"Of course."

"Did your boss get along with his partner, Yang?"

"Sort of."

" 'Sort of'?"

"They seemed to get along okay. I wasn't with them much when they had meetings."

"What about Mr. Yang's security people? Do you know them personally?"

"A couple of them."

"I understand that you or your colleague didn't especially like your boss."

"Why do you say that?"

"We've been told that one of you said you wished him dead."

"That's ridiculous."

"It comes from a good source."

It was true. Harry Flynn was not the sort of man who would fabricate such a thing.

The questioning continued for another half hour with little useful information elicited, at least from my perspective. Haggerty asked Uri what he thought.

The big Israeli shrugged. "They both fell down on the job of protecting the victim," he said. "Did one of them kill him? Possible."

"What do you think, Jessica?" Haggerty asked.

"At least they confirmed that Kim and Betty LeClair weren't getting along. I did find it interesting that the problems between them didn't start until last week, around the time that Yang was killed and the diamond stolen. Was that what they fought about?"

"Maybe we should ask Betty," Haggerty suggested as we left the room.

"I will," I said. "I'd planned to swing by her new cabin anyway. I'll raise it with her. By the way, I received another note about curiosity, this one a quote from Eleanor Roosevelt."

"Did you? Probably some fan of yours having fun."

"Well, it's not my idea of fun."

"Mrs. Fletcher?" It was Uri.

"Yes?"

"I didn't want you here, but thanks for

your help."

"You're welcome, but why didn't you want me here?"

"Haggerty and I are professionals. You're not."

I started to respond, but he held up a thick finger to silence me.

"As long as you're involved," he said, "please watch your step. Whoever killed Kim won't hesitate to kill again."

CHAPTER TWENTY-THREE

Rupesh was carrying a tray down the hallway when I knocked on Betty's door and received no response.

"She isn't there, Mrs. Fletcher. She left fifteen minutes ago."

"I thought she was supposed to remain confined to her stateroom for the duration of the crossing," I said. Haggerty had suggested she stay in her room. Perhaps he wasn't forceful enough. She hadn't been expressly forbidden from leaving.

"She left with another woman," Rupesh said, setting down the tray.

"Who was it?"

"I don't know. She knocked and went inside. They left together a few minutes later."

"Can you describe her?"

He looked at me quizzically, as though questioning why I should want him to do that. "She is — how can I say it? — I have seen her on the ship. She is about my height but bigger." He pulled his arms apart to show her width. "She keeps her hair very short, and wears black, all black. She looks like — well, should I say it? — she looks maybe a little bit like a man."

Kiki Largent.

"Thank you, Rupesh."

Betty went off with Kiki Largent?

I called Haggerty's cabin and told him what I'd learned from Rupesh. "It has to be Kiki Largent," I said, "based upon his description of her."

"Where did they go?" he asked.

"I don't know."

"Where's Jennifer Kahn?"

"I don't know that either, Michael. She left after breakfast with Dennis. They were going to take a walk on Deck Seven."

"I'll meet you there at the Outdoor Promenade, the one off Stairway B."

"I doubt Jennifer and Dennis are still there," I said, consulting my watch. "And I don't know if that's where Betty went with Kiki. It's a big ship, Michael."

"We'll check anyway."

I tried to process the potential meaning of Betty having gone off with Kiki. As far as I knew, they were strangers before having met on the ship. Unless, of course, they'd forged a relationship revolving around the jewelry theft. There could be no other explanation.

"Have you seen them?" Michael asked when he arrived at the promenade.

"No. I just got here."

We headed toward the bow, which had us bucking the tide of passengers getting their exercise and otherwise enjoying the lovely weather. A few people stopped me to chat about my lectures and books, and I as politely as possible kept our interactions brief, motivated in part by the frustrated expression on Haggerty's face. We passed Kings Court and the Winter Garden, one of many bars and lounges, and paused outside the Canyon Ranch Spa, where I'd intended to indulge myself with an afternoon of treatments, another best-laid plan unfulfilled.

I was about to suggest that we head in the other direction when I caught sight of Betty out of the corner of my eye. She leaned on the railing looking out over the ocean, while Kiki, who stood at her side, appeared to be berating her. One thing was certain: Whatever Kiki was saying wasn't pleasant.

"Should we barge in?" Haggerty asked.

"I don't think so," I said, drawing him behind a jog in the ship's structure. "Better for her not to be aware that we know she left her stateroom. She might become even more evasive."

"You're right."

I pulled up the hood on my jacket, and Michael turned up his collar, both of us angled slightly away from the pair as we continued to watch them. With so many people on deck, it was not difficult to fade into the crowd. A few minutes later, Kiki stomped away and walked past without noticing us. Betty continued to hug the railing, her attention set on some faraway place. Eventually she left the rail and disappeared through a door.

"What do you make of it?" Haggerty asked as we retraced our steps to where we'd exited to Deck Seven.

I'd been pondering the answer from the moment we saw them together. "I think we're in the midst of a cabal," I said, "a den of thieves — Kim, Betty, Kiki Largent, and undoubtedly Jennifer Kahn. The bigger question is how to prove their connection in some tangible way."

"And you have an idea how to do that?"

"I'm beginning to develop one, Michael. Let's find a quiet place for a cup of tea and I'll lay it out for you."

Haggerty and I sat for almost an hour as I sketched out the conclusions to which I'd come, and some tentative ideas about how to proceed. When I was finished, he said, "The problem is, Jessica, we're under considerable pressure to wrap this up prior to reaching New York. Stanton said if he doesn't locate the gem before we dock, it'll disappear in a city of eight million, never to be found again. Plus, it'll be a lot harder to round up everyone for more questions once they've scattered. We've got the rest of today and tomorrow, and two more nights at sea."

"And I have a lecture to deliver this evening."

"Tonight?"

"They don't usually schedule lectures at night, but my previous programs have drawn big crowds. They feel it would be a fitting end to the crossing, at least from an entertainment perspective. But I'll never make it without a nap."

Agreeing to touch base later, we parted, Haggerty to a meeting with the staff captain and I to Betty's suite again. This time she answered my knock and invited me in.

"Have a good morning?" I asked.

"Yes. You?"

"Very nice. The weather is beautiful."

"So I see, although I don't have much of a chance to enjoy it."

"You should get out on deck," I said. "No reason why you can't."

"I thought I was supposed to stay in the cabin," she said.

"I'm sure they wouldn't mind if you sneaked out for an hour as long as you're comfortable doing it. Your safety is the main consideration. There's still a murderer somewhere out there."

"You don't have to remind me," she said, shuddering.

"Betty, what were you and Kim fighting about?"

"Fighting? We weren't fighting."

"Several people have remarked on it. And even I saw you leave your cabin so furious you didn't even acknowledge me."

"Oh, I'm so sorry if I was rude."

"I wasn't looking for an apology. What made you so angry with Kim?"

"It wasn't anything important," she said, going to the mirror to check her appearance. She picked up her hairbrush, slapped her palm with the back of it, then put it down. She looked at me in the mirror. "You know men, Jessica. They can be so bossy."

I didn't say anything, waiting for her to continue.

She turned to face me, her eyes stormy now, a frown creasing her brow. "He was a real chauvinist, you know, always telling me what to wear and when to talk and not to

298

talk. 'Keep quiet, unless I tell you to speak.' No one's going to tell me to keep quiet. I didn't come on this trip to be arm candy. If I have things to say, I'll say them." She drew in a deep breath and let it out. "I'd just had it up to here, that's all." She raised a hand to her chin. "Anyway, you can see it was nothing really important. My feelings were hurt. But now that he's gone, I wish I had been nicer to him. I really did love him, and I know he was devoted to me." She pushed a strand of hair behind her ear, and stole another look at herself in the mirror.

"I see."

She nodded. "Would you like to have lunch with me here, Jessica? It's lonely not having anyone to talk to."

"Thank you, no, Betty. I can't right now. Is there anything I can do for you before I leave?"

She shook her head. "Thank you for all you've done for me already."

"I haven't really done anything at all," I said. "I'll check in on you later."

"I'll look forward to your visit."

Even though I wasn't privy to many conversations between Betty and Kim, I suspected her explanation of the reasons behind their disagreements was a fabrication. And I highly doubted that she was lonely and longed for my company. That she wasn't about to admit to her trip to Deck Seven with Kiki Largent only compounded the mystery surrounding their relationship. They must have known each other before meeting on the ship. We knew Jennifer and Kiki were last-minute additions to the ship's passenger list, but how far in advance had Kim Chin-Hwa made his reservations? I made a mental note to ask George if he knew or could find out.

After a wonderfully refreshing catnap in my cabin, I arrived at lunch precisely at noon and was surprised to see Harry Flynn, Dennis Stanton, and Jennifer Kahn already seated. Harry got to his feet and greeted me. Dennis smiled broadly. Jennifer's greeting was pure frost.

"How is everyone?" I asked.

"Did you know?" Jennifer snapped.

"Know what?"

"What a phony that Wendell Jones is."

I drew a breath. The ship's rumor mill had reached her.

She didn't wait for me to answer. "Harry just told me that Jones is not who he claims to be. He's some kind of cop who's been put in charge of the investigation of Kim's murder."

I said nothing.

"Well, did you know?" she demanded.

"He's an old acquaintance of mine."

"It seems everybody on the ship knew except me."

"I didn't know," Stanton lied.

"Then that makes two of us. What an insult to be toyed with like this."

"I hope I haven't let some cat out of a bag," Flynn said. "I assumed everyone knew."

"It's not any fault of yours, Harry," I said. "Mr. Jones — Michael Haggerty — he has his reasons for traveling under an assumed name."

"What reasons?" Jennifer asked.

"I think that's a question to ask him," I said.

"Actually," Harry said, "he's a British intelligence agent."

"A *what*?" Jennifer said.

I saved Harry from having to explain further. "Mr. Haggerty is a former agent for British MI6. He's retired now."

"So why the phony name if he's retired?" Jennifer asked.

"As Jessica has suggested," Harry said, "we'd better ask him, and here he is."

We all turned as Haggerty entered the Princess Grill and approached the table. Jennifer, whose appetizer had just been served along with a drink, stood and stormed out, coming so close to Haggerty that he had to move aside to avoid physical contact.

"What's gotten into *her*?" he asked, taking his seat.

"I'm afraid I spilled the beans," Harry said dejectedly.

"Nonsense," Stanton said, slapping him on the shoulder. "It's not a state secret anymore, now, is it?"

I reinforced his message with a smile at Harry.

Harry's presence held Haggerty, Stanton, and me in check. We wanted to discuss what had been happening but were restrained by his presence. As nice as he was, Harry was a big talker. We couldn't trust him not to pass along a good story, so instead we made small talk during the meal. In the end, he didn't stay very long. He didn't look well, and when I questioned Harry, he said he was feeling tired and just needed a nap.

"I took a nap earlier," I said, putting a hand on his arm. "You'll feel a lot better later. I can guarantee it."

"I hope so," he said. "We're in for a rough evening." He waved at the view through the huge windows.

He was right. What had been a sanguine,

sunny day at sea had changed over the past hour. It was now misty and overcast, the bottom of the clouds an ominous charcoal. The swells had begun to increase, causing a slight but discernible motion of the ship. "I checked with the weather officer," he said. "We're headed into a nasty cell, a real gale."

"He feels bad about telling Jennifer who you really are," Stanton said to Haggerty after Harry had left.

"Does she know about you?" Haggerty asked.

Stanton shook his head. "I'm sure she doesn't," he said.

"Let's keep it that way," Haggerty said.

At Haggerty's urging, I filled Stanton in on what had occurred with Betty LeClair, and her clandestine meeting with Kiki Largent. I also summarized what I'd told Haggerty earlier that day, my thoughts on the matter and the conclusions to which I'd come. "I think the three of us are now up-to-date on everything."

"You're right," Haggerty said, "but what do we do with what we know?"

"I have an idea," I said.

I spent the early part of the afternoon in my cabin going over lecture notes for that evening's presentation in the planetarium.

The ship's entertainment director called to say that he expected a full house, and to inform me that my final book signing, which usually occurs immediately following a lecture, would be held the following morning at ten.

At four, Harry Flynn called.

"Feeling better, Harry?" I asked.

"Somewhat. Jessica, I was wondering whether you'd join me for a drink."

"I won't be drinking," I said, "not with my lecture coming up this evening. But I'd be happy to meet you."

"Terrific! The Commodore Club, say, at five?"

"Yes, that will be fine. You won't be meeting with the others for drinks before dinner?"

"I'm not sure. But I do want to spend some time with you without all this talk of murder and the intrigue that goes with it."

I laughed. "I couldn't agree more," I said.

Before meeting Harry Flynn, I went to the staff captain's offices, where I spent a half hour outlining ideas I had about identifying Kim Chin-Hwa's murderer, and as a bonus hopefully locating the missing Heart of India diamond. He was skeptical at first that my approach would work, but eventually agreed to cooperate.

Harry was already at the Commodore Club when I arrived. He was as nattily dressed as usual, in a pale blue blazer, white slacks, multicolored striped shirt, and white loafers.

"You look like you're ready for a party," I said after he'd stood and kissed my cheek.

"On cloud nine, Jessica. Always ready for a party. Do you know where the expression 'on cloud nine' comes from?"

I laughed and assured him I didn't.

"Years ago they classified clouds into ten types. Number nine is the cumulonimbus, you know, those tall, fluffy clouds, some of them towering forty or fifty thousand feet above us. They look so peaceful and happy, like people said to be 'on cloud nine.' Of course inside those happy-looking clouds can be violent storms."

"So people who say they're on cloud nine might be hiding something tumultuous inside."

"Exactly. Thank you for joining me."

"I was pleased that you called."

"You never know whether you'll see someone again on a huge ship like this before reaching port, and I didn't want to miss the opportunity to spend some quiet time with you. I decided years ago that when I meet someone who is especially nice and caring,

305

someone with intellect and an appreciation for a variety of things, including man's many foibles, it's almost a sin to not tell that person of your feelings."

"I wouldn't argue with that," I said.

"Well, then," he said, "I am simply following through on my promise to myself to never let such an opportunity pass by. You are a lovely, sensitive woman who I am sure does not suffer fools easily but who is always looking for the best in people. You are obviously also a trustworthy person of sterling character."

"That's very flattering, Harry."

"Which is not my intention, I assure you. In other words, Jessica Fletcher, you have been added to my not very extensive list of white hats who have enriched my life by their sheer presence. I wanted you to know that."

I blushed. "I'm afraid, Harry, that for me to now tell you what a delightful gentleman you are would sound hollow."

"Say it anyway, Jessica."

I said through a smile, "All right, Harry Flynn, you are a delightful gentleman."

"I like that," he said. "Now, let's toast to having met."

I didn't want a cocktail or wine with my lecture looming, so Harry ordered a bottle of sparkling apple cider. We clicked the rims of our flutes and laughed.

"It's a nasty storm we've entered," he said, pointing to the vast stretch of roiling water ahead of us. "It will get worse before it gets better." Sheets of seawater splattered the large window that afforded a panoramic view of Mother Nature's fury.

"Funny," he said plaintively, "how I actually prefer weather like this to smooth sailing."

"In your blood?"

"Undoubtedly."

We sat in silence watching the scene through the window until I announced that I needed to leave.

"Thank you for joining me," he said, standing, taking my hand, and kissing it.

"The pleasure was all mine, sir," I said. "You'll be at my lecture?"

"I'm sure you'll knock 'em dead, as the saying goes."

"And the origin of that phrase is?"

"I haven't the foggiest notion. If for some reason I'm unable to attend, please know that I'm with you in spirit."

I thought it strange that he didn't commit to being there. He'd attended the two previous lectures and seemed to enjoy them.

"Thank you for the cider but especially

for the kind thoughts, Harry," I said. "Coming?"

"No. I think I'll sit here for a while and enjoy the view. There's something majestic about an angry sea that stirs my imagination. You run off and do what you must to prepare. Lecture well, Jessica Fletcher."

I returned to my stateroom and called Dennis Stanton to check on whether his role in that evening's lecture was in place. He assured me that it was. My next call was to George Sutherland's cell phone.

"How are things going?" he asked.

"All right, I think." I outlined for him the plan I'd fostered with the help of Haggerty, Stanton, and the *Queen Mary 2*'s staff captain.

"It's a bit of a long shot," he said when I was finished.

"I know that, George, but time is running out. It's worth a try."

"I wish I were there with you," he said.

"I do, too, but we can't change that. You still can help me. Can you think of anything to add to what I've decided to do?"

"I can't think of anything at the moment, but if I do, I'll get back to you. I'd wish you good luck, lass, but I have confidence in your abilities."

"Good luck is welcome, too. I'll certainly

need plenty of that," I said.

"Then good luck and have a care."

My final call before dressing for dinner was to the staff captain, who'd assumed responsibility for the final piece in that night's puzzle.

"It's all worked out quite nicely," he said.

There was nothing left now to do but wait until it was time to take the podium.

CHAPTER TWENTY-FOUR

That night, Dennis Stanton took Jennifer Kahn and Kiki Largent to dinner at Todd English, a specialty restaurant on the ship created by its namesake, one of the world's most celebrated and charismatic chefs.

Michael Haggerty avoided the Princess Grill and had dinner in his stateroom.

Betty LeClair was escorted from her suite to a private dining room, where she dined with the ship's master and a select group of his officers.

Kim Chin-Hwa's two bodyguards ate in Kings Court.

In another private dining room, Richard and Marcia Kensington were the guests of the ship's uniformed hotel manager and his staff. The couple had been told that it was the custom on the *Queen Mary 2* to host newlyweds enjoying a shipboard honeymoon. No such custom existed, but the event had been choreographed by the staff captain to accommodate me. I didn't want any of these people coming into contact with one another until my lecture, assuming they'd all be there. Making sure they showed was the responsibility of various people who'd been enlisted as part of the plan for the evening. As skeptical as the staff captain had been at first when I outlined what I intended to do, he pulled out all the stops once he'd signed on, and his cooperation was appreciated.

My plan was to start with dinner in the Princess Grill, which would give me another opportunity to chat with Harry Flynn before the night's program. Much to my surprise he didn't show up, but I would catch him later. He'd probably be in his regular seat at the lecture. I ate light, a special selection from the Canyon Ranch Spa menu. I knew our waiters were puzzled by my lack of dining companions, but they said nothing, and neither did I.

Following dinner I went to the planetarium and secluded myself in a small room reserved for lecturers. The entertainment director poked his head in the door.

"All set?" he asked. "I don't think we'll have a vacant seat in the house."

"That's wonderful," I said.

He lowered his voice and moved into the

room. "I get the feeling that something unusual is happening."

"What gives you that idea?"

"Just a vibe I'm getting."

"Well," I said, "I admit that I've decided to abandon my original lecture plans and take a different approach."

"Really? Different in what way?"

"I've decided to use a real murder as the basis for my talk. I thought it might be fun for the audience to see how a mystery writer creates a story using real life as its basis."

"I'm sure they'll be fascinated by that, Jessica." He looked back to make certain no one else was listening. "Especially considering the tragedy that's occurred on the ship. Did you hear about that? We've been trying to keep it quiet, but I know rumors are circulating."

"Yes, I've heard one or two," I said, drawing a series of deep breaths. "I'm ready any time you are."

He went to the podium and introduced me, adding as a final line, "And I'm sure you'll find Mrs. Fletcher's final lecture to be unique and exciting. Please welcome back to Illuminations — Jessica Fletcher!"

I walked to the podium and looked out over the audience. The entertainment director had been right. Every seat in the massive planetarium had a body in it, and the overflow crowd sat on the steep steps leading down to the stage. The applause was loud and sustained, which, of course, heartened me. I held up my hands to quiet the audience and looked up at the planetarium's faux sky and its multitude of twinkling stars. I smiled and said, "I feel as though I'm delivering this talk in heaven. You are all very kind in your greeting, and I truly appreciate it. So I'm going to take advantage of your forbearance. I trust you'll allow me to deviate from my originally advertised program to speak about something considerably more immediate — real-life murder and how it might influence a writer of crime novels. I'll be taking you through a writer's thought process as she — in this case me — bases a fictitious murder mystery on real life."

I paused, and there were murmurings from the crowd. Some people must have connected my opening remarks with the rumors they had heard. I took that moment to scan the faces in the crowd in search of those individuals whom I counted on being there.

I saw Haggerty standing at the back of the room, arms folded. Next to him was Uri Peretz.

To my right, Stanton had an aisle seat halfway up the steps; sitting next to him were Jennifer Kahn and Kiki Largent.

A glance to my left confirmed that Richard and Marcia Kensington were flanked by two members of the hotel manager's staff.

And directly in front of me, in the first row, was Betty LeClair, with Kim's two bodyguards on one side and two uniformed crew members on the other.

All present and accounted for.

"Let me begin," I said, "by recounting for you a murder that has intrigued this writer. Let us say hypothetically that it happened right here on the *Queen Mary Two.* Let's assume one of our fellow passengers was found stabbed to death in a whirlpool on Deck Thirteen. He was a successful businessman and he'd had a partner, a wealthy gentleman in London. Recently his partner had purchased a rare and expensive diamond, the Heart of India. Deep blue, its history steeped in mystery and violence, it carried with it a legendary curse; those who possessed it would attain only one of two possible futures in their lives, either great happiness or great tragedy. Unfortunately the curse came true for its new owner. Thieves broke into his home, stole the diamond, and brutally killed him in the process.

"Now, if I were concocting a novel based upon that occurrence, I would begin by creating a cast of characters who had some connection to the partners, our two victims."

I looked again at those people in the audience who'd been enticed to come to the lecture under false pretenses. Betty squirmed in her seat; the expression on her beautiful face said that she preferred to be anyplace but there at the moment. If Jennifer and Kiki wanted to leave, they would have to crawl over Dennis Stanton, who occupied the aisle seat. Haggerty and Peretz hadn't moved. Members of the staff captain's security staff now stood at the entrances to the planetarium.

I continued. "Police reports revealed that whoever stole the diamond and murdered its owner knew precisely when he would take the precious gem from his safe. Why had he removed it? Evidence points to someone having been with him, and in all likelihood it was a woman. There was the lingering scent of an expensive perfume. I'm not an expert on perfumes, but I've heard of one called Shalini that is expensive and distinctive, so that's the one I'll use in the novel. One of the victim's security staff told the police that his boss often entertained women in his private study, and when he did, he left instructions that he was not to be disturbed. Let's suppose that he removed the precious diamond from the safe to show it off to his visitor.

"That leads me to speculate that the woman he was with was acting in concert with those who broke in. At least that's how I would structure the plot for my book. Please bear in mind that I'm talking about creating a work of fiction using actual events as a blueprint."

I had their undivided attention.

"Now," I said, "let's move on to the topic of rare gems and the underground market for stolen goods. The Heart of India was reported to be worth more than ten million dollars. And during the same week it was stolen, three posh London jewelry stores were broken into with millions of dollars of gems taken. Were the subsequent robberies carried out by the same gang of thieves? Or were they the work of others who were sure the authorities would be distracted investigating the theft of the Heart of India? Either way, the thieves who stole the precious stones had to have a way of spiriting them out of the country, and were then faced with the problem of selling them without being detected.

"As the writer of this novel, I would conjure a scenario in which these things could be accomplished. My story really doesn't need any further embellishment — the theft of a diamond worth ten million dollars coupled with the brutal killing of its owner is gripping enough. Add to those elements the fact that the victim's partner was also murdered — right here on the *Queen Mary Two.*

"But it would be appealing to me as a novelist to add yet another dramatic dimension to the plot. What if the potential buyer of the gems was a terrorist group that would use profits from the sale to further its evil agenda? That possibility would capture the attention of various intelligence agencies around the world, especially in those countries that represent prime targets for terrorist activities.

"And so we have two separate but equal agencies — law enforcement and intelligence — interested in solving both murders and thwarting any attempts to use the stolen gems to advance terrorist aims."

I said through a sardonic laugh, "Our novel is now taking shape quite nicely, isn't it?"

There were verbal agreements from members of the audience, and one gentleman in the second-row center loudly asked, "Do you know the ending before you start writing?"

"I usually have a good idea when I start how the pieces will fall into place at the end, but the story and some of the characters often go off in their own directions as the writing progresses. But in the case of this particular novel, I've come to conclusions that will form the basis of my denouement. Sometimes I struggle to reach this point, but in this instance I believe that a resolution has become clear."

"So?" the same man asked. "Who did the dastardly deed?"

His question spawned laughter.

"I'll be getting to that," I said. "But before I do, let's add another dollop of drama to the story. The murder victim on the ship — I haven't decided what name to give my fictional character in the novel — is accompanied by a beautiful woman. Naturally she's bereft at the death of her companion, as any of us would be."

I looked down at Betty, who glared at me. She started to get up, but one of the bodyguards placed his large hand on her arm and gently restrained her.

"I'm sure the real woman upon whom I've

based my character won't take offense at being used as a model for my fictitious character, which, as I've said, is only a creative exercise on my part."

I waited for the buzz to fade.

"It struck me that it would enhance my novel if such a beautiful woman was not only romantically involved with the murder victim on the ship but also his partner. She'd been having an affair with the owner of the Heart of India, and had been the woman in his study the night he was killed. Of course, that would make her an accomplice to the crime. Why would she do it? If my flight of literary fancy is correct, she would likely be the recipient of money generated from the private sale of the Heart of India, because such a treasure could never come onto the open market unless it was recut, significantly lowering its value."

I stole a glance at Jennifer Kahn and Kiki Largent, neither of whom seemed to be contemplating leaving. Good! The Kensingtons sat placidly, Richard with his perpetual scowl, slumped in his seat, and Marcia nervously fiddling with the strap of the binoculars that she seemed never to be without, although she hadn't raised them to get a better look at me.

"Let's see," I said. "Where was I? Oh, yes,

once I've decided to move forward with a plot that involves a beautiful woman, I then have to decide how to structure the spiriting of the stolen Heart of India and the other jewels out of Great Britain. A friend of mine, an intelligence agent, told me that some jewel thieves these days prefer to travel with their contraband on ships rather than by air. That makes sense. Ships like this, with more than two thousand passengers, make it relatively easier to get lost. Of course, that doesn't guarantee unimpeded passage, but the odds against being intercepted are more favorable than going through, say, Heathrow or Kennedy airports.

"Savvy, professional jewel thieves, not your garden-variety burglars, continuously seek ways to stack the deck in their favor, pardon the pun. Before boarding this ship for the crossing to New York, I was given a DVD of a new documentary about the smuggling of drugs from Africa into the United Kingdom. One of the smugglers was interviewed on camera, his face blurred, of course. He said one of the most effective ways to avoid interception by authorities is to choose individuals to carry the drugs — they call them 'mules' — who are least likely to be suspected of engaging in such behavior. That makes sense to me, and if I were smuggling drugs — or stolen jewelry — I would certainly follow that advice, which means that's how I would have the jewel thieves in my novel do it."

My gaze dropped to the seat usually occupied by Harry Flynn and across the sea of other faces. Harry had attended each of my previous lectures, but I didn't see him in the audience for this one. Since he hadn't appeared at dinner, I wondered if he wasn't feeling well. I hoped that wasn't the case and that he'd simply decided to eat elsewhere and try his hand again at the casino's craps table. I did, however, see another familiar face in the crowd. Rupesh had entered the planetarium and stood near Michael Haggerty and Uri Peretz. He was out of uniform, dressed in jeans and a T-shirt. Did room stewards get an evening off?

"Is everyone still following me?" I asked.

A chorus of "Yes" answered my question.

"Good. So far I've put together the elements for a pretty solid murder-mystery novel, or, as my British friends prefer to term them, 'crime novels.' It has everything going for it — a beautiful woman, ruthless killers, expensive diamonds and other precious gems, terrorists, and government intelligence agencies — and I'm now ready

321

to start writing. But —"

The gentleman in the second row interrupted again. "But do you know how it ends before you start?" he repeated.

I paused for effect, cocked my head, placed an index finger on my chin, and replied, "Yes, I think I know how it ends."

That answer fostered a flurry of comments between members of the audience.

Richard Kensington stood and yanked at his girlfriend's arm.

"You aren't leaving, are you?" I said, directing my comment at them.

Everyone turned to see whom I was addressing.

"Before you go," I added, "you might want to hand over the binoculars you're wearing to one of the uniformed crew members stationed at the doors."

Richard pulled Marcia to her feet and tried to drag her up the aisle. She dug in her heels and said, "No! I won't do it anymore!"

Richard released his grip and proceeded toward an exit but was stopped by the ship's security crew. He struggled, but they easily subdued him, one on either side, his arms firmly in their grip.

"Why don't you come up here with me," I said to Marcia.

The commotion had left audience members in the dark, and they verbalized their confusion. I waited for Marcia, who now stood trembling in the aisle, to decide what to do. Slowly, using the backs of seats to steady herself, she approached the podium. When she drew near the podium, she halted, her expression fearful.

"May I?" I said, holding out my hand.

Slowly she lifted the strap that held the binoculars from around her neck, and placed them in my hand. I glanced at Jennifer and Kiki, who sat with Stanton. I expected some sound of protest from either of them, but they remained silent.

I faced the audience again and held up the binoculars. "In the novel I'm writing, I've decided that these binoculars will have a function aside from bringing things closer. If I'm wrong, then, well, I'll have to come up with a different ending."

People leaned forward in their seats as I fiddled with the twin lenses in search of a way to open them. One wouldn't budge, but the other opened easily. I unscrewed it, tipped it over my open hand, and let out an involuntary gasp when my fingers closed over a small black velvet pouch.

"What is it?" someone yelled.

I emptied the pouch and held up the blue

stone. The Heart of India caught the spotlights trained on the podium and set off a dazzling light show, a breathtaking display of brilliance and fire. Oohs and aahs filled the spacious planetarium. One voice cut through. "Is that real?"

"Yes," I said. "It's the Heart of India, the diamond stolen in London, the one a man was killed for, that man who was the partner of the murder victim on this ship." I motioned to a pair of security guards, who took possession of the diamond and the binoculars and, accompanied by the *Queen*'s purser, left to secure them in the ship's safe until the ship docked in New York and they could be handed over to the proper authorities.

I waited for the multiple voices to wane before continuing. "In order to be fair to my readers, I'm obliged to explain how I came to suspect the binoculars might be used for more than their usual purpose. This young woman, like many of us, was eager to look out over the waves in hopes of catching a glimpse of whales or dolphins. I'd noticed that whenever she raised the binoculars to her eyes, she would look over them, more than through them. That struck me as odd, although I might not have connected it with the theft of the Heart of India had it not been for the behavior of her male companion, Richard Kensington.

"Richard and Marcia were posing as honeymooners. Why would they do that? Remember the DVD I mentioned, the one about smuggling drugs? If I were smuggling a diamond aboard this ship, who would be the perfect person to carry it, someone considered unlikely to become involved in such a nefarious undertaking? A honeymooning couple! How perfect.

"Of course, I have to come up with a reason for this person to have agreed to smuggle something in the first place. Richard held the clue. What if he's the disgruntled son of the executive director of an insurance company, the insurance company that held the policy for a famous diamond? What better way to get even with a parent you hate than by taking something that will hurt him both personally and professionally? And the bonus is getting paid handsomely at the same time by the jewel thieves? That works for me."

I turned to Marcia, whose crying had subsided. "How much were you being paid to pretend to be married to Richard?"

She shook her head. "I wasn't being paid," she said. "I love Richard. We really are engaged to be married; we're just not married yet."

"You jerk!" Richard Kensington shouted. "You stupid — I was never going to marry you." A yank on both his arms by the security officers ended his tirade.

Marcia flew up the aisle after him. "You promised! Don't call me a jerk. I'll tell them everything I know about you." She trailed after Richard and the officers as they escorted him out, screaming at her former fiancé.

I said softly to the audience, "Characters in my novels often do things for love that all the money in the world wouldn't entice them to do."

An audience member spoke up: "So he and his girlfriend stole the diamond from the character in your novel and killed him." Another asked, "Is she the beautiful woman you referred to earlier?"

"Bear with me a little longer. We're not finished yet," I replied. "No, in my novel, this young man and his love-struck girlfriend only serve to smuggle the Heart of India into the U.S., hiding the diamond in plain sight in a pair of binoculars, as common a tourist accessory as you can find. They aren't murderers; they were the mules. It's very possible he had *her* carry the diamond so that if they were intercepted by customs agents, she'd take the rap, and he could claim to know nothing about the gem."

A few people booed Kensington, evidently not for being involved in the scheme but for his lack of concern for Marcia.

"So," someone said, "who killed the passenger and the guy in London who owned the diamond?"

I looked at Kiki Largent and Jennifer Kahn. "Would you like to help me answer that question?" I asked them.

Without warning, Kiki scrambled over Stanton and ran up the aisle in the direction of Haggerty and Peretz, who braced to intercept her. But she stopped short of them, grabbed a young blond woman from her aisle seat by the hair, and pulled her into the aisle. Kiki then pulled a knife from beneath her black sweater and held it to the woman's throat.

"Get out of my way," she snarled at Haggerty and Peretz.

"Don't be foolish, Kiki," I said into the microphone. "We're at sea. There's no place you can go."

"Move!" Kiki told Haggerty and Peretz.

"Let her go," Haggerty said.

Kiki's answer was to pull the terrified young woman closer and to hold the knife up to her face. "You move or she dies," Kiki said.

Haggerty and Peretz held up their hands as a gesture that they were complying and stepped aside. Members of the ship's security staff did the same as Kiki maneuvered her hostage, whose face reflected her abject fear, toward the closest exit. I came down from the podium and approached Betty. "You don't understand," she said to me.

I ignored her, content that those with her wouldn't allow her to leave, and went up the opposite aisle to the back. Rupesh looked at me but said nothing. Kiki appeared to be unsure of what to do next. She'd reached the exit doors but hesitated.

"Don't compound what you've done by hurting an innocent bystander," I said.

Kiki's square face was a mask of anger and resolve, lips a thin, tight line, eyes wide as though reacting to a harsh light, the knife's steel blade reflecting the planetarium's lights. The hundreds of men and women in the audience looked on in shock as the tableau played itself out.

"We can take her," I heard a security officer say to a colleague.

"Please don't," I said. "It's not worth the risk; we don't want anyone hurt."

Kiki made her next move. She herded the

woman out the door and into the reception area. We followed — Haggerty, Peretz, Rupesh, an assortment of uniformed officers, and me. Kiki headed for the elevators off Stairway A, which wasn't far. Passengers who stood waiting for an elevator gasped as they saw Kiki and her hostage appear, and ran from the area.

The elevator arrived. Other passengers stepped from it, only to be confronted by a woman dressed in black holding a knife to the throat of a young blonde. They got out of the way as Kiki forced the woman into the elevator and pressed a button. The doors slid closed. We watched as the numbers above the doors indicated her ascent — four, five, six, and seven, where it stopped. Security officers ran up the stairs, followed by Rupesh. Haggerty and I frantically pushed the up button. Seconds later the empty second elevator arrived and we got in it. I pushed seven; the trip to Deck Seven seemed to take an eternity.

We reached it and stepped out. Kiki now held the woman against one of the heavy doors leading to the outside promenade. You didn't have to be outdoors to know that we were in the midst of a raging storm. Harry's prediction of a gale was accurate. Violent streaks of lightning reaching from the sky to the ocean cast bizarre slashes of light. The wind picked up the rain and flung it against windows and doors and sent anything loose on the deck flapping, as though the *Queen Mary 2* were being whipped by an angry god.

Our collective impotence was palpable. All we could do was stand and watch. Kiki had the upper hand. I didn't have a doubt that she would go through with her threat to kill the blond woman if anyone tried to take the knife from her and wrestle her to the ground. But where could she go?

My mind raced. Would this saga that had resulted in two murders end with a third?

I pleaded with Kiki to let the woman go.

"Shut up!" she said. With that, she pushed the woman against the door with such force that it opened against the wind's fury; windswept rain blew through the opening, spraying Kiki and her hostage.

They were gone, out the door and to the deck, where in fair weather thousands of happy passengers enjoyed the exhilarating experience of soaking in the vast Atlantic Ocean's vistas.

Everyone looked at one another, confused as to what to do.

Rupesh bolted from my side, raced to the door, laid his weight against it, and tumbled out onto Deck Seven, where Kiki stood at the railing holding the blonde from behind, one arm around her neck, the other pressing the knife against her temple. She saw Rupesh in her peripheral vision and turned, the woman between her and him. He extended his hand to Kiki. Although we couldn't hear what he said, it was obvious that he was attempting to coax her to give up.

"Somebody help him," a security officer said.

Before anyone could react to his order, Kiki pointed the knife at Rupesh and loosened her grip. The blond woman broke free and threw herself across the deck away from her captor. That left Kiki, who held the knife, and a weaponless Rupesh. We watched with trepidation as Rupesh stepped closer to her. The security officers went into action and burst through the door. But they were too late. Rupesh had grabbed Kiki's wrist when she lunged at him with the knife; he twisted her arm and flipped her onto her back on the deck. The officers swarmed on top of her, pulled her to her feet, secured her arms behind her, and led her inside, followed by a dripping wet Rupesh, his arm supporting an equally wet, but very relieved and grateful, ex-hostage.

CHAPTER TWENTY-FIVE

Fifth Day at Sea

It seemed I'd just gotten to bed at three o'clock that morning when my wake-up call sounded at seven. I resisted the temptation to answer the phone, hang up, and climb back under the covers. Instead, I staggered through my morning ablutions and emerged from the shower partially refreshed and somewhat ready for a new day.

Kiki Largent had been secured in the ship's brig for the duration of the crossing, which would end in New York early the following morning. That such a genteel giant as the *Queen Mary 2* would have a brig came as a surprise to some, but it makes sense. On any given day the ship contains more than two thousand passengers and a thousand-plus crew members, the population of a small city. Rare as a seagoing crime is, having a secure facility in which to hold lawbreakers is a pragmatic necessity.

Betty LeClair proclaimed her innocence and balked at being sequestered in her suite with two crew members guarding her door twenty-four hours a day. There was no legal mechanism under which to charge her while at sea, and she posed a dilemma to the ship's senior officers. But Haggerty used his MI6 intelligence credentials to establish priority and called the shots when it came to handling the various suspects. He alerted law enforcement officials in New York and London that there were individuals aboard with possible (and plausible) connections to two murders, as well as to the theft of the Heart of India and other recent jewelry heists.

Richard Kensington and his former fiancée and reluctant accomplice, Marcia, were sequestered in their cabin with guards to enforce that decree. But Marcia refused to stay with him — I applaud her for that — and was given a separate cabin in which to spend the final day and night of the crossing.

Jennifer Kahn posed a different sort of problem. Although she and Kiki traveled together, there was scant evidence to link her to any of the crimes, including the murder of Walter Yang and the theft of his Heart of India diamond. Marcia had been kept in the dark as to who else was involved in the conspiracy. Richard kept mum as to who recruited him to be the carrier of the diamond. Jennifer vehemently denied any knowledge of the jewel theft and expressed dismay that her "dear Kiki" could have murdered anyone. Apparently she was secure in the knowledge that her assistant would continue to protect her, even at the risk of her own life and liberty.

Haggerty and Stanton wanted to search her cabin, but without a proper warrant, there was concern that any contraband seized from Jennifer might be inadmissible in a court of law. But Haggerty wasn't to be put off. He, Stanton, two members of the ship's security staff, and I went to her stateroom. Haggerty knocked.

"Who is it?"

"Ship security," an officer replied. "Please open the door."

The sound of someone scurrying about inside could be heard.

"What do you think she's doing in there?" Stanton asked.

Haggerty's response was to knock again, harder this time. As the minutes passed, I was convinced that someone would have to break down her door, something I was sure would not please the ship's officers.

Haggerty pounded again, using a key ring on the door for emphasis.

There was the sound of the door being unlocked, and Jennifer opened it, a wide smile on her finely etched, perfectly made-up face. "What's this all about?" she asked.

"We'd like to search your cabin," Stanton said.

"Why didn't you just say so?" she said, stepping aside to allow us to enter. "There's no need to make such a racket."

We entered the room. The two security officers didn't participate in the search. They stood to one side as Haggerty and Stanton started going through things, opening drawers, and pulling things from the bathroom medicine cabinet.

"Open the safe," Haggerty ordered.

Jennifer laughed. "It *is* open," she said. "The blind leading the blind."

Haggerty ignored her sarcasm and looked into the open safe, which was empty.

Jennifer sat on the bed and watched placidly as the two men continued their hunt for something incriminating. I went to the balcony more to stay out of their way than anything. I sat in one of the chairs and allowed the breeze to wash over me. It felt good. I heard Haggerty say, "All right, that's enough. There's nothing here."

Jennifer said in a mocking tone, "Of course there's nothing here. What did you expect to find, diamonds or something?"

I got up and was about to rejoin them inside when something on the floor of the balcony caught my eye. It was roughly the size of a peanut, but it sparkled. I picked it up and held it in my hand. No question about it. It was a diamond. I took it inside and showed it to Stanton.

"What's this?" he asked Jennifer.

"I haven't the slightest idea."

"It's a diamond," Stanton said.

"Oh, let me see," she said, getting up and going to him. "It does look like a diamond," she said. "Imagine that, a diamond on my balcony. I knew this was a first-class ship, but I never expected them to go to this length to impress passengers."

Stanton, Haggerty, and I looked at one another before Stanton led us to the balcony. He looked down into the waters of the Atlantic and shook his head. "I never expected this," he muttered. He turned to Jennifer, who stood in the doorway. "You tossed them overboard," he said.

"I haven't the slightest idea what you're referring to," she replied calmly and with a hint of victory in her voice.

"You threw millions of dollars' worth of diamonds into the ocean," he said, his tone now angry.

"Are you crazy?" she said. "What woman do you know who would do a dumb thing like that? Diamonds are a girl's best friend. Don't you know that? Or aren't you familiar with popular songs?"

I handed the small gem I'd retrieved from the balcony floor to Stanton. "Sorry," I said. "This is all that's left."

Despite her professions of innocence, we all knew that Jennifer had been up to her neck in every aspect of the case, including the theft of the Heart of India, the murder of Walter Yang, and the break-ins of the three London shops that same week. She had used the term "murder" to me when discussing Kim Chin-Hwa's death. She claimed to have heard that he "drowned," but I believe she was simply trying to throw us off. Making the assumption that his death was a murder was a big misstep, taken long before the rumors had circulated widely as to the nature of his death. But I had the sinking feeling that while the others involved in the plot would be brought to justice, it was entirely possible that Jennifer Kahn would walk away a free woman.

In order to spare me, Michael, Dennis,

and Uri from intrusion by curious fellow passengers, we were given a small private room in which to take our meals. When I walked in at eight that morning, I was surprised to see Rupesh there. He was dressed in a trimly tailored blue suit, white dress shirt, and muted red and blue tie.

"Good morning, Mrs. Fletcher," he said, smiling broadly.

"Good morning to you," I said, "and congratulations on your heroics last night. I remember now that your cousin Maniram said you taught karate, a useful skill to know."

His smile widened even further as he said, "You can thank Agent Peretz for that."

"Oh?" I said, taking my seat at the table. "Why?"

"He's been my handler since I joined RAW."

My face mirrored my confusion.

"RAW," Uri said, "the Research and Analysis Wing of India's government intelligence apparatus. It's their lead agency, as good as they get. I've been Rupesh's handler since he joined."

"I received much of my training in Israel, including martial arts," Rupesh said. "Mossad trains many of our agents, as does your

CIA. In fact, RAW was patterned after the CIA."

"And you are on the ship as an agent, not a cabin steward?"

"Yes, that's correct," he said. "We had received information through the Israelis that jewel thieves might be transporting their stolen goods by ship, and that proceeds were going to terrorist groups through intermediaries in New York. We've stationed agents on a number of ships, including this wonderful one."

I couldn't help but laugh. "I don't know how effective an intelligence agent you are, Rupesh, but you certainly are a top-notch cabin steward."

"I'm a fast learner," he said.

"I'll vouch for that," Uri said in his characteristic low rumble of a voice.

I looked to Dennis, who sat back in his chair, hands folded on his lap, a Cheshire cat's grin on his face.

"I can understand why you're so contented this morning," I said. "You've saved your insurance company a huge payout now that the Heart of India has been recovered."

"True," he said, "but there's millions of diamonds from the store heists that are, as the mob likes to say, 'sleeping with the fishes' hundreds of feet below the Atlantic."

"Well, at least you got back the big stone," Haggerty said, "and you can thank Jessica for that."

"Oh, I am well aware of that," Stanton agreed, tossing me a salute.

Haggerty raised his glass of orange juice. "Here's to you, Jessica," he said.

The others joined him in the toast.

"What I find amazing," Stanton said, "is that the young woman, Marcia, was walking around the ship, going to meals, and all the while she was carrying a diamond worth ten million dollars in her hollowed-out binoculars. Pretty gutsy."

I said to Uri Peretz, "The night you followed Kiki on the ship, the night when she met someone on the deck in the storm, I was following *you*."

Uri laughed. "You're good at tailing people, Mrs. Fletcher."

"It wasn't difficult. I'm assuming that she met Richard Kensington that night and gave him the Heart of India. I spotted Marcia up there while the exchange took place. Leaving the gem in the cabin, even in a safe, would have made them nervous. Better to have it in the hands of an innocuous young woman. After all, she and Richard had been tapped to carry the diamond off the ship because they would likely be beyond suspicion by authorities. Might as well also take advantage of that while the ship was at sea."

Following breakfast, Haggerty asked what my plans were for the rest of the day.

"To relax," I replied, "a facial and massage in the Canyon Ranch Spa, a walk on the deck now that the weather has cleared, certainly a nap, and finish a book I'd started before we left Southampton." I was about to get up but remembered the two notes having to do with "curiosity" that had been delivered to me. I pulled them from my purse. "I suppose I can toss these away," I said.

"What are they?" Stanton asked.

"Two notes I received. Probably from an Irish fan of mine having fun."

Haggerty reached for them. "Give them to me," he said.

"Why?" I asked, handing them over. "Because they're yours?"

He looked chagrined. "How did you know?"

"When we talked in your cabin, you tossed your cummerbund over some papers. I lifted it to see what you were concealing. There was an envelope, which had been typed with the same machine. Why did you do it?"

"Oh, just to keep you intrigued and working with me. I thought that if you were receiving strange notes, your interest would be piqued." He laughed and tore them in half.

"You devil," I said.

"Looks like it worked," he said. "You didn't lose interest for a minute."

I was tempted to throw the rest of my English muffin at him but thought better of it.

"No harm done," he said. "Now that you've solved that puzzle, what else is on tap for you today?"

There was no sense in being angry at Michael. It wouldn't have accomplished anything. I said, "I want to swing by the Princess Grill to see if Harry Flynn is still at breakfast. He must be wondering why all his tablemates have abandoned him. I haven't seen him since we had a drink together before dinner last night, and he wasn't at my lecture."

"He's an active guy," Stanton said. "Keeps him young, I suspect."

"And I suspect you're right. I'll catch up with all of you later." I turned to Rupesh. "Have you called your mother?"

He laughed heartily and assured me that he had.

Haggerty walked me from the room.

"I have a question for you," I said.

"Which is?"

"It's about Uri. I somehow don't see him as an intelligence agent. He's — well, he's so big, so visible."

"He's out of his element in this case, Jessica. He's usually behind a desk back in Israel sifting through intelligence. He's brilliant at it. But since he's Rupesh's handler, they wanted him on the scene." Haggerty laughed. "He admitted to me that he searched my cabin."

"Why?"

"To see whether I'd come across anything that he didn't have. Happens all the time. We trust each other but only to a degree."

"You operate in a strange world, Michael."

"And it gets stranger all the time."

He kissed my cheek, and I headed for the Princess Grill. Harry wasn't there, nor had he shown up for breakfast, according to our waiter. I was worried about him, and went to his cabin. My knocks on his door went unanswered.

I returned to my stateroom, where I placed a call to George Sutherland's cell phone.

"Jessica!" he said. "You did it again."

"I did?"

"Don't be modest now, lass. I've been briefed on everything that's occurred on the ship. You've broken the Heart of India case wide open."

"With plenty of help, George. Where are you?"

"In New York."

"You *are*? Why?"

"To help facilitate extradition proceedings. We want to take into custody the suspects you're holding. I'll be waiting at the pier when you arrive."

Knowing that I'd be seeing him again in less than a day did what no nap would. My spirits were already elevated because of what had transpired the night before, and the contemplation raised them even further. "I can't wait to see you," I said.

"I'm eager to see you, too, lass," he said. "Stay out of trouble for the duration of the crossing. No more murders."

"That's a promise," I said lightly, and we ended our conversation.

I walked out on my balcony, stretched out my arms, and took a deep breath of the briny air. I felt as though a thousand-pound weight had been lifted from my shoulders. I hadn't realized how tense the previous days had been. With all the "bad guys" stashed away, I saw things in a totally different light. Life was good again.

The sound of someone knocking drew me

inside again. I opened the door to find a crew member from the purser's office holding an envelope. I'd meant to stop by to thank the staff captain and his staff. My ruse at the lecture would never have been possible without his cooperation. The crewman handed me a fat manila envelope with my name handwritten on it.

"What is it?" I asked.

"I don't know," he said. "Another passenger left it for you with instructions that it was to be delivered to you personally."

"Who left it?" I asked.

"I'm sorry. I don't know," he replied.

I thanked him, carried the package back out on the balcony, and opened it. Inside were two envelopes, one addressed to me and the other to a name I wasn't familiar with. I opened mine to find a note and a sheaf of hundred-dollars bills, lots of them. I fanned them out; there had to be at least forty. I dropped them on the glass-topped table and unfolded the note. The handwriting was precise and legible, almost printed. I started to read:

My dear Jessica Fletcher,

When you read this, I will have done something of which you might disapprove. In fact, many will disapprove.

But I have a suspicion that you'll understand, if only because you are such an understanding and nonjudgmental person. You see, I haven't been completely honest with you. Despite my outward appearance of a hale and hearty fellow in the pink of health, you've been spending time with a dying man. The doctors told me that I had, at the most, only a few more months to live. Cancer, of course. Bad cancer.

I knew I'd have to end my final days in a hospital or hospice, but I couldn't put my daughter through that, and frankly, I didn't much like the idea for myself either. I admit to being a bit of a coward when it comes to death. I'm also the sort of man who abhors being a burden. No, Jessica, I decided that I would leave this world on my own terms and under conditions palatable to me.

I've spent almost my entire life on the sea. The oceans of the world have nourished my soul and inspired my visions. There is no place I would rather be than on the water, looking up into God's heavens, breathing in the salt air and marveling at this world in which we live. My life has been rich, Jessica, rich beyond what any man should expect.

I've spoken to you about my daughter, Melanie, the apple of my eye, as the saying goes. She's a bright, caring person who has put up with her seafaring father for all of her life. That she's turned out as wonderfully as she has is a tribute to her mother, although I'll take a modicum of credit simply for having been there at the beginning. I would not want her to see her father wasting away in some medical facility, although as a nurse she spends her days in just such places.

And so, Jessica Fletcher, I've elected to join all those men and women whose lives have ended beneath the oceans of the world. It's where I prefer to be, considering the circumstances. I have regrets, of course. I would like to have learned how all the intrigue turned out. Having had the privilege of spending my final week on earth with you was a delightful and totally unexpected treat. My passage on the *Queen Mary 2* was to provide one last moment of luxury and sheer pleasure, which it was. Having you as a sailing companion was icing on my cake, as it were.

I now ask a very large favor of you. I have enclosed with this note the winnings from my sojourns to the ship's craps table. I would like Melanie to have it. Would you be so kind as to deliver it to her? I realize that this is an imposition, but I somehow feel that you won't take it that way. You have my eternal gratitude for doing this for me.

I must now admit to having had a fleeting yen for some hanky-panky with you, Jessica. Do you know the origin of the term "hanky-panky"? Years ago it was the name given to a concoction of brandy and ginger. After consuming one too many, certain men would make amorous advances to the nearest woman, thus said to be engaging in hanky-panky. I hope I haven't bored you with my trivia, dear lady.

May you have warm words on a cold evening,

A full moon on a dark night,

And the road downhill all the way to your door.

Your friend,
Harry Flynn

CHAPTER TWENTY-SIX

I sat on the balcony and cried until my tear reservoir was empty. There were so many things I wanted to say to him, so many questions to ask. I'd loved the pride he took in knowing the origins of sayings and expressions, and his *joie de vivre.* Could his love of life ever be reconciled with his decision to end it? Of course it could, I decided. He was a man who believed in living his life on his terms and schedule. And he was right about me. I would not be judgmental.

I stood at my balcony's railing and peered into the Atlantic's blue, sometimes aqua water, depending upon how the light hit it. Harry Flynn had decided to go "home" to a final resting place beneath the ocean he loved. "Sleep well," I said, a gust of wind capturing my words and blowing them out to sea, perhaps to where he could hear them. And then I added, "And enjoy the diamonds, Harry. They're yours now."

I gathered the money, Harry's note to me, and the envelope addressed to his daughter and went to the staff captain's office, where I found him busy with paperwork.

"I'm sorry to bother you," I said, "but there's something you should know about one of your passengers." I handed him the note written to me and waited while he read.

"How tragic," he said, dropping the note on his desk. "You're certain Mr. Flynn went overboard."

"I don't have any reason to doubt it," I said.

"Well," he said, rubbing his eyes against an obvious lack of sleep. "This has turned into quite a crossing, unlike any we've ever experienced before."

"And hopefully never to be repeated. I will, of course, carry out Mr. Flynn's wishes and deliver the note and the money to his daughter in New York."

He managed a small smile. "I'm sure Mr. Flynn's faith in you, Mrs. Fletcher, has been well-placed. Thank you for the news. I'll follow up on it immediately, including arranging for his daughter to be notified."

I also broke the news to Haggerty, Stanton, and Peretz at lunch in our private room.

"I liked him the minute we met," Stanton said.

"I did, too," Haggerty chimed in. "You'd never know that he was that ill."

"Because he was determined to not let it show," I said. "He wanted to be very much alive right up until the moment he decided it was time to end it. I miss him and his stories already."

And I knew that I would continue to miss Harry Flynn for the rest of my days.

I used my remaining time on the *QM2* pursuing all the wonderful amenities I had neglected up until then. My spa treatments were welcome and soothing. I left feeling rejuvenated and positive. While enjoying a massage, I had decided to spend the rest of the time on the *Queen Mary 2,* as brief as it might be, thinking of Harry as testimony to the joys of life, and making every moment count. I had dinner in my stateroom, packed and left my suitcases in the hallway outside my door as instructed, and watched some TV, including the oft-repeated instructions about what to do when witnessing a fellow passenger going overboard. Had I seen Harry prepare to take his dive into the Atlantic, I would have followed those instructions — yelling loudly "Man overboard" and looking for a lifeline to toss to him — knowing that he would have been annoyed that I had.

I finished the book I'd been reading and climbed into bed early. We'd be approaching the Red Hook section of Brooklyn at approximately four the next morning and I didn't want to miss our arrival, sailing beneath the Verrazano Bridge, whose span the ship's funnels would clear by only ten feet, passing the Statue of Liberty, and seeing the Manhattan skyline grow closer as we approached. I'd enjoyed that experience on previous arrivals on the *Queen Elizabeth 2* and never failed to be awed by the spectacle.

I was on my balcony at four the following morning. Once we were nestled up next to the pier that had been specially constructed to accommodate the size of the *Queen Mary 2,* I went to the Grand Lobby, where I'd agreed to meet Michael, Dennis, Rupesh, and Uri.

"Well," I said, "here we are. Have the suspects been taken off?"

"They're in the process of doing that as we speak," said Haggerty. "Half of New York City's police department is waiting for them along with a contingent from Scotland Yard."

Including George Sutherland. That thought warmed me.

"For your information," Haggerty said as

352

we disembarked, "Ms. LeClair has decided to cooperate. She's admitted that she was the one with Walter Yang when he was killed, and that she'd set him up. She's looking for some sort of plea deal. I doubt if she'll get it."

George was there on the pier when I left the ship along with my four colleagues-in-crime. They watched as we embraced.

"Gentlemen," I said, "this is a very, very dear friend, Inspector George Sutherland of Scotland Yard."

"Jessica did quite a job helping me break the case," Haggerty said.

I said nothing.

"I don't doubt that for a moment," George said. "She always does."

We all stayed over in Manhattan that night and had dinner together. It was a lively gathering with much laughter and good-natured kidding. As we parted in the lobby of the hotel in which we were staying, Haggerty took me aside.

"Do I sense more than a friendship with your handsome Scotland Yard buddy?" he asked, thickening his Irish brogue for effect.

"We're — we're fond of each other," I said.

"You know how to break a man's heart," said Haggerty. "I thought that once we hooked up again that we might —"

"Think again, Michael. It's been lovely seeing you and Dennis again, and meeting Rupesh, and I have to admit that being involved in bringing murderers and jewel thieves to justice has been satisfying. But I'm heading back to Cabot Cove in the morning, where I intend to settle in to write my next novel. The only crimes I intend to confront will be committed by my characters. As for George . . ."

"Yes?"

"I'll let you know if I ever decide to do something rash. Good night, Michael. It's been fun."

I met George for breakfast the next morning. My flight to Boston was scheduled for three that afternoon; George's flight to London left at six. But we had an important mission to accomplish before catching planes. I'd told him about Harry Flynn's request that I deliver money and a message to his daughter, and asked him to accompany me, which he readily agreed to do.

Melanie lived on a pretty treelined street of four-story brownstones on Manhattan's East Side. I was relieved that the staff captain had arranged for her to be notified of her father's apparent suicide; I would not have wanted to be the one to break the sad news.

Melanie greeted us at the door. She was a tall, striking woman whom I judged to be in her early fifties. She wore tan slacks, a burgundy turtleneck sweater, and sneakers. Her brunet hair was long and secured in a ponytail that reached her waist. No doubt about it: She was Harry Flynn's daughter. His strong genes had been passed to her.

I explained why we were there. She seemed at first to not understand what her father had done to cause our arrival, but when I said that the money represented his winning at the ship's craps table, she laughed. "That devil," she said. "The last time he was here, he ran off to Atlantic City and lost a bundle. He promised he'd never play again."

"He evidently felt lucky," I said, "and he was."

She opened the sealed envelope and read what her father had written in the note it contained. She began to weep softly halfway through. When she'd finished reading, she wiped her eyes and forced a smile. "I never saw much of him," she said, "but he always made sure my mom and I never wanted for anything. The money always arrived on time along with a silly letter filled with sayings and jokes and —"

"And the origins of nautical phrases and myths," I said.

"You heard a few of those?"

"Oh, yes, and enjoyed every one of them."

She made us coffee and served pound cake and a bowl of fresh fruit. We stayed for more than an hour. When we were readying to leave, she handed me a five-by-seven color photo taken recently of her father. "Would you like to have this?" she asked.

I looked at the man in the picture: nattily dressed, standing erect, his steel gray hair carefully combed. What was most striking was his smile, wide and genuine and with a hint of playfulness in it.

"Thank you," I said. "I'd like it very much."

George saw me to my flight at LaGuardia.

"I feel as though I haven't even seen you," he said.

"That's because it's true," I said. "This could hardly be called a reunion."

"We have to remedy that," he said. "Go on, now — they've called your flight, and I have to get over to Kennedy for mine."

Needless to say, we reluctantly parted.

Rupesh's Cabot Cove cousins were astonished when I told them of his heroic feat, but I left the information that his latest job was with India's top intelligence agency for him to share with his family. "And by the way," I added, "he did call his mother at my urging."

Michael Haggerty and Dennis Stanton stayed in touch and kept me up-to-date on the fates of Jennifer Kahn, Kiki Largent, Betty LeClair, Richard Kensington, and his lady friend, Marcia. All had been returned to London to face an assortment of charges and still awaited trial.

The photo of Harry Flynn now stands in a leather frame on my desk, next to my other family photos. Whenever I feel down, I look at it and a smile returns to my face and infects my spirit. Harry had included a verse in his note to Melanie that I think of often when gazing at his picture.

May the leprechauns be near you,
To spread luck along the way.
And may the Irish angels
Smile on you this day.

And may they smile on you, too, Harry Flynn.